POSSESSED

A reverse harem bully romance

STEFFANIE HOLMES

D1596358

Cover design: Amanda Rose

ISBN: 978-0-9951302-6-5

❀ Created with Vellum

JOIN THE NEWSLETTER FOR UPDATES

Get bonus scenes and additional material in *Cabinet of Curiosities*, a Steffanie Holmes compendium of short stories and bonus scenes. To get this collection, all you need to do is sign up for updates with the Steffanie Holmes newsletter.

www.steffanieholmes.com/newsletter

Every week in my newsletter I talk about the true-life hauntings, strange happenings, crumbling ruins, and creepy facts that inspire my stories. You'll also get newsletter-exclusive bonus scenes and updates. I love to talk to my readers, so come join me for some spooky fun :)

A NOTE ON DARK CONTENT

This series goes to some dark places.

I'm writing this note because I want you a heads up about some of the content in this book. Reading should be fun, so I want to make sure you don't get any nasty surprises. If you're cool with anything and you don't want spoilers, then skip this note and dive in.

Keep reading if you like a bit of warning about what to expect in a dark series.

- There is some intense bullying in the first couple of books, but our heroine holds her own. Our heroes have been born into cruelty and they'll need to redeem themselves.

- This series deals with themes of inequality and cycles of violence – there may be times where this is tough to read, especially if it hits too close to your lived reality.

- This is a reverse harem series, which means that in the end our heroine, Hazel, will have at least three heroes. She does not have to choose between them, and sometimes her heroes like to share. Although this book is set in high school, I'd call it R18 for sexual content.

- Subsequent books contain violence, threat of sexual violence (that doesn't succeed), and cruel and capricious cosmic deities.

Hazel and her friends are deep in a cruel, bloodthirsty world. It's not pretty, but I promise there will be suspense, hot sex, occult mysteries, and beautiful retribution. If that's not your jam, that's totally cool. I suggest you pick up my Nevermore Bookshop Mysteries series – all of the mystery without the gore and trauma and violence.

Enjoy, you beautiful depraved human, you :) Steff

To James,
Who didn't just stand up for me,
but taught me how to stand up for myself

CHAPTER ONE

I paced the length of my cell (they called it a room, but I prefer to name things what they were, and it was cold and damp and the door was locked and there were bars on the window, so it was a fucking cell), rubbing the spot on my arm where they'd injected me. It had taken me some time to realize that if I didn't bite the nurses, they'd ease up on the drugs and I'd get my mind back to myself.

For a while, at least.

We just want to help you, Hazel, they said as they shot me up with something that made my head spin and tiny invisible bugs crawl under my skin.

Poor thing. You don't know how sick you are. But we're going to make you better.

I hoped so. Because I couldn't stand the me they'd brought in here. I thought I was someone who knew right from wrong, who would fight tooth and nail for what she believed in and for the people she cared about. But I didn't know how to go to war against myself.

I might have been losing that battle for longer than I realized.

Maybe that was why everything and everyone I cared for went up in fire and flames.

Trey. Quinn. Ayaz. Greg. Andre. Dante. My mom. Their faces flashed in front of my eyes, wreathed in a halo of fire. They were all lost to me now.

I was lost to myself.

I turned up the cuff of my grey hoodie and rubbed the spot on my wrist where I'd once worn a tattoo of the Elder Sign. Only I'd never had that tattoo. But it felt so real – I could recall perfectly the tearing sensation as Ayaz dragged the needle over my skin. Like a cat's claws gnashing into me.

Only it wasn't real. I'd hallucinated the whole thing. The tattoo, the teachers sacrificing students on behalf of the shadowy Eldritch Club, the cosmic god waiting in his prison of shadow, awakening from an eons-long sleep beneath the school where I was supposed to be getting the finest education.

And the Kings of Miskatonic Prep – I thought they meant something to me, that we shared a bond deeper than anything I'd ever felt before. But I invented that, too. Everything else I could believe was psychosis – my garbled account of the god invading my dreams and the cavern beneath the gym and the shadows that chased me sounded pretty damn crazy. But everything I felt for those three guys still coursed through my veins. All the moments we shared when they'd let down their defenses and shown me pieces of their souls... all of that was too powerful, too raw and painful to be fake.

But it was fake.

Dr. Peaslee wanted to get to the bottom of what caused my psychosis, but I didn't need inkblots and drugs and therapy to know what had fucked me up. And it was all of my own doing.

It all went back to the fire at our Philly apartment.

But maybe I'd imagined that, too. Maybe the fire that tore my life apart only happened inside my broken mind. Maybe the unforgivable thing that haunted my soul was simply a nightmare made real by my subconscious.

Ayaz said we were never together. He said he'd never degrade himself to be with someone like me. But I recalled every touch, every word, every caress, as though it had happened yesterday. I could still feel the ghost of his arms around me, his teeth digging into my shoulder, his lips brushing mine. How could I have invented something that still burned in my body and turned my heart to mush?

And how could I remember something that never happened so vividly and yet have forgotten the horrible things they said I did? *Did* I torment Courtney and her friends? I know I used the superglue and exchanged their beauty products with chemicals that peeled their skin, but that was a pale shade of what they'd done to me, to Greg and Andre, and especially to Loretta.

I felt nothing but satisfaction for those two acts. For months, I lived in fear of the monsters of Derleth Academy, of the bullies who hated me because I wasn't like them. Now I knew that they were right – I was different. *I* was the only monster.

Full fucking circle.

There was a knock at the door. I didn't move from the bed as Nurse Waterford entered, balancing a tray piled with styrofoam cups. Behind her stood the orderly with the beefy arms they always brought to deal with me since the biting incident. Just in case I didn't cooperate. The orderly took his place at the end of the bed while Nurse Waterford plucked a cup from the tray and handed it to me. I shook the cup, listening to the pills inside clatter against each other. She passed me a bottle of water with no lid and stood back to watch while I swallowed.

I peered inside the cup. Today I had one red pill and two pale blue. I hated the blue pills the most. They turned my brain to sludge. The world stretched around me as I slid through time like an elastic band stretched too tight.

The orderly's eyes narrowed. He reached his giant flipper hand toward me. I tipped the container into my mouth, catching the pills on my tongue as they went down. I swallowed a mouthful of water and fog – but it was the fog that was supposed to make me see clearly.

"Fifteen minutes until lights out, Hazel." Nurse Waterford backed toward the door. I didn't need a reminder – I'd been counting the minutes. There wasn't anything to do in my cell. I wasn't allowed to interact with other patients (inmates) in the TV room and I didn't have library privileges yet (and likely wouldn't get them. Dr. Peaslee seemed to think even a paperback could be a weapon in my hands. He wasn't wrong.) so there was nothing to do but stare at the cell walls and pore over the remnants of my life, wondering what was real and what I'd invented.

Was it the fire that pushed me over the edge? Did the fire even happen? Are my mother and Dante still alive somewhere? Why haven't they come to save me?

My cell door slammed shut – the echo clattering through the bare room. I dropped back against the sheets, tucking my knees to my chest and curling into a ball, angling my face toward the bathroom to capture the faint breeze from the vent. The fresh air feathering my face made me think of Ayaz's kisses.

Ayaz cupping my cheeks in his hands, bringing my face to his to sear me with his kiss. His body pressing against mine, desperate to close the space between us, to press hot skin to skin. My nails scraping his back, clawing for purchase as we slid together, trying to crawl inside each other's fire...

No. I squeezed my eyes shut, waiting for the fog of the drugs to pull me under. *You're not real,* I told the vision of the Turkish boy with black diamond eyes and dazzling smile. I imagined myself wriggling out from beneath him, pushing him away, grabbing my clothes and pulling them on. I pictured him biting his lip, his dark eyes sweeping over me in concern. He reached out to grab me again, to pull me back into my delusion. I shoved Ayaz out of my room and slammed the door in his face.

Dr. Peaslee said now that I understood my delusions, I had to confront them. I had to force myself to kick Ayaz out again and again, as many times as I needed to until I rewrote the memory into something that approached the truth.

Because it couldn't be true. Not if Ayaz was in Ms. West's office, violent eyes focused on me, shoulders tense as he told me I was nothing to him.

My bed creaked as I stretched out on the narrow foam mattress. The single lightbulb in the ceiling flickered out as the timer clicked over. Dread clenched my stomach as a familiar drug haze pooled in my toes, slithering up my legs, reaching with sickly fingers to clutch my body and drag me into sleep.

Sleep brought fresh horrors – the nightly visitations from the god that wasn't supposed to exist. And in the morning, I could remember nothing of my dreams except that they filled me with an unsettled horror.

Did my dreams hide answers, or were they more lies?

The fog slithered down my arms, touching my fingers with sickly warmth. It wrapped around my neck, glissading over the planes of my cheeks to dribble through my eye sockets into my mind. I slid into the troubled darkness of my dreams.

But it wasn't the god who visited me this time.

It was Trey.

He stood outside Derleth Academy, on the grass in front of the gymnasium wall. Behind him, the enormous penis we'd graffitied there in red paint glowed under the moonlight. He ran a hand through his dark hair, and the light streaked it with crimson. His stark beauty drew my breath – the weeks of starvation from the sight of him had made me desperate.

But he wasn't real – he was only my mind trying to betray me.

"Get out of my dreams." I folded my arms, wondering as I did with the faint detachment of one who dreams, how I knew I was dreaming, how I thought that I had any control in this place.

I'm dreaming because Trey is here. Not only that, but he was looking at me like he actually gave a fuck. The concern in his icicle eyes made my chest constrict. Even though I knew it wasn't real, I couldn't stop faint hope glimmering at the edges of my mind.

"Hazel." Trey's eyes swept over me, and the look on his face called me to run to him and throw myself into his arms. It took all my self-control to cement myself in place.

"I'm not supposed to think about you anymore. I can't get better if I cling to this idea that you and I—"

"Just shut up for a moment and listen. I don't know how much time we have." Trey strode toward me, his long, toned legs covering the field between us in a few steps. He didn't stop until he stood in front of me – dangerously close, his body calling to me with intense heat. "You haven't exactly been easy to reach."

"What do you mean?" I said the words carefully, testing them on my tongue. In the dream world, the fog no longer claimed my limbs or my mind. I could move freely, talk freely, but I wasn't allowed to believe anything that happened here. "Why have you been trying to reach me? I'm nothing to you."

Trey's eyes swam with desperate anger. "I don't know what my father has done to you or where he's taken you, but we're working on a plan to bust you out. Can you tell me anything about where you are?"

"No. You're a figment of my disturbed mind, trying to get me to resist treatment. If I tell you anything, you'll just twist it all around and make things worse for me, because that's what my mind does now—"

I yelped as Trey grabbed my wrist. He yanked me forward, dragging me off balance so I staggered against him. His chest pressed against mine and his powerful scent – his fresh blossom and cypress tang touching my tongue like a drug. My heart leaped as the heat of his body seared me through my blazer. His heart raced alongside mine, thudding in my ears. "Does *this* feel like a figment of your disturbed mind?"

"Yes," I whispered, my defenses slipping. Trey's eyes burned with a fire that consumed the ice inside him.

"Fuck," he growled, and his lips met mine with fury and fire. He wrapped his hand around my neck, pressing my face to his, devouring me like he'd walked across a desert and I was the first water.

As we kissed, warmth rose through my body, starting in a deep spot between my legs and flaring through my stomach to dance across my chest. A flame inside me that had been cold and dead leaped to life once more. The flame soared through my limbs, pooling in my palms, building to a fiery force that burst through my skin, soaring across the sky.

And I *knew*.

This dream *was* real.

Somehow, I was really outside the school, kissing Trey Bloomberg. He was speaking to me and touching me through my dream. His strong hands caressed my arms. His lips drew fire across mine with urgent need.

I broke the kiss and pulled away, my eyes wide. A burning grass smell itched my nostrils, and the crackling sound distracted me from the heat in my arms. Trey turned to see what I was looking at. He jumped at the trail of flame that snaked across the grass, moving toward the wall.

"Fuck." He glared at me. "What have you done?"

I put my hands on my hips. "Don't blame me. You're the one in my dream. How is that possible, by the way?"

A smile tugged on the edges of Trey's hard mouth. He dragged me toward the edge of the field, his fingers digging into my arm. "I've been praying."

"Huh?"

That smile made the fire inside me flicker to life again. "I prayed to the god. I figured it worked so well for Christians and Muslims all these years, it was about time the guy downstairs owed me something for what he'd taken away. I was lying out here under the stars, praying that I could talk to you, that I could know that you were alive. I must've fallen asleep, because the next thing I'm kind of floating through all these weird thoughts and visions that weren't mine. It was all these random faces – Ayaz and Quinn and some dude with a gap-toothed smile and paint on his face and a woman who looked like an older version of you, only she was screaming. And then they all kind of melted together and I was back here and so were you."

"The god sent you into my dreams." I still didn't quite believe it.

"Yeah, and I'm never doing it again because your head is *really* messed up."

I laughed. "This is the nicest dream I've had in a very long time. If you really are Trey, then why are you kissing me?"

"Because..." his mouth twisted, as though there were things he wanted to say but he couldn't find the words. He sighed. "I don't know how much time we have. We need to share what we know. After you jumped out the window, my father grabbed your phone off the table. He took me away to some dark corner of the school. He tried everything to get me to tell him where you were. He even tried to bargain with me. And when that didn't work, he..." A shudder ran through Trey's body. "You don't want to know what he did. But neither Quinn nor I would give them anything, I swear. They didn't like that. We're still here at school, but they took away all our privileges – our rooms, our Club membership, our access to the common room, everything."

"What about Ayaz?" My breath hitched.

Trey didn't answer. "It's not important now. Where are you? Did you get to Zehra?"

"No. There was a cave-in. Zehra wasn't there. She could've been caught in it... I waited all night. That's why I came back."

Trey shook my shoulders so hard my brain wobbled inside my skull. His eyes blazed. "You never should have come back. But where are you now?"

"I'm in the Dunwich Institute, of course. Because I'm cuckoo bananas."

Trey swore. "You've been right here in Arkham this whole time? Fuck my father."

"Gross. No, thanks."

Trey's cold smile lit up my heart. He drew himself back from the rage that threatened to carry him over the edge, squaring his shoulders and tightening his jaw – that look he always got before he blew everyone away in class. "Agreed. Okay, so you're at Dunwich. And they haven't hurt you?"

"Not really. They restrained me after I bit a nurse, but it probably hurt her more. She bled everywhere." Trey looked aghast, and I laughed. "They just give me lots of drugs. They're fixing all my broken memories."

"What broken memories?"

I poked him in the ribs. "Like you. Like Ayaz. He told me we'd never been together, but I have all these feelings..."

"Of course. That makes sense. They can't hurt you physically because they don't want to hurt the god, but if they alter your mind, they can control you." His thumbs dug into my shoulders. "Hang in there, Hazel. We're getting you out."

"How do you plan on doing that? You can't leave the school, unless that's another of my broken memories."

"I'll find a way."

He said the words with such fierce assurance that I believed him. I believed this dream boy who I'd created in my mind would come and save me. My chest soared with hope I knew I shouldn't feel.

I shook my head. I couldn't indulge this. Dr. Peaslee said it wasn't healthy. "Don't bother. I'm here because I'm sick. They're going to make me better. I had all these hallucinations about you, about us, about gods and monsters and rats in the walls—"

"They weren't hallucinations. They were real." Trey kissed me again. "What we have is real."

"Of course you'd say that. You don't want me to take the drugs and stop hallucinating you—"

"Is this a hallucination?" Trey grabbed my arm and swung me hard against him. His fierce kiss burned through my soul, his lips rough, possessive, burning with unchecked need, with a desperation that pulled me under his spell...

I woke up, my whole body drenched in sweat, the ghost of Trey's kiss sizzling across my lips.

I replayed the dream in my mind. Trey's touch had felt incredibly real. Moving slowly, swimming against the tide of drugs sweeping across my mind, I held up my wrist. My fingers trailed over crescent-shaped dents where his nails had dug into my skin.

Real.

But then, dreams always felt real, didn't they? According to Dr. Peaslee, my whole life since I arrived at Derleth Academy was one weird-ass dream. The drugs they had me on probably made Trey seem more real, more Technicolor.

I rubbed at the crescents. A faint, familiar smell wafted across my nostrils. Spring herbs, wild-blossoms, fragrant cypress wood – light and airy and calming.

Trey's scent.

I sucked in a breath, letting the taste of him linger on my tongue. Through the high, barred window, the moon traced a path over the cinder-block walls, illuminating the pits and scratches from the other inmates who'd had this room before me.

For the first time, I truly *saw* the great deception. I'd fallen right into their trap.

Trey was right. I wasn't crazy. I'd been set up by Vincent Bloomberg to get me out of the way without breaking the oath Ms. West had made with the god. By making me believe that I was insane, they could nullify me without having to hurt me at all. It was genius. Top marks to Vincent for his imagination.

I slotted the pieces together to form a grotesque image. I'd had those dreams where I'd seen myself as the bully terrorizing the school. Ms. West had convinced me that was what happened, but she did have a god who could control dreams on her side.

They knew I wouldn't believe them unless one of the guys turned on me. If they'd threatened Trey and Quinn, they would have put the screws to Ayaz as well. I couldn't believe he would bow to them, but maybe he'd had no choice.

Or maybe he wanted to hurt me. Maybe this was his plan all along.

I stared down at my blank wrist, where the Elder sign tattoo had been. That was the one part of the deception I couldn't put together. No one except the guys had touched me before they dragged me to Ms. West's office. How could they remove a tattoo without me even noticing?

Ayaz is the one who gave me the tattoo.

I pressed my finger to the scar from the fire – that remnant of my past that reminded me of what I was capable of. I drew strength from what I knew now – that Trey and Quinn were fighting for me, that evil people thought they had beaten me, and that I wasn't crazy. At least, not in the way they expected.

It was time for Vincent Bloomberg and the Deadmistress to learn what happened to people who crossed Hazel Waite.

CHAPTER TWO

Now that I could see the deception for what it was, I couldn't throw myself into therapy with my previous abandon. I tried to pretend everything was normal, but every time Dr. Peaslee probed into 'the demons of my past' and the 'traumatic experiences I'd suffered,' all I could see was Vincent Bloomberg leering over his back – the puppetmaster pulling the strings. I wasn't giving that bastard any more ammunition to use against me.

This was *war*.

Even though I was a decent-enough actor, Dr. Peaslee literally had a degree in sniffing out deceptions. He spotted my change in temperament after a couple of sessions and ordered me into his office.

"You were doing so well, Hazel. I don't understand what happened. You can't keep resisting treatment. When faced with overwhelming proof from teachers, friends, and classmates that you've been suffering delusions of persecution, you refuse to let go." He clasped his hands in front of him, tilting his head to the side in this way he did to make himself feel more approachable.

I'm sick of fucking fake people pretending to be on my side.

I refused to meet his gaze. Instead, I watched the monitor

behind his head, which he'd foolishly angled in such a way as to give me a sideways view if I leaned back in my chair ever so slightly. The screen was divided into squares, and each square showed a video feed from an inmate's cell. It was too far away and too slanted for me to identify individuals, but I recognized the rounded safety furniture and bare block walls.

No privacy. Nothing sacred. Something about seeing those video feeds reminded me of Trey's room at school, of the college prospectus I'd pulled from his bedside table, the one where he'd scrawled NO FUTURE. NO HOPE. NO TOMORROW across the photographs of happy students. Derleth was a prison where Big Brother watched every move, where even the Kings of the school had to hold their secrets tight.

Dr. Peaslee was still talking. "...Ms. West has placed you in my care, and I made her a promise that I would cure you of these delusions. As your medical professional, I have no choice but to recommend a more permanent treatment."

My eyebrow lifted. "What treatment is this?"

"Researchers at Arkham General Hospital are on the fore-front of medical research in the area of the brain. They've been able to connect a specific area of the frontal cortex to specific mental conditions, including the kind of trauma-induced halluci-nations and delusions you're experiencing. By removing those areas, we've able to completely cure the patients of their psychosis."

His words sent a chill down my spine. "You're talking about... a lobotomy?"

Dr. Peaslee chuckled, as if jamming an icepick into my brain was somehow a laughing matter. "No, no. We don't use that word today. Lobotomies, as performed by Victorian doctors like Free-man, were barbaric and unsafe. Now, we understand much more about how the brain works. The procedure is entirely safe and performed under anesthetic. I will be the doctor operating, and I have one of the highest success rates in the country."

"The highest success rate in experimental lobotomies? No thanks." My head swam. No fucking way was this guy getting anywhere near my grey matter. "I refuse this treatment."

"I'm afraid that since you're a minor and are no longer of sound mind, you cannot make medical decisions for yourself. Your guardian has approved the procedure."

"My guardian?" I snorted. "I don't have a guardian, unless you've somehow found the sperm donor who impregnated my mother."

Peaslee steepled his fingers. "When you entered Derleth Academy, the state of Pennsylvania signed over your guardianship to Ms. Hermia West. She feels this operation would be in your best interests."

Of course she does. It was another way to get around the pact we made. According to the rules we'd agreed to, she wasn't allowed to hurt me until the end of the year, but that didn't mean this guy couldn't come in with his ice pick. She must've decided it didn't matter how much that hurt the god as long as I was out of her way.

Which meant I was an even bigger threat than I realized.

A familiar rage bubbled up inside me. It started in my stomach as a slow simmer, the heat rising through my chest to settle over my heart. That someone who was supposed to be looking out for me – for all her students – had the power to do this and that fucking weasels like Peaslee let them all get away with it made my blood boil.

They're not going to get away with it for long.

"So carving up my brain is in my best interests? Some guardian." I stood up. My palms burned with heat. "I'm not doing it."

"This isn't a matter for discussion, Hazel. Your operation is scheduled for two weeks time. I'll be visiting you within the next couple of days for some preliminary tests. I suggest you use the interim to get used to the idea. I can give you some information leaflets to read, if that will help you come to terms with it?"

The heat buzzed against my skin, flames licking the undersides of my palms. "You think a fucking leaflet is going to make this *okay?*"

"Hazel, you look distressed. Perhaps I should have someone take you back to your room. You can skip therapy today—"

The heat burst from my palms. The rage flared inside me, rushing along my arms and hurtling from my fingers, completely beyond my control.

Dr. Peaslee's computer sparked. He shoved his chair back just as flames leaped from the keyboard. A burning plastic smell filled the room.

Satisfaction replaced the rage as I watched Peaslee cower in the corner, his eyes wide as sparks rained from his monitor like some kind of fucked-up fireworks display. Smoke billowed from the unit. A shrill alarm buzzed in my ears.

The satisfaction didn't last long. Dr. Peaslee moved his hand to a panel on the wall. I didn't have time to wonder what he was doing before he pushed a button and two orderlies barreled into the room, pinned me on his desk, and stuck a needle in my arm.

CHAPTER THREE

Two weeks.

That was all the time I had left before they permanently altered my brain and I believed the lies they were trying to force down my throat.

Two weeks until I lose the only weapon I had that could destroy the god and free the students of Miskatonic Prep.

Two weeks until I could no longer remember what was real and what made me who I was. They would take the only beautiful memories I had left and twist them into something ugly. They would erase Trey and Quinn and Ayaz and turn them back into my tormentors.

And that wasn't even the worst thing. Only I knew just how tightly I clung to my last shreds of sanity. Just beneath the surface, I hid something dark, something dangerous. Something I didn't understand and had hoped to banish forever.

But I couldn't hide from myself. Not any longer. Not with everything that was at stake.

The only way out of this institution was to stop trying to brace myself against the madness. I had to embrace it. I had to become someone I'd always feared, someone I'd locked down deep, because acknowledging her existence meant accepting the monster inside me.

Possessed by fire.

Whether I wanted to acknowledge her or not, my time at Derleth had revealed the cracks in my system. I couldn't control the monster when I was around Trey, Quinn, and Ayaz. When they were my bullies I'd been able to stay cool, but that was because I was used to life shitting on me. Now... they were so much more to me, and I had this warm hope flickering inside me. And that made me dangerous.

I needed a plan. I needed control.

My glimpse at Dr. Peaslee's computer screen showed the cameras in our rooms were angled in such a way that there was one small corner they didn't quite reach – in our bathroom stalls, down beside the toilet. I figured there was probably some law about not being able to film patients (inmates) while they went to the bathroom.

That meant I had a private space where I could practice.

As soon as the orderlies locked my door and I heard their footsteps fade in the hall, I went into the bathroom, locked the door, and sat on the toilet as though I were going about my business. Casually, I snaked my hand up the wall and pushed on the air vent. It had always been open a tiny crack, just enough to send a faint breeze through the room when the wind picked up outside. That wasn't enough for my purposes. I pushed on it, but it wouldn't give any further. I gave it a good hard shove, but the thing wasn't moving. I'd have to try another way.

I flushed the toilet, washed my hands, and laid down on the bed. The mold patterns on the ceiling swirled in front of my eyes, resolving themselves into the twisted shadows that had followed me in the gymnasium. I still had no clue what those shadows were and why they had attacked me that day – if that was even what they were doing.

Miskatonic Prep had so many mysteries still to unravel. Why

did I hurt the god? Why were there so many rats scrabbling in the walls, but I'd never seen a single rodent? If the god ate souls, why were Trey and Quinn and Ayaz still so... human? But there were only two mysteries I *needed* to solve – how could I stop the Eldritch Club from sacrificing more innocents? How could I find a way to give back what was taken from the students of Miskatonic Prep?

The key in my door turned. Nurse Waterford walked in, accompanied by the beefy orderly. She held out my cup of medication. I noticed a small white pill inside that had never been there before.

She handed me the uncapped drink bottle.

"Thanks. Um... it's so stuffy in here," I waved my hand in front of my face, then pointed to the small, barred window high up on the wall. "Is there any way we could open the window? I'm feeling faint."

Nurse Waterford exchanged a lingering glance with the orderly. She wasn't the empathetic type, but she might have heard about what happened in Dr. Peaslee's office and assumed I was shaken up. She shook her head. "Not in this room. But James will open the vent in your bathroom. That's the best I can do, I'm afraid."

Fine by me. I tipped the cup of pills into my mouth as the orderly fiddled with the vent and finally managed to crack it open. Now I had ventilation. Hopefully, it would be enough to get rid of any smoke before it set off the fire alarms.

I set down the water bottle. The orderly checked my open palms, then grabbed my neck and wrenched my head back. Nurse Waterford nodded. Satisfied I'd swallowed every last pill, they let me go. The door slammed behind them.

As I listened to their footsteps disappearing, my fingers fiddled with the edge of my sleeve, touching the tiny pills in their hiding place. It hadn't occurred to them to check up my sleeve, where I'd unpicked a few stitches and slipped the pills inside the hem. Just one of the sleight-of-hand tricks Dante taught me.

I hopped down from the bed and sat on the toilet again. *Plink plink plink.* I dropped all the pills into the water. Trey's voice trembled against the inside of my head. I wondered if I'd dream of him tonight.

I hoped I would.

But dreams could wait. I needed to practice. This monster was going to learn some self-control.

CHAPTER FOUR

I started small, tearing off squares of toilet paper, laying them on the cold tile floor, and thinking about things that made me angry until my palms felt hot. It wasn't difficult, not when I pictured Ayaz's cold eyes and the way he had turned on me, throwing the night we'd shared back in my face.

Square after square of toilet paper went up in flames before my eyes. I stopped when I could smell the smoke in the air. Even with the vent open, the smoke alarm was only by the door, and I couldn't risk setting it off. I rubbed my palms together, trying to shake off any residual heat, then crawled into bed. I closed my eyes, hoping Trey would visit my dreams. Or Quinn. My heart ached for his silliness and total disregard for rules or propriety. I longed to hear him called me 'Hazy' in his carefree way.

But I couldn't sleep. All night I tossed and turned, thinking about those squares of toilet paper immolating, thinking about another fire that started with a spark and a whoosh of rage and flame and ended with two urns filled with ashes.

The next day, I had to wait until after breakfast and an inane arts and crafts class that reminded me painfully of Ayaz to be left alone in my room. First, I tried individual squares again, making sure yesterday's progress wasn't a fluke. Next, I practiced with the same-sized squares, but moved further away. I needed to understand how close I needed to stand to start a fire. I leaned against the shower stall, watching the orange flame flicker and go out as the fire consumed its fuel. How far away could I be and still summon a flame at will?

It turned out, I could control the fire from two feet inside my bedroom. Interesting.

By the end of the week, I was sending up toilet paper pyres from the farthest corner of the room, without even looking in the direction of the bathroom. I no longer had to have visual sight of my target. I just needed to visualize it in my mind and BOOM – up in smoke it went.

Inside me, the monster clawed at my skin, its fire burning bright and hot. I'd always had some sense of the monster, some inkling of a secret hidden inside me. But I'd been running from it my whole life, trying to escape its grasp. Now, for the first time, I'd deliberately dug it up and fed it on my rage.

My mother and I had always lived on the edge of my fire, moving one step ahead of the flames. Memories flooded me as I focused on my task – Age three; I lay on the couch, listening to my mother entertain one of her clients in the tiny bedroom we shared, while down the street his car burned out. Age six; a teacher told me I wasn't allowed a second cookie, and her hair caught fire. Age ten; Mom scrimped and saved to buy us a car, but we had to sleep in it for two weeks after her deadbeat boyfriend kicked us out. One night she couldn't afford dinner for us. I got angry. The engine exploded. We were lucky to escape with our lives. The car wasn't so lucky.

I spent my whole life trying to suppress the fire, knowing that with my anger came a power that would destroy everything good that came our way. I'd never tried to test the limits of what I could do. I didn't even know if there *was* a limit.

Mom never mentioned the fires to me. We just didn't talk

about them. She kept everything light and fluffy – trying to build a fantasy world for me that would distract me from my empty stomach and the bruises on her arms from her clients. But sometimes... I'd catch her watching me with wary eyes, like she suspected me. Like she didn't know me. I never told Dante – I never had to, because when I was around him I never felt like burning anything to the ground. He made everything better.

Until I destroyed him, too.

I'd already destroyed all that was good in my life. But was I, Hazel Waite, burner of things, destroyer of worlds, powerful enough to burn an entity from across space and time? It was possible, but I needed to know for certain.

I needed to test my fire on something bigger. I needed to know how powerful I was. And I needed to know *soon*. The clock was ticking – just four days left until I was rushed off to have my brain sucked out through my nose.

During breakfast, I started a grease fire in the kitchen that sent billows of smoke over the cafeteria and caused us to be evacuated into the garden. Then, I made Dr. Peaslee's car battery explode, taking out the two cars parked either side of him in the parking lot.

Bigger. Bigger.

The more I burned, the more the flames crackled beneath my skin – a deep rage that had been bubbling for decades, for longer than I'd been at the mercy of Ms. West and Miskatonic Prep.

I wanted to burn it all.

I would have my chance.

The next afternoon, three days before I went under the knife (and probably never came back) our schedule allowed for an hour outside. Nurses would escort us around the grounds or get us involved in games of tetherball or other inane things. I was assigned to Nurse Craig, who usually opted to hand out scraps of bread for patients to throw at the apoplectic-looking ducks while she snuck away for a cigarette. Or possibly to write a romance novel. No one had ever thought to ask.

I crumbled my bread through my fingers while I watched Nurse Craig back away toward the path, hiding behind a topiary to light up her cigarette. A pile of dead leaves had been swept into the corner of the path by the gardeners.

Ten feet away, Nurse Craig rolled her head back in ecstasy, the smoke dangling from her fingers.

I turned back to the ducks. The last of my bread grew hot in my hand, the edges blackening as the heat seeped through my skin. I dropped it in the water with a splash as I flicked my hand out and aimed the flare of heat behind me. I kept walking around the lake, feigning delight as the ducks dipped and dived for the bread (clearly the institution hadn't got the memo that bread wasn't healthy for a duck's digestive system) and *thinking* the fire into being.

A whiff of burning caught my nostrils.

I didn't turn around until the commotion started. The hiss of a hose dousing the flames. The cries of the inmates, startled by orange flames leaping from the leaves. The topiary roared, as if possessed, before the flames consumed the last of their living nourishment.

"Nurse Craig, how could you be so careless?" Nurse Waterford shouted as she sprayed water over the ruined topiary. "You can't smoke outside near the leaves."

"But I wasn't anywhere near the leaves," Nurse Craig shot back. "I don't see how any ash could have possibly reached that pile."

"It was careless, not to mention against the rules. You shouldn't be smoking around the patients. I'll be informing Dr. Peaslee about this infraction." Nurse Waterford stepped back, her sodden uniform clinging to her body. She panted hard as she stared at the charred circle on the path.

I'd set that fire from a hundred feet away, from across the

other side of the pond, and it hadn't felt like any great effort. I was confident that I hadn't even touched the limit of what I could do. As soon as the flames left my hand, they no longer listened to me – but I didn't need them to.

All I needed them to do was burn a path to freedom.

CHAPTER FIVE

I had two more outdoor exercise sessions before my operation. On the next one, I begged to be put into the group who would walk a circuit of the grounds. Nurse Waterford looked skeptical, but Dr. Peaslee patted me on the shoulder.

"Hazel has been a model patient these last couple of weeks," he said. "I think she deserves a treat before her big stay at the hospital. Isn't that right, Hazel?"

I hope you choke on a diseased dick. I nodded. "Sure. That'd be nice. Thank you."

I trailed behind the group, my arm linked with a slight girl of around twelve named Naomi who dragged her feet and stared around with vacant wide-eyed innocence. Was she a victim of Peaslee's not-a-lobotomy? I tried not to shudder as I held her cool skin.

"Pretty," Naomi said in a breathless whisper, but I didn't know what she referred to. I followed Naomi's gaze as the nurse pointed out opening flowers and animal statues hidden in the bushes. While the other inmates exclaimed over a tiger statue they'd seen a hundred times before, I scanned the perimeter for a weakness I could exploit.

A high stone wall surrounded the institute, overgrown in places by centuries of creeping vines. Patients must have tried to scale it in the past, because a line of barbed wire encircled the top of the wall. *Yeah, right, we're not prisoners here.* I wasn't escaping that way unless I could get my hands on some wire cutters.

Twin iron gates barred the front entrance, and a guard on duty 24/7 checked every vehicle that came in or out. I indulged a brief fantasy of hiding out in Dr. Peaslee's car with a weapon I'd point at his throat, forcing him to drive me out of the compound... but then we stepped into the kitchen garden to see the herbs and vegetables the inmates tended, and I saw the perfect escape route.

The institute's kitchen was a modern steel and concrete extension sandwiched between the old asylum building and the boundary wall. At the rear of the building, a small loading area for supplies was currently occupied with a delivery van. The kitchen staff unloaded crates of milk and instant mashed potatoes. The driver shut the doors and drove out through a small gate.

A *wooden* gate.

Beside me, Naomi whimpered. I relaxed my grip, realizing I'd been squeezing her hand so tight I'd crushed her fingers. Nurse Waterford frowned at me, and I plastered a huge smile on my face. This time, it wasn't even a fake smile.

Back in my room that night, I dropped my pills into the toilet again. *Plink, plink, plink.* For the first time since I'd been imprisoned here, I imagined the faux concern of Ms. West and Vincent Bloomberg as they manipulated me to be their scapegoat, and I allowed myself a tiny smile at their expense.

You thought you rendered me powerless, but you're about to find out just how wrong you are.

Trey appeared in my dreams that night, but I couldn't reach him. I watched through a window at school as Ms. West dragged him into a classroom. Inside, his father loomed over him, his face twisted with malice. Behind him stood Damon Delacorte, grinning a smile that lacked all of his son's warmth as he brandished a baseball bat.

"Trey, no!"

My fingers clawed at the window, but it was locked tight, the glass unyielding to my fists. Damon advanced, and the lights flickered out. Inside the classroom was darkness – the kind of darkness that had form and malice, that we had all been taught to fear. I banged on the window and called Trey's name until my voice was hoarse. But I couldn't penetrate the darkness...

I woke in a cold sweat, my hands coiled into aching fists, my throat scratchy, not sure where my dreams stopped and reality began. Was Trey all right? Were they hurting him? Did the lights go out so Damon could have his fun in the darkness, or because the god was there in the shadows, watching and waiting?

I have to get out of here. I have to save them all.

I dressed in my grey institution slacks and hoodie, tapping my feet with impatience while I waited for the orderlies to unlock the door. At breakfast, I scraped my porridge bowl clean and asked for seconds. Naomi saw me at the table and scooted away from me. In arts and crafts, I drew a picture of a nurse burning at the stake. *Let Dr. Peaslee analyze that.*

During therapy, Dr. Peaslee noted with satisfaction that he'd seen me walking around outside. "You seem to be accepting your place here, Hazel."

Like fuck I am. I shrugged. "I've been thinking about what you said, about the surgery. I'm scared, but I don't want to fight. I want to be better."

He could barely keep the pleasure out of his voice. "You are remarkable, Hazel. I admire your strength and willingness to embrace the process, even when you feel afraid."

"Thank you, sir." I flashed him a smile worthy of an Oscar. "After the operation, will I get to go back to school?"

I didn't mistake the flicker of deception in Peaslee's eyes as he smiled again. "Of course. Maybe not right away – we'll have to bring you back here to monitor for a few weeks. But there's no reason you can't finish out the year with your classmates. I bet they'll be glad to see you're okay."

You're lying. I had no idea how much Peaslee knew about the school and what went on there, but he was definitely covering up whatever vile thing they planned for me next. Luckily, I wasn't going to stick around to find out what it was.

Warmth itched in my fingers as I rejoined the other inmates and we were led outside for our exercise. Again, I asked to be in the group walking the perimeter. I needed to time this just right.

I tried to join hands with Naomi again, but she shrunk away, so I was stuck with an elderly guy named George who drooled a lot and had fits. I sat next to George in art therapy, but he gave no indication he remembered who I was.

As we wandered down the path toward the duck pond, my hand in George's clammy one, I drew up all the rage I'd hidden inside me. It wasn't difficult – all I had to do was recall the horrors of Derleth Academy and heat flared along my arms, reaching into my fingers and swirling around the tips. It pooled in my palms like raindrops finding the cracks between cobbles, until it grew uncomfortable for George and he yanked his hand away. "Too hot," he mumbled at his shoes.

I pictured Ayaz's face twisted with contempt, the way he'd looked at me as if I was a bug – so insignificant I wasn't even worth squashing. They had taken one of the most precious things in my life and twisted it into something ugly, and for that, I would feel no remorse for what I was about to do. I held that image in my mind until the fire burned it to ash. When there was nothing left of me but my anger, I directed my palms toward the dormitories and remembered the way my sheets twisted around our legs as Ayaz held me in my dorm that night, the way the old mattress groaned under his weight as he'd climbed on top of me, the warmth he brought to that cold, damp cell and my even colder heart.

I *pushed* with my mind, driving the memory into the flames until it smoldered with my rage. And I thought of other mattresses I'd seen – narrow beds in cells that held the broken bodies and minds of my fellow inmates. And I thought of what they might have been forced to endure under the care of Dr. Peaslee – all in the name of silencing their cries.

And just like that, the heat burned through my palms, leaving my body and flying like a hot wind of change toward the dormitories.

I had no way of knowing if it had done what I'd sought out to do. My fingers cooled, and I took George's hand again, trying to resist looking up at the building as we moved along the path. We passed under an arch of roses, stopping so inmates could stoop to sniff the fragrant flowers. I lifted my chin and bent towards a red rose – the color the same crimson as the highlights in Trey's hair when they caught the light.

The color of blood.

I sniffed the air. Beyond the cloying scent of the rose was something acrid – the faintest whiff of burning on the breeze.

That was my first clue. We continued our walk, passing through the entrance to the kitchen garden. The cook stopped snipping the rosemary bushes as the alarm sounded from inside. Nurse Craig stopped in her tracks, unsure of her next move.

Nurse Waterford burst from the fire exit, a trail of black smoke snaking around her heels. She sprinted across the court-yard toward us, waving her arms.

"Don't go near the buildings!"

"What's happened?" Nurse Craig called.

"What does it look like? Get the patients under the rotunda." Doors banged as the orderlies and other staff exited the building, pushing patients in wheelchairs toward the rotunda that served as the emergency meeting point. I cast my eyes up to the second story, where the first tendrils of smoke curled from the narrow dorm windows, turned black from the chemicals in the mattresses. "The fire department is on their way."

"But what happened? How could we have a fire?" Nurse Craig seemed rooted in place, frozen by the improbability of the event.

"It doesn't make any sense!" Nurse Waterford cried, her usual stoic facade shattered. "Every mattress is ablaze. It's completely impossible."

The scream of the alarm buzzed inside my head. The nurses shoved us back toward the lawn. I pressed my burning palms together, and the large oak tree over the rotunda burst into flame.

What people never tell you about fire is that its power is mostly in its invisibility. Sure, the leaping flames tearing through the oak were frightening, but it was the heat that seared the air and robbed the oxygen that was the true malice. A wave of heat rolled off the tree, engulfing me, squeezing sweat from my body. It reminded me of the oppressive embodiment of the god's darkness – the way he could be *felt* even though he had no form.

The tree crackled as branches snapped and splintered off, ancient wood succumbing to immolation.

Nurse Craig screamed. Patients and orderlies ran in all directions as a flaming branch snapped off and crashed to the ground. In the chaos, I slipped away from the group and ducked back through the gate into the kitchen garden. I crouched behind the rosemary bush and sent a ball of fire at the wooden gate. The guard on duty leaped back as the flames made quick work of the wood. He barreled across the lawn towards the others, barking orders into his walkie-talkie. I flattened myself against the wall, my heart pounding against my chest. As soon as he was out of sight, I ran for it.

The flames had torn a hole in the wood large enough for me to pass through, if only I could get close enough to handle the heat. I sucked in a breath and lunged for the gate. Heat rolled over my body, a hand of caution pushing me back, reminding me what fire could do when it touched skin. I steadied myself, closed my eyes against the wall of flame, and sprinted through the hole.

Heat engulfed me, bringing with it pain that tore at my chest and roared in my ears. I imagined I saw my mother's face at the window, her mouth open in a silent scream as an orange halo framed her head. I reached through the flames toward her, desperate to pull her to safety. But she was unreachable. Gone to the angels, where they could place a real halo on her head while I burned up down below.

And then I lurched forward, releasing myself from the fire's possession.

My eyes flew open as I rolled across gravel. I lay in the middle of a narrow access road, flanked by towering trees. Sirens screamed from the village. Behind the walls, the Dunwich Institute burned. Good fucking riddance. I was on the right side of the fence.

I was free.

If I wanted to stay free, I had no time to stop and smell the roses. I crawled into the shadows of the trees, checking my body over for injuries. Apart from another burn on my wrist just above the scar of the first, I was untouched. Now I had to figure out what to do next.

It would take the firefighters some time to put out the blaze since it had started simultaneously in multiple rooms. By now the nurses would have realized I was missing, but I hoped they'd assume I'd run back inside or hid on the grounds and wouldn't send out a search party for some time. I needed to be as far away as possible when that happened.

I hauled myself to my feet and headed deeper into the forest, walking downhill in the direction of Arkham. The town nestled on the curve of the coast at the mouth of the peninsula, surrounded on three sides by dense forest and one side by that cold, unforgiving ocean. It was one of the earliest settlements in the area – not quite as old as Salem, but practically contemporary. In many ways, Arkham functioned much as it always had – the fishing industry provided much of the town's employment, and I got the vibe from what Ayaz told me that the residents still regarded Parris' home on the peninsula and the elite who came through with distrust. I could expect no help from the town, but I was never one to ask for help when I could do something myself. Arkham was closest, and it would have the supplies I needed immediately.

As I walked, various options of what to do next played out inside my head. I could hitch a ride to the West Coast. I could go across the border to Canada. Hell, I could try Mexico or Ireland or even Romania. Romania could be cool. As soon as an idea appeared, I held it in my head, pleased for a moment to consider how easily I could slip away from this cursed place and disappear completely, before dismissing it.

I didn't have options. I had people that needed me – Greg and Andre and Trey and Quinn and the rest of the Miskatonic students. And Ayaz. Maybe he needed me most of all.

I couldn't leave Arkham until I achieved what I set out to do.

They would all have this taste of freedom if it was the last thing I did.

The black smoke of the fire trailed down the valley after me, blanketing the village with stripes of darkness. I ducked from garden to garden, hiding behind flower pots and under porch swings, staying out of sight as much as possible until I found my way to the main street. I wandered into a corner store and pretended to be engrossed with a display of cabbages near the counter. When the shopkeeper turned her back to help a customer, I plunged my hand into the "Pennies for the Elderly" jar and drew out as many bills as I could grab. Right now, I needed it more than they did.

The next stop was a thrift store across the road. I discarded my grey clothes in the changing rooms and walked out in faded jeans, a black t-shirt, and an oversized black hoodie. When they came to look for me they'd be after a girl wearing the grey clothing of a Dunwich inmate. I wouldn't give them the chance to spot me.

I couldn't do much to change my hair right now, but the hood would hide it until I got to my next destination – Zehra's RV. I needed to know for a fact if she survived that cave-in. If she did, we could work together to bring down the entire Miskatonic Prep institution.

If not, I was on my own. What was fucking new about that?

But first, I needed to pay a visit to my jailer.

When Ayaz and I were working on our Salem project, I'd borrowed a library book about the history of Arkham, hoping it might have information about Parris and his home. It only had a couple of paragraphs about the house, but it spent an entire chapter describing the Arkham Grand – a fancy hotel on the main street. The book even spoke about the hotel receiving important guests while rich parents visited their children at Miskatonic Prep. It would be the only establishment in the town that Vincent Bloomberg would deign to stay in. I had a hunch he'd be in town for my lobotomy – he'd probably leer over my hospital bed during the operation, relishing his victory.

Not anymore.

And there it was – the Arkham Grand. I crouched behind a flowerbed, staring up at the hotel facade. The three-story building with the Georgian columns dwarfed the surrounding shops and diners. It looked a little worn around the edges now, the paint peeling in places, the windows on the upper story streaked with dirt. Like everything Vincent Bloomberg touched, it would eventually turn to ruin.

I slunk into the front lobby behind a small group of Chinese tourists wearing "I Love Massachusetts" t-shirts and ducked into the hallway before the bellman caught sight of me. In my thrift store getup, I looked more like a hoodlum than a hotel guest, and

I didn't want them to kick me out before I located Vincent's room.

I was just pondering how to figure out where he was staying when a loud voice boomed from the lobby. "I want an espresso delivered to my room. And not lukewarm like it was last time. The standards in this place have slipped to an appalling level."

"Certainly, Mr. Bloomberg." The bellman sounded harried. "We'll bring that for you right away."

I peered out from the hallway. There he was – the man who'd tried to convince me I was crazy, who'd tried to have me lobotomized, who'd hurt his own son in a hundred unforgivable ways just to hold on to power that wasn't even his. Trey's dad stood in front of the reception desk, his suit immaculate, long fingers brushing through dark hair that caught crimson highlights beneath the grimy chandelier.

I peered closer. Was Vincent Bloomberg... going grey? The sweeps of grey above his ears hadn't been there before. His face appeared older, too – more lines around his eyes, and his cheeks had a slightly sunken quality, like he'd been losing weight.

Hmmmm. Interesting.

I remembered last time I'd seen him, when he'd come to the school to complain to Ms. West about me, he'd seemed older then, too. I thought maybe it was just the harsh lighting in Ms. West's office. But he'd aged another ten years since that visit – changes too drastic to have happened in only a couple of weeks.

Is it me? I assumed that the power the god gave to the senior Eldritch Club members not only gave them their influence over others, but it also kept them young. That made sense since the god had effectively stolen life from their children via their souls. Perhaps it gave some of that youth back to their parents. That sounded insane, but it made as much sense as anything else that has happened since I came to Derleth.

But now, for whatever reason, that power was waning, and

Vincent wore that evidence in his cavernous cheeks and crinkled eyes.

Something... or someone... is disrupting the god's power.

I wondered if, despite their efforts, my time in the Dunwich Institute had been hurting the god. Did a cosmic deity respond to psychological torture in the same way it did to physical? Apart from when I saw Trey, I hadn't felt the god's dreams – perhaps because of my distance from the school or the drugs they'd been giving me – but Vincent's grey hair gave me hope that I was still influencing the deity in some way.

"And a copy of the *New York Times*, one that's not stained with sticky fingers like this morning's *Wall Street Journal*," Vincent barked. He spun on his heel, turning toward me. I yanked my head back behind the column, but not before he strode with purpose in the direction of the hallway.

Shit.

His room must be on this floor. If he walked past me he'd be certain to recognize me. He had to know by now that I'd escaped. That was probably what he was so pissed about.

I spied a maid's closet and raced toward it, yanking the door open and diving inside just as his footsteps approached. I buried myself in a pile of starched linen, peering out through the cracked door, my breath in my throat. He stomped by, so close I could have reached out and grabbed him. The thought gave me a perverse thrill, but I held back. I had something worse in store for him.

As soon as Vincent's footsteps faded around the corner, I stepped out of the closet and crept after him, pressing myself up against the wall and leaning out just far enough to see him open the door to room 6. He slammed it behind him, the *BANG* shattering the silence along the quiet hall.

I ducked back behind the wall, my heart hammering. I looked both ways, and seeing no one else about, I stepped out into the hall, crossed to Vincent's door, and pressed my ear against the thick wood.

I didn't expect to be able to hear anything, but Vincent's angry voice carried. "She's not dead. We would know it if she was dead. So she must have escaped."

There was a pause before he said, "I don't need you to explain it. I don't give a fuck about your excuses. I just need you to sort it out. Do what you have to do. I'll make sure you're shielded from any fallout. But Hazel Waite must be found. I'll have my security team call you. They'll set up a perimeter. She can't have got far, but we need to make certain she doesn't leave the state."

More silence. He was on the phone, probably to Dr. Peaslee. My knee ached and the burn on my leg smarted like fuck. I adjusted my position, crouching lower, straining to hear more as the flame inside me licked at my skin once more.

The fire became an itch inside my skin, a desperate possession by my rage that sought release though the only possible avenue – burning Vincent Bloomberg to ash.

Soon. Soon. But first I need to know what he's saying. I need to know if Trey and the others are in danger.

Vincent barked into the phone again. "That's a terrible idea. The police will make a mess of it, and I'm not making any public appearances right now. I need this gone without drawing attention to the school. I'm a busy man, Peaslee. I've told you what needs to happen. Just get it—"

"What are you doing?" A voice behind me demanded.

CHAPTER SIX

The bellhop peered down at me from behind a stack of towels. I jumped. My shoulder slammed into the door. Inside the room, Vincent Bloomberg swore. The phone clattered on its cradle.

Panic sliced through me. I opened my mouth to make an excuse, but there was nothing I could say. The bellhop must've noticed my deer-in-the-headlights expression, or maybe he'd just had an earful of Vincent Bloomberg bossing him around. He pointed down the hall. "There's a fire exit on the right. Go. I'll distract him."

You don't have to tell me twice. Heart hammering, I fled down the hall and shoved open the fire exit just as Vincent's door slammed open and he started shouting that he'd have the bellhop fired.

I hit the woods on the edge of the town and accepted their sheltered embrace, moving between the trees as I headed out along the main road.

Why didn't you burn him?

I turned the question over and over in my mind as the fire blazed beneath my skin, flaring up and dying away as my anger at Vincent, at my own actions, waxed and waned.

When that bellhop startled me, the fire dropped its possession of me. I took his offer of escape without hesitation because he was innocent, and I didn't think I could set Vincent alight without hurting others inside the hotel.

Controlling the fire was more than just pointing it in a direction. I had to master my emotions or more innocent people would be hurt.

But is anyone truly innocent? The fire bit back at me. I didn't have an answer for that. All I knew was that Vincent Bloomberg was still alive, for now, and that meant I was still in danger.

No cars passed me as the road narrowed and started its climb up the peninsula, but I didn't step out from the trees until I came to a sign that read, "Arkham Camping and RV Park." *Hopefully, this is the place.*

A path sloped down toward a small stream surrounded by a few dilapidated RVs and a couple of tents. A woman slumped in a beach chair in front of her tent, her eyes vacant as she peered down into the stream, a limp fishing line fixed between her legs. The place was eerily quiet, apart from the faint sound of David Bowie singing from behind one of the locked RV doors.

As I passed by the David Bowie RV, I noticed a small Turkish flag in the window of a battered Airstream parked under a bent oak. My heart skipped. *This must be it.* Not knowing what I'd find on the other side of the door, I knocked.

No one answered.

I cupped my hands against the glass window and peered inside. Everything looked dark and static. The shadows remained silent and still. "Zehra?" I called, knocking again. "Are you in there?"

Nothing. My chest tightened. I remembered the cave-in, the way the ground rumbled as a rock shelf collapsed, blocking the cave entrance. Zehra was supposed to be there, but she wasn't. Did she just not show up, or was she trapped behind the stones, or had something else happened to her...

"Zehra, it's Hazel. I need to talk to you. I need to know what happened at the cave—"

"She's gone, kid."

I whirled around. The fishing woman stood behind me, leaning against a cane made of driftwood. Green eyes swept over me, no longer vacant but sparked with intelligence. "She hasn't been back to that RV in several weeks."

Several weeks? My heart plunged further. I knew why. I'd waited and called for her after I discovered the cave-in, but Zehra hadn't come... because she'd been there already, in the cave, waiting for me. I'd kept myself awake all night hoping Zehra had been delayed somehow, that she'd escaped deeper into the tunnels and found a way out. But if she hadn't come back here...

Finding her RV had been a long shot, but I pinned so much hope on it. Zehra was the only one who could do something with the information I had. The keys we'd cast for Ms. West's laboratory were probably long gone. I'd left them in the lockbox on the cave – I supposed I could go back to look for them, but not right now. Fuck that. If I could have spoken to Zehra and found out the name of the woman she'd contacted, then we might have had a chance...

If the Eldritch Club hadn't killed her in that cave-in.

I squeezed my eyes shut, willing the rage to simmer down. Burning down Zehra's RV wouldn't help bring her back. And there might be something here that could help me.

How long was I inside the Dunwich Institute? What had happened at the school since then? Were Greg and Andre okay? What about Trey and Quinn and Ayaz? I needed to know.

Angry tears pricked at the corners of my eyes. Zehra didn't deserve to die like that. She had been on the run since she was a teenager, because she was the only student to ever escape

Derleth. She'd only just found her brother. She was a fucking cool person and I'd wanted her as a friend. I'd never had a girlfriend before. And now I never would.

Yet another innocent person dead because of me.

I shouldn't have come here.

No. Don't do that. Don't wallow in self-pity. You didn't kill her. Vincent Bloomberg did, somehow.

I didn't believe for a single moment that cave-in was an accident. I left the phone on the coffee table in Trey's room. On it, the text message I sent to Zehra, telling her to meet me and when. Maybe they had that trap laid for years. Maybe the god was the one who shook the earth and made the stones fall, or maybe Vincent had dynamite. But either way, they'd killed Ayaz's sister to stop her getting the information I had.

I slumped against the screen door. The handle caught against my waistband and flipped down. The door swung open, sending me toppling inside.

"She left this open?" I glanced back at the woman, but she'd wandered off to check on her fish, cackling under her breath.

I peered around Zehra's home. Her bubbly personality came through on every surface, from the bright green and yellow flags strung across the kitchen to the half-finished crossword puzzle on the table. I pulled open drawers and cupboards, shifting through bright plastic bowls and cups and a mountain of books – art history, medical journals, popular novels in English and Turkish.

I sucked in a breath between my teeth. Zehra had left everything in a jumble, like she'd be back any moment. Her life – frozen in time. Because of Vincent, she'd never got to have a real life. She'd outsmarted assassins and lived under the radar when she should have been batting her long eyelashes at besotted guys in college.

Ayaz. She'd done all this for Ayaz.

Now she was gone, and it was up to me to pick up where she'd ended. Even if it ended up destroying me, even if it broke me into a million pieces, I had to save the boy who tried to doom me.

At least there were things here I could use. I pulled open drawers, inspecting neat piles of warm clothing – leggings, thermal sweaters, woolen socks. Boxes of condoms torn open (at least she'd been having some fun). I stuffed clothes into a backpack, adding candy bars and packets of ramen noodles. A hunting knife. A torch. Underneath her bed, I found a small, locked leather suitcase.

What's this?

The combination lock had four rows of letters. I tried the word AYAZ. It opened with a click, revealing a stack of articles, academic papers, scribbled notes, old books, and what looked like occult drawings. A handwritten letter on top caught my eye.

> If you have possession of this case, I am dead. That sucks, but I hope at least I made a beautiful corpse and no one brings me back as a zombie, like they did to Ayaz. Here is all the research I have on Rebecca Nurse and her magic and what went down at Miskatonic Prep. Please, use it to help my brother.

I spread out the documents on the floor, holding each one up and trying to discern its significance. Zehra had made it easy, sticking Post-it notes in the books to highlight certain pages and writing her notes across the documents.

Zehra had been tracing the family lineage of Rebecca Nurse – particularly along the female line, which couldn't have been easy since history didn't exactly keep accurate records of the lives of women. From what I could make out, Rebecca left Parris' coven and Arkham somewhere in the 1750s. She seemed to move around a bit – there were records of her appearing all along the west coast. Rebecca wrote occult pamphlets about souls as magical energy and how magicians could manipulate them, which she distributed through underground networks. Zehra had two of the originals in the box, their corners torn, the yellowed paper crumbling to the touch. According to the receipts also nestled in the box, she'd paid a pretty price for them. Zehra had even more pages photocopied and bound together, but of course, beyond identifying the sigil I'd seen in the cave, I didn't understand a word of it.

Rebecca was arrested at least three times on suspicion of witchcraft and blasphemy, although acquitted. She died along with twenty-five in a fire that consumed a church in the settlement of New Cambridge.

Fire. The flames always seemed to follow me.

Rebecca had two daughters who both married. I ran my finger down pages of Zehra's loopy handwriting as she traced both family trees. I flipped right to the end of her pad and found a page of eleven names – all women, all with birthdates in the last sixty years, all alive and living in the United States. The descendants of Rebecca Nurse.

Darkness fell as I read until my eyeballs scratched against my lids, fighting against the dying light. The bottom of the box contained material about Ms. West and Miskatonic Prep – internal hospital memos about disturbing trends with flatlining patients, followed by garbled witness statements about strange things going on in the morgue. I read the dismissal letter for Ms. Hermia West, where she was promised 'neutral references' should she be employed by another hospital. I saw minutes of Miskatonic Prep board meetings, where Ms. West's qualifications were discussed in-depth and it was decided to offer her the Headmistress' job. I saw evidence from the Teachers' Association that those qualifications were fabricated. Hermia West had never trained as a teacher.

I remembered something Trey had said last quarter. He'd wondered if the fire hadn't been an accident, if the senior Eldritch Club members had been planning something for a long time. At the time, I dismissed it because it seemed impossible –

how could so many parents conspire to do something so evil? Looking at these documents, I saw the evidence of what we'd long suspected – that Vincent and the other parents had brought Ms. West to Miskatonic deliberately, three years before the fire.

I couldn't say anything for certain. But I knew who might be able to. I flipped back through the hospital notes, searching for a name that might denote Zehra's contact. The forensic pathologist, Dr. Deborah Pratt, had given a particularly chilling eyewitness statement when she'd found Hermia West in the lab at night, conducting experiments on cadavers. Beside her report, Zehra had stuck a Post-it note with an address and phone number and initials. *This must be her.*

Deborah Pratt. The name sounded familiar. I shuffled through the other papers until I found the list of Rebecca Nurse's descendants. Sure enough, Deborah Pratt was one of the last names on the list, along with her younger sister Jessica. *That can't be a coincidence. This is all connected in some way, but how?*

I leaned against the fridge, rubbing my eyes. What was I going to do now? I could go find this Deborah woman and tell her about the icehouse laboratory, and maybe she could figure out how to reverse whatever evil Ms. West had done to the students. But that didn't solve the problem of the god under the gymnasium, or the Eldritch Club manipulating the world behind the scenes. Not to mention the fact that I didn't exactly want to help any of the Miskatonic Prep students right now, especially not the ones who betrayed me.

Ayaz's dark eyes flashed before me. How had I read him so wrong? He'd convinced me he cared about me. I'd lost my virginity to him, for fuck's sake. In the end, he had been the one to betray me. How deep was the spell Ms. West had him under?

No. I couldn't entertain the idea that Ayaz's betrayal was a trick. I didn't need that kind of hope clouding my judgment. He betrayed me just as everyone else in my life had betrayed me, and

I'd fallen right into his trap. That was what happened when you allowed yourself to care about people. You became weak.

I held up two of my fingers. A tiny flame danced between them. I watched the shadows bend around it. I would never be weak again.

CHAPTER SEVEN

I slept in Zehra's RV that night, although 'sleep' was a wildly generous word for staring at the ceiling while wild thoughts raced around in my head. I'd placed a knife from the kitchen drawer beside my pillow, but even that didn't make me feel safe.

At some point, I must have drifted off, because the next thing I knew I was back in the underground cavern of the god. Apart from its oppressive presence in its cage far below, I appeared to be alone. Flickers of sickly light played off the alien mineral veins crisscrossing the walls as I stepped out of the shadows and made my way to the edge of the platform.

I reached up, touching the ropes where they'd suspended Greg at Ms. West's command. A cold hatred pulsed in the jute. These ropes had known so much pain.

Beneath my feet, the wooden boards creaked as they swelled against their bonds. The padlock jerked as the god rattled and railed against it.

This is a dream. None of it is real.

It was supposed to frighten me, but I wasn't afraid. What could this god in this school do to me that it hadn't already done? I wanted to fuck with them. I wanted to cause a little chaos.

I bent down and slid the bolt free.

The doors fell open, clattering against the platform. A shadow rushed forth to surround me. Darkness blanketed me, of the beginning of the universe. From inside the shadow, form and substance stretched from another dimension to rake at my flesh, rolling over my body, invading every pore and orifice. I longed to slink away, but I stood my ground.

You hurt me, it seemed to be saying, although there were no words, only a sensation of speech touching the edges of my mind.

"What are you?" I screamed into the hatred. "What do you want?"

I want what you want. You and I are the same.

"I'm nothing like you! I don't steal the futures of innocent kids."

I don't understand—

A thump startled me from my dream state. I bolted upright, my breath catching in my throat as I remembered where I was. In Zehra's RV, in the woods, with no cosmic deities present. I fumbled for my knife, my fingers closing with satisfaction around the handle as I listened hard. *What was that sound?*

The still night closed in around me. I dropped the knife. *I must've imagined it. There's no one...*

Thump. Scrape... scrape.

Fuck shit fuck.

Someone... or something... was outside the RV. Right outside. I could hear breathing, heavy and hard. I palmed the knife handle again, sliding out of bed as silently as I could and flattening myself against the cabinets. My breath hitched as a shadow moved across the window, obscuring the square of pale moonlight.

A voice cursed as they tripped up over the stoop. A man.

It's probably just a drunk trying to find his way to his RV in the dark, I told myself, but I didn't believe it. The god's presence still scratched behind my eyelids. I wasn't safe anywhere, not even inside my own head.

Whoever it was, I wasn't going to wait for him to come in and rape me. Or worse.

I crept as silently as I could toward the door. Zehra's research I'd left spread everywhere muffled my steps. The man outside tried the handle, tugging it so hard the entire RV rocked, but the door remained locked. *Idiot.*

The man let out a grunt of defeat. His footsteps shuffled away, probably to try the window. I raised the knife above my shoulder and slid my hand across the door, turning the lock and pushing down the handle as silently as I could. With a click like a gunshot, the door unlocked. The shadow lurched toward the noise, and I threw the door open, barging out with knife raised and fire rising through my chest.

"Arrrrghh!" I wailed like a banshee, lunging at the man. He raised his hands to cover his face, dropping a satchel into the dirt. The moonlight caught high cheekbones and wide, terrified eyes. The knife froze midair, and I gaped.

Cowering under the window, wearing a black death metal hoodie pulled tight over a rumpled Derleth uniform... was Trey Bloomberg.

CHAPTER EIGHT

The knife clattered from my hand. Trey jerked back as the blade bounced down the steps. I managed to force air into my lungs long enough to form the words, "What the fuck are you doing here?"

"Hello to you, too." Trey tried to shove his way past me into the RV. I blocked the door with my body, which meant he pressed himself up against me instead. My breath hitched as he sizzled against me, his fingers hot as they brushed the back of my hand. Even now, he could make me feel completely turned about.

Well, fuck him.

Trey was a revenant who wasn't able to leave the school, which meant this wasn't Trey. It was an apparition, or a trick of the god, or some new horror sent from Vincent and Ms. West to torment me—

I lunged for the knife, but Not-Trey was too fast, his fingers closing around my wrist and pressing it against the wall. Heat sizzled beneath his fingers, jolting straight down my arm to warm my core.

"I'm not here to hurt you," he growled.

"Funny. You could've fooled me," I shot back, but the words

came out breathy, thick with lust. It smelled like Trey – fresh herbs and sweet cypress. It *felt* like Trey – hard and hot and immovable. I had so many questions, but my eyes fixed on those pouty lips, and I struggled to form the words.

"Hazel, it's me."

"You're not Trey. It's impossible."

"Oh, I assure you, I'm me." There was that familiar voice, thick with scorn but dripping with barely-concealed desire.

Focus, Hazel. This can't be happening. Trey can't be here. How is he here? How did he get outside the walls of the school?

"Let me inside." Not-Trey's breath brushed against my ear. "I don't want to risk anyone recognizing me."

I weighed my options. I didn't have the knife. Not-Trey had me pressed against the wall, and yet he was asking permission. Sort of. If he'd wanted to hurt me, he could've done some serious damage by now.

And Trey *did* come to me in my dreams, back at the Dunwich Institute. Maybe this was a dream. A very realistic, very lustful dream. I bit my lip and nodded.

Trey released my hand and stepped back, panting hard. I took in the sight of him – dressed in his Derleth uniform, usually immaculate but now torn at the knee and streaked with dirt. Twigs stuck out in all directions from his dark hair.

Questions burned inside my head. Fire sizzled in my veins. Who was I kidding – I wasn't going to tell him to piss off. I stepped back into the RV and held the door open. Maybe-Trey picked up his satchel from where it had fallen and stepped inside, slamming the door shut behind him.

"Thanks for—" he started, but I cut him off.

"If you're Trey, how did you get outside the walls of the school?"

Trey dropped his satchel on the RV's tiny table. It made a heavy *thump*. He folded down the edges to reveal an enormous chunk of stone, engraved with a circular sigil about the size of a dinner plate.

"You cut this out of one of the caves?"

He nodded. "It was Ayaz who figured it out, although he doesn't know it yet. He did a presentation for alchemy class about a magician who used a sigil to trap a demon inside. The magician then moved the sigil all over the world, bringing the demon with it so it other covens could use it in their rituals. I wondered if I moved the boundary sigils, I could extend the boundary of the school as far as I wanted."

"Clever."

Trey dared a smile.

"I didn't mean you. I was talking about Ayaz." I leaned against the wall and folded my arms. "It must've taken some serious muscle to chip out that sigil."

Trey grunted. He held up his hand. I gasped at the lattice of scars across his palm and fingers. Hands that were usually smooth and soft, used to being waited on, now bore the marks of manual work. It was a sign of his desperation. "I've been working it free ever since I found you in your dream. I stole a chisel and hammer from the maintenance shed, but it took so long to walk out to the boundary I could only do a bit at a time before I had to head back to school."

I touched the edge of the stone, feeling the bumps of the chisel marks beneath my fingers. My chest tightened in that way it did when I was around the guys, when one of them did something that might've been considered sweet if I wasn't so completely fucked up.

I wasn't the girl guys chisel sigils out of caves for.

But apparently I was. Because there was the sigil, and there was Trey fucking Bloomberg, standing in the RV in vivid Technicolor, and he smelled *so good*.

"Why did you come looking for me? I'd have thought the first thing you'd do once you were free was to go on a complete bender or apply for college."

"Why did I come for you?" Trey rested a hand on the wall behind my head. His breath feathered my face. That fire inside me leaped and danced against my chest. "Because I heard Dunwich burned down and you'd disappeared. I had to see if you were okay, and I figured if you escaped you'd try to find Zehra. Fuck, Hazel. After everything we've been through, you still don't trust me?"

His words pinched in my chest. I tried to slide out from beneath him, but his bulk blocked my path. "Zehra's *dead*, and I just escaped from an asylum your dad threw me in. They were going to lobotomize me, and it was Ayaz that put me there – your best friend. I think I've earned the right to be skeptical—"

Trey's lips pressed against mine, and any protests I'd been formulating died on my lips. I wrapped my arms around his neck, clinging to him. All those nights alone in Dunwich, I'd thought of this moment, of seeing him and Quinn and Ayaz again. And now... Trey's lips on mine were achingly real. The moan that escaped his mouth tore through me like a forest fire.

This kiss... this kiss... *I can't think... I can't...* Trey pulled me under. I tore my mouth from his. He had me pinned against the doorframe. I couldn't duck around him, so I bent my neck back as far as I could, breathing hard. My lips tingled, my body aching with heat for whatever he wanted to do to me.

For whatever I wanted to do to him.

He came all this way... for me. He chipped away at that stone so he could reach me.

"Does that answer your question?" Trey traced a line along my jaw.

"Not entirely." I tugged him toward the bed. The fire inside me flared high, drowning out any last warning.

I had to *know*. I couldn't explain it, but I needed Trey's scarred hands on me. I needed those lips on mine, I needed to hear him moan with need again. Maybe with him, I could erase Ayaz's betrayal from my mind.

We crashed down onto the narrow bed in a fury of limbs. Trey's teeth scraped my lip. I tasted the tang of blood, but it only made me press against him harder, clawing at his body, trying to crawl inside him. The fire inside me longed to burn the clothes from his flesh, to destroy every barrier that held me from him.

I restrained myself, barely, tugging his hoodie over his head and moving my hands down his chest, tearing at the buttons on his rumpled shirt. He clawed at my clothes, dragging them from my body, his hands searing my bare flesh. Trey rolled on top of me. In the tiny space, our feet pressed against the wall. Hands and mouths and skin connected. All Trey's hard corners came apart as he unleashed himself – the desperate boy, the reckless boy, the possessive boy.

More than anything, I wanted to be possessed by him.

He shoved his hands under my ass, pushing down my jeans and panties with a single swipe. Before I could do anything, Trey plunged his face between my legs. This was nothing like before, with Ayaz, who'd been kind and gentle. This was hot and needy, an attack on my clit with his tongue. I surrendered to Trey, giving myself over to the raw fury of the fire he stoked inside me.

Trey thrust two fingers inside me, pressing them against the wall, pushing me harder against his mouth as his tongue spelled out all the things he couldn't say. The tension that had twanged between us ever since the day we met stretched tight, tugging us together, burning his heart against mine.

He added a third finger, stretching me, demanding more. He sucked my clit into his mouth, pounding the end with his tongue as he sucked. It was the most exquisite torture. The orgasm that tore through me rocked the RV on its wheels.

I slammed my fist into the wall as a scream escaped me. Trey stretched a hand up, trying to cover my mouth, reminding me that we were trying to stay secret, remain hidden. But I was gone, somewhere far away, where Vincent and Ms. West and the fucking Great Old God of dreams couldn't touch me.

I was in Trey Bloomberg's arms, and that was the only place I wanted to be.

Trey slid up the narrow bed, cupping my face in his hand once more. I tasted myself on his lips, sweet and tart and intoxicating. His other hand stroked my breast, pinching my nipple as the fire inside me begged for release. I fumbled for Zehra's condoms. The thought flew through my head that Ayaz would be pissed if he found out his kid sister had a sex life, but I pushed it aside. I couldn't think of Ayaz now.

I hooked my fingers into Trey's boxers and slid them down. Trey's icicle eyes watched me as I took in the sight of him... of all of him. He laughed low in his throat, this earthy growl that did strange and wonderful things to my insides.

"Your eyes are bugging out of your head," he grinned.

"Um." That was all I had. Trey was bigger than Ayaz, if that was possible. I tossed the condom at him. "Is that... even going to fit?"

"Sure." Trey tore open the package and rolled it down with one hand, the other brushing my breast. His thumb slid over my nipple. I tried not to think about how experienced he was, about how many times he'd done this before with girls like Tillie who knew what to do with a guy like him. He pushed my shoulder, turning me over so I was facing away from him, my back pressed against his chest, that enormous cock rubbing between my ass cheeks.

Trey held my face in his hands, bending me back so he could plunge his tongue inside my mouth. His hand slid down my thigh, fingers light on my skin as he hooked my leg over his. He adjusted himself and pushed inside me, hot and hard and urgent.

My back arched back against him. Trey plunged his hand between my legs, rubbing my clit as he thrust wildly. In minutes, another orgasm built inside me. Our hard edges ground against each other until pieces of our souls chipped off.

With a growl that was more animal than human, Trey's body finally shuddered with release. He collapsed against me, his arm draped over my chest, his lips pressed against my shoulder.

I wanted to lie there forever. I wanted to pretend this was how it could always be – hot, needy sex, no pretenses, no evil school or Great Old God shadowing our happiness. But as my eyelids fluttered shut, I caught the faint glimpse of the stone on the table. The lines of the sigil glowed with faint blue light.

The glow of a flame.

CHAPTER NINE

"Can you see that?" I tried to sit up, but Trey held me down, wrapping his arms around my shoulders, his breath hot on my ear. He squeezed me against him, driving out the air in my lungs with the force of his hug.

"Stop thinking for five minutes and just enjoy this," he whispered roughly in my ear. "I've only been dreaming about it every night since second quarter."

And maybe I was an idiot because instead of boxing him around the ears and going to inspect the sigil, I sunk deeper into his embrace and breathed deeply of his herbs and heather scent. For just a few minutes.

But of course, my brain wouldn't stop. Only now, it had completely forgotten about sigils and Great Old Gods and had turned back into a teenager – a whirling ball of angst and hormones. I'd gone from a virgin to sleeping with two different guys in a matter of weeks. Neither of them was my boyfriend. At least, we'd never had any kind of conversation about commitment. I had this vague sense that I was supposed to feel offended by their treatment, that I should be wallowing in a desperate need to tie one of them down into a relationship. That sleeping with two guys – two best friends – was going to label me a slut, and that I should care about that. But I didn't.

Maybe I am my mother's daughter.

Or maybe it was just so low down my list of problems I didn't even care. Both guys were *dead*. I wasn't just a slut, I was a zombie slut.

Zombie slut. I'd have to tell that one to Quinn. He'd love it.

Quinn. I missed him. Maybe that was a weird thing to think after I'd just slept with Trey, but I was definitely past caring that my thoughts weren't normal. Quinn was the first of the Kings to ever be nice to me, to give me a glimpse at the real person that hid behind his mask. I missed the way he lightened every situation and had some crazy comeback ready to go. Trey and I were both too serious – our competitive natures meant that we'd always crash against each other. We both wanted to win, to be first, to be the best. Quinn didn't care about any of that – he just wanted to make people laugh. He made everything fun.

I hoped he was okay. I hoped whatever they were doing to him at school hadn't dimmed his light.

Speaking of light... I twisted my head to look at the sigil. Yup, still glowing with that faint line of flame, the way Rebecca Nurse's seal had back in the cave when Zehra and I had seen it. Trey hadn't seen the flame then, either.

But what did that mean?

Trey's fingers traced the line of my jaw. "I thought I lost you."

His words dripped with emotion that tightened my chest. I wasn't ready to face what Trey was trying to tell me. I pulled a Quinn, turning to him with a grin and saying, "Turns out you can't get rid of Hazel Waite that easily."

Trey sat up, his jaw tightening. He wasn't going to be dissuaded. "Hazel, you have to tell me what happened. Last time I saw you, you swung out my window like a monkey. You were going to see Zehra and tell her about Ms. West's lab. How did you end up at Dunwich?"

"What happened was that Ayaz betrayed me." I told Trey everything that happened, from the cave-in to what went down in Ms. West's office, how they told me that I was emotionally unstable, that I'd been bullying other students and pretending the three Kings were my boyfriends.

"They wanted me to believe it. They've been planning this for some time. Ever since Quinn and I overheard that conversation between your fathers and Mrs. Haynes and Ms. West, I've been having these vivid dreams. I didn't say anything because I assumed it was just a side effect of the god's interest in me... but now I think it was part of your father's plan to deal with me. They wanted me to doubt my sanity, so... achievement unlocked. I thought I was nuts until you turned up in my dream. Thanks for that, by the way. You pray almost as good as you fuck."

Trey jabbed me in the breastbone with the tip of his finger. "I think that was all *your* doing – you and the god have some kind of connection. That's why you keep seeing all this stuff when you sleep. I just got caught in the middle."

I snorted. "Yeah, well, the god likes to mess with my dreams, but I don't think that makes me special. Greg had nightmares all last quarter after his run-in with your deity."

Trey shrugged. "Yet another mystery we can't solve. Go back to your story. You saw my father at Dunwich?"

"No. I went to the Grand Hotel in Arkham. He's staying there. I listened outside while he told the doctor who treated me at Dunwich it was his job to find me. He admitted he masterminded the whole thing." Trey looked flabbergasted at what I'd done. I leaned back and flashed him a smile, a little bit proud I'd managed to render him speechless. I decided not to tell Trey what I would've done if the bellhop hadn't shown up. "What I can't figure out is why Ayaz went along with it or how they managed to do *this*."

I rolled back my sleeve to show Trey my wrist, where the tattoo had disappeared.

My skin tingled where Trey's fingers grazed it. He turned my wrist over, his beautiful lips twisting into a frown. "Your tattoo is gone."

"Yup."

"This I don't understand. How can a tattoo just disappear?"

"I've asked myself the same question every day since. It was on my wrist when I went into the exam room. I remember seeing it when I was throwing stones at Quinn's window. But when Ayaz grabbed my wrist in Ms. West's office, it was gone."

I thought I was crazy. I touched my fingers to the burn on my wrist, to remind myself that I as much as I wanted to spill my feelings to Trey, the dark secrets I carried needed to stay buried deep. I bit back the words that threatened to leave my lips. *You're the one who brought me back to reality and made me realize that everything had been an illusion. You're a beautiful, dead boy, and you're the only thing in my life that feels real.*

Trey bit his lower lip. He peered closer. "This looks as though it's been lasered off. See, there's a burn here—"

His fingers grazed the scar on my wrist. I whipped my hand away. "Not that. That's old."

Trey sighed. "Hazel, I *know* that scar is old. You touch it every time something happens you don't want to deal with. I'm talking about the scar next to it. Look for yourself."

I held up my wrist to my face, squinting at my skin in the light. There was the scar from the fire, but I couldn't see...

No, wait... there it was, just a tiny discoloration at the edge of my scar. It wasn't there before I'd gone to Dunwich, I was sure of it. I'd stared at this wrist enough times to know.

"But... isn't laser painful? How could they have done that to me at school without me noticing?"

Trey's eyes darkened as he considered it. "Shit, okay. I might know. At Dunwich, they gave you drugs, right?"

"Ooooh yeah. All kinds of drugs. Enough to make a Philly dealer weep."

"Maybe they knocked you out with drugs when you got there and you were under long enough for them to permanently remove the tattoo? If they had already decided to do that, it would just be a matter of tricking you for a couple of minutes in Ms. West's office."

I frowned. "Correct."

"Well, I was backstage at rehearsal getting some touch-ups a week before this shit went down. Ms. West came around, talking to students, seeing how the production was going. I overheard her asking Lauren about the stage makeup. She specifically asked if it was heavy enough to cover dark features like tattoos. Do you think it's possible someone in that room could have swiped your wrist with makeup without you noticing?"

I remembered the orderlies lunging at me and my frantic fight to escape. Once Ayaz walked into the room, they could've swiped makeup on my wrist or even cut off my whole arm and I wouldn't even have noticed. "I can't believe Ayaz would do that to me. He knew it was all lies."

"Not Ayaz." Trey's jaw set hard. "This is all my father's doing."

But I know your father is evil. Ayaz was supposed to be my... was supposed to care about me. "Why would Ayaz help him?"

"I don't know." A darkness crossed Trey's eyes. "He won't talk to me or Quinn. We're bottom feeders now, stripped of our standing and all our privileges, and he's top of the school. He's been trailing around after Courtney like her personal lap dog ever since you left. I can't get close to him without the other monarchs fending me off."

"What about Quinn? Is he okay?"

"He's fine." The set of Trey's jaw told me there was something he wasn't telling me. My stomach tightened. "He's been more helpful than normal. He's holding down the fort at school while I try to find you."

"And Greg and Andre? They're okay, too?"

Trey nodded, but the storm in his ice-blue eyes bothered me.

"You're not telling me everything." I glared at him. "You can't do that. This situation is dangerous enough without keeping secrets. It was a secret that led to this whole horrible mess in the first place."

"I agree," Trey shot back, his thumb reaching out to touch the burn on my wrist. "We can't keep secrets from each other anymore."

My blood turned to ice. *No.*

You're not getting that secret out of me. That's mine to take to the grave. That's my guilt to bear.

"Fine." I drew away. "Don't tell me. I'm just going to find out anyway when I go back to school."

Trey snorted. "Don't be stupid. You can't go back there. They'll just throw you back in Dunwich, or worse. It's already halfway through the year. Ms. West doesn't have to wait much longer until your bargain comes due."

"Don't you think I know that? But I'm not just going to run away while all those evil things are still going on, not until I know Greg and Andre are safe and you guys are free."

"We'll never be free," Trey's jaw tightened. "You need to let go of the idea of saving us. We're already dead – and now we're just frozen in time. We can't go backward, and there's no future for me, Hazel. There's no future for *us*. You need to get out while you still can."

"Nope. Not accepting that." I swiped my toe through Zehra's papers on the floor. "Somewhere in here is the answer."

Trey shook his head. "I promise we'll get Greg and Andre out. And then the three of you will get as far away from Derleth Academy as possible. That's the plan. It's the only possible plan. Everything else is hopeless."

"You have hope, Bloomberg. Otherwise, you wouldn't be here.

Otherwise..." I held up the empty condom wrapper we tossed on the floor. "This wouldn't have happened."

"It shouldn't have happened," Trey growled.

"Why not?"

"You know why not."

My heart pattered. "Because Ayaz and I..."

Trey's fingers curled through my short hair. "I don't care about that."

"How do you not care? Isn't being a King of Miskatonic Prep all about taking what's yours, coming first, winning at any cost?"

"It used to be. And then you arrived on campus and shot us all to hell."

"Then why are you saying this shouldn't have happened?"

"Because I should be stronger than this. Because you're going to go off and have an amazing life and probably rule the world someday. Because I'll have to say goodbye to you, and now it's going to be so much harder."

I shrugged his hand off my shoulder and sat up, glaring at him. "If you know me at all, you wouldn't even say that shit. I'm not leaving you, and I'm not leaving Ms. West to continue to sacrifice scholarship students. End of discussion."

An awkward silence descended between us. A hundred things I wanted to say beat against my lips. I bent down and grabbed a handful of Zehra's papers, shoving them into his arms. "Can you help me make sense of all this?"

"What is it?"

"Zehra's research. Do you remember what she told us in the cave, that she knew someone who might be able to help reverse what happened to you?"

Trey nodded.

I held out the Post-it note. "I think this is her – Dr. Deborah Pratt. She was a pathologist who worked with Ms. West at Arkham General. She's where we need to start. But there's so much information here, mostly about Rebecca Nurse and her family tree. I don't know if any of it is important, or..."

I slumped down on the floor and spread out the papers around me, creating a kind of barrier between me and Trey's fiery, magnetic presence. Unspoken between us was the fact that Ayaz would be the best person for this job. Ayaz who spoke several dead languages, who had a fascination with the occult and who knew more about the history of witchcraft and Great Old Gods than any of us.

But if I couldn't have Ayaz, then Trey was the next best option. He bent over the papers, wearing that same hard, focused expression he had whenever he tackled any activity, whether it was getting a perfect score on an exam or tormenting some scholarship student.

Unable to tolerate the chaos of the pile, Trey immediately set about organizing. He pulled out the newspaper articles about the fire and set them aside. "We already know everything we need to know about this."

Trey's description of the fire and of digging his way out of his own grave still burned fresh in my mind. The articles couldn't tell me anything his recollection wouldn't. Trey made separate piles of the Rebecca Nurse genealogy and the occult stuff. He bit his lower lip as he sifted through the pile, and his shoulders relaxed. He enjoyed putting everything in order.

As I sorted the papers onto Trey's neat stacks, I picked up a page I hadn't noticed before. It contained lines of symbols made of lines and triangles. They looked like the imprints of chicken feet walking across the paper. The symbols formed three columns down the page and were scrawled on both sides of the paper, and several sets were crossed out or circled, or had question-marks or notes in another language (possibly Latin) written next to them. At the top of the page, Zehra had added a Post-it note.

"Stolen from Ms. W office. ???"

"Does this mean anything to you?" I handed the paper to Trey. "She must've taken it before she left Derleth."

Trey took the paper, frowning as he ran his hand down the page, his full lips pursing as he whispered unknown words under his breath. His muscles twitched, nostrils flaring.

"Trey?"

He curled his fingers into a fist and slammed it into a cupboard door. Wood splintered, and I ducked, covering my head as cups clattered to the floor around us.

"Fuck. What did you do that for?"

Trey shoved the paper in my face. "Do you know what this is?"

"No. Duh. That's why I asked you."

Trey's face was white. I'd never seen him look so... out of control, like there was all this rage inside him and it had nowhere to be. "It's proof of exactly what I suspected. It's a code commonly used in the Eldritch Club – cuneiform, an ancient Mesopotamian script that's common among practitioners of magic. We can all read it."

"So it's a spell? Or like, minutes for a club meeting?" I put on a snooty English accent. "'Jeeves, we're out of fifty-year-old Scotch.'"

Trey looked at me like I was insane. "I thought I'd get a break from Quinn, but apparently, he's rubbed off on you. It's a list. A list of all the students of Miskatonic Prep." Trey slammed his fist into another cabinet door. *"Fuck."*

I snatched the paper out of his hands before he could destroy it. "Okay, so it's like a class roll or something? I'm not sure exactly what that proves—"

"This is the minutes from an Eldritch Club meeting. It's dated four years before the fire, the year before my dad enrolled me in Miskatonic Prep." Trey's whole body trembled with rage. "Every powerful family in the country has contributed a child to this list."

"What are you saying?"

"I'm saying that the fire wasn't an accident. They planned exactly when it would be, and exactly which students would be killed that night." Trey's eyes blazed. "Our families chose us to be sacrificed."

CHAPTER TEN

Fuck.

Well, that's dark.

I mean, I wasn't surprised. I'd believe anything of Vincent and his Eldritch Club cronies. I'd certainly believe it of Ms. West and her Dr. Frankenstein lab.

Even though Trey had suspected for some time, seeing proof of what his parents, all the parents, had done wiped him out completely. He punched a few more cupboards and then collapsed on the bed, a dishtowel wrapped around his bleeding fist.

I let him be. That was some heavy shit to deal with, even in the context of the shit that Miskatonic Prep had thrown at us. I finished sorting and reading through all of Zehra's material, but nothing was as damning as that page of names. My stomach growled, so I pulled some ramen out of the backpack and found two bowls Trey hadn't broken – a dinner fit for a King.

After we'd eaten we lay side-by-side on Zehra's narrow bed – the bed where we'd had frantic, desperate sex only a few hours earlier. Trey held up the paper and turned it over and over, the tension in his shoulders growing with every rotation.

Eventually, I snatched it off him. He tried to explain what

each symbol meant, how the different chicken's feet represented sounds and how they could be used to represent modern names – like Quinn, Courtney, Tillie. He pointed to his own name, right at the top of the list, as if his father couldn't wait to get rid of him.

My palms itched to melt Vincent Bloomberg's smug face. *I should have incinerated that bastard while I had the chance.*

Trey and I slept cradled in each other's arms. Well, Trey slept, his body shuddering as he settled into a string of violent nightmares. I held him tight, bracing his body against the onslaught, and stared at the ceiling. The light was still on in the RV, but I couldn't bear the thought of shifting Trey's weight to get up and turn it off. Moths battered themselves against the windows, desperate to get inside to worship their faux sun god.

As soon as the real sun peeked over the horizon, I shook Trey awake. We gathered up Zehra's research and all the candy bars and condoms we could find into the backpack I'd started yesterday, then stole out of the RV and walked into Arkham. Trey kept a lookout while I hotwired a car and drove us to the state line. We dumped the car, changed our clothes again (stopping at a nondescript thrift store for something to fit Trey), and got on a bus that would take us back across the state in the opposite direction to a small town about forty miles from Arkham, where this Deborah woman lived.

Thankfully, the bus was mostly empty. We found a seat at the back. Trey dropped the satchel at his feet. It made a loud clang as it hit the metal floor.

"What you got there, son – a bag of rocks?" The man across the aisle peered at the satchel through reading glasses smeared with grease.

"Mind your own business," Trey snapped.

No one talked to us after that, for which I was profoundly grateful. My stomach twisted in knots. We'd found a couple of paperback novels at the thrift store, but I was too stressed out to read mine. Every time the bus lurched around a corner I expected to see Vincent with a roadblock or an armored car, ready to take us both back to that hellhole. I stared out the window, thinking hard, while Trey read a fun-looking romantic heist book by Katya Moore called *The Siren Job*. Occasionally, he'd stop me to ask about something in the text – he was missing twenty years of cultural references and technological advances.

At some point, the gentle sway of the engine and the scent of stale potato chips shoved in the creases of the seats must've lulled me to sleep, because the next thing I knew I was back in the god's cavern.

And the god was *pissed*.

The room groaned under the force of its fury. Slivers of rock fell from the ceiling, shattering against the polished floor. The veins of strange, alien mineral seemed even more oppressive as they loomed inward, as though at any moment they would topple like dominoes to squash me.

But I didn't think the god was interested in me, judging by the circle of hooded figures that crouched in reverence around the scaffold, their hands attempting to shield their skulls from falling debris even as they refused to move from their vigil. Voices chanted the god's strange tongue in high, hesitant voices, wavering with fear each time a new sliver of rock crashed to the floor.

The figure nearest the trapdoor lifted its head, rolling its body away as a particularly large lump of rock toppled down right where it had been lying. Its hood fell away and I recognized Ms. West, although she looked considerably less well-put-together than usual.

"You have to understand," Ms. West said, her voice swooning in that dramatic tone. "She was hurting you by being here. We sent her away until it was time for you to take her. This way we'll be able to figure out how they could affect you—"

But the god didn't have to understand anything. From within his prison, he howled and wailed and gnashed his teeth made of galaxies. Like a child throwing his toys out of the crib, he wanted something he couldn't have.

He wanted *me*.

"We gave you the other girl," Headmistress West said. "Remember what happened after you took her? It will be worse with Hazel. We need more time to understand—"

She yelped and leaped back as a long sliver of rock fell from the ceiling and penetrated the floor directly where she had been standing, sending up a spray of shards.

"This is ridiculous," she snapped to Dr. Atwood, who'd torn off his hood to run to her aid. "Vincent was the one who wanted to try this disastrous plan. *He's* the one who lost Hazel, and yet we're the ones answering to the god's wrath."

"Isn't that the way it's always been?" Atwood sighed.

"Well, maybe it's time we had some changes around here." Ms. West yanked her hood over her hair and hurried to the edge of the room, sheltering under one of the alcoves.

"What are you suggesting?" Atwood ran after her, arms over his head, shielding his face as more rock fell from the cavern. The other figures picked themselves up and raced after them.

"I'm merely saying that if Mr. Bloomberg's power has been stripped, I see no reason why we should continue to take orders from him. if you want something done, you need to do it yourself."

A wide grin spread across Atwood's gaunt features. He bent his head toward Ms. West, and they whispered something together. I lurched forward, trying to hear more of their conversation, but the god buckled the ground beneath me. I pitched forward, my body jolting as the god shook me with invisible hands...

"Hazel... wake up." Trey's voice called me. I flung myself out of my seat with a jolt, hitting my head on the luggage rack as I stumbled down the aisle.

"Fuck! Ow." I rubbed my head. We must've stopped to pick up

more passengers, because twenty pairs of wary and curious eyes watched me from previously unoccupied seats.

"What happened?" Trey helped me back into my seat. "You were calling out something, and thrashing about. People were staring."

"I was there, in the god's cavern." A cold shiver rocketed down my spine. "The god knows that I was taken away, and he's not happy at all. He's about to bring the roof down on the faculty. And there's more. It seems Ms. West doesn't want to work with your father."

Across the aisle, a woman watched me with a wary expression. She lifted her child out of the seat beside her and bounced him in her lap. The man in the seat in front of us got up and moved to an empty bench at the front of the bus.

Trey bent over so his forehead touched mine. He brushed a strand of hair from my cheek, and the tenderness of his touch made my chest tighten. Trey had never been taught how to show love, how to be caring, and so this was foreign territory for him. He was nothing if not a fast learner.

"Tell me exactly what you saw," he whispered. "Do it quietly. We don't know who might be listening."

In tangled whispers, I explained about the cavern and the falling rock and the anger of the teachers. "Ms. West said that they gave him 'the other girl.' She had to be talking about Loretta. But the way she said it, it was as though Loretta and I were similar in some way – like Loretta had hurt the god, too."

Trey shook his head. "Loretta's the same as every other sacrifice. She went to the gymnasium with the teachers, and she came back one of us. Are you okay to walk? The next stop is ours."

"I had a dream. I didn't break my hip," I snapped, but I gripped Trey's shoulder as he led the way off the bus. "And there is something different about Loretta. She went back to school instead of becoming one of the maintenance staff. And she's changed. Even though you supposedly don't have a soul, there's a warmth to you that shines through. You still care. You still *feel*. But there's nothing behind Loretta's eyes."

"I thought that was just who she was. She was kind of dead inside when she arrived at school. If anything, being a revenant has made her more lively. And she's only a student because Courtney wanted to use her to torment you. And what Courtney wants, she gets, especially from Ms. West."

"Why is that?"

"Because Courtney's mother has more money than any of the other Eldritch Club members, and I think she's best buddies with the headmistress." Trey's expression hardened. "Gloria Haynes hardly ever visits the school, but Ayaz said he'd often heard Ms. West speaking with her on the phone, and he said there were pictures of the two of them together in her chamber."

Thanks for reminding me that Ayaz used to do the nasty with the Deadmistress. I fought the urge to gag.

Don't think about it. Focus on why you're here – to find out what Deborah Pratt knows.

Deborah lived at the end of a small row of wooden houses backing onto the forest. Colorful dog statues lined the path to her door, and a green glass suncatcher tinkled in the breeze as we rang the doorbell. It certainly didn't look like the home of a pathologist, let alone one who was involved in dark magic.

I rang the doorbell. From deep inside the house, the theme song from a Disney movie played. A short woman in her midforties with a round face and vivid hazel eyes and the same dark skin and thick, kinky hair as me answered the door. "Are you selling cookies for the dog charity?" she asked. "I'll take two boxes. I just want to help all the poor puppies."

"Are you Dr. Deborah Pratt?" I asked.

"I am, love. Who's asking?"

"I'm Hazel Waite. You were speaking with my friend Zehra Damir. I think..." the words caught on my tongue. "I think something terrible has happened to her. And we need your help."

CHAPTER ELEVEN

Deborah's home was exactly as I expected it to look from the outside, filled with hand-stitched quilts and colorful rugs and even more dog statues. She led us into a living room with a sliding glass door overlooking a small balcony and the forest beyond. Two elderly poodles luxuriated on a giant bed by the window. Outside, a Jack Russell puppy pawed at the door, his eyes wide and as he followed Trey's and my movements across the room.

"That's Roger. I won't let him inside," she said, indicating the Jack Russell. "He's quite excitable, and I want us to be able to speak without interruption. Please, take a seat. I'll make us some tea."

Trey and I sank into the sofa while Deborah bustled into a kitchen at the rear of the house. I tugged stuffing from a tear in the leather while Trey cast a disapproving eye around the dog portraits and porcelain plates hanging from the walls.

"Are we sure this is the right woman?" Trey flicked his eyes to the kitchen, where Deborah hummed while crockery clattered. "She seems a few galaxies short of a cosmic god—"

"Arf!" One of the poodles loped over and placed his head on Trey's knee, wide brown eyes staring up at him, imploring him.

This interested me – dogs have an excellent sense of smell, and can even be trained to locate dead bodies. So why didn't these dogs act as if Trey was dead?

Hope flickered in my chest, before dying again. I had all the evidence I needed that Trey was a smokin' hot walking corpse. *Just because a dog likes him doesn't mean he's alive like I am.*

Trey recoiled, his body stiffening. "The dog is touching me."

I laughed at the rich boy who'd never had any kind of affection in his entire life. "I think he wants you to scratch his ears."

Reluctantly, as if he was afraid of being electrocuted, Trey reached out a hand and placed it on the dog's head. The dog shuddered in pleasure from human touch, its tongue panting in ecstasy. Trey's mouth wavered. He stroked his fingers through the dog's curly fur. "He's so soft."

"I think he likes you," I smiled. Trey scratched the dog behind its ear. The dog placed a second paw on Trey's leg, lolling its head to the side. Trey's shoulders relaxed, the tension fleeing him as he shared this moment with his new friend. All his life, any love he'd been shown had been conditional. He didn't know what it meant not to have a price.

"Leopold is very picky about people," Deborah said from the doorway. She set a tray of tea and homemade cookies on the table. "You must be very special for him to take a liking to you."

"I doubt that," Trey said, but he didn't stop stroking Leopold's fur.

Deborah handed me a cup of tea. I plucked a shortbread from the plate and bit into it. "Zehra has gone missing. I was supposed to meet her in a cave to share some information with her that she was going to pass on to you. There was a cave-in, and I think she was trapped or... or something else."

"Straight to the point, I see." The woman chuckled as she sipped her tea. "I like that. Zehra was the same – she said she'd been waiting for ten years to figure out what happened to her brother, and she wasn't going to waste another minute."

"When was the last time you heard from her?" I couldn't help the flicker of hope that danced in my chest.

"She sought me out about six months ago, and we've had regular conversations via phone and text, which stopped about five weeks ago. I've tried calling her, but her phone goes straight to voicemail."

I squeezed Trey's knee. I didn't want to think about what this meant. *She's not dead until I see her body, and knowing the god, maybe not even then. I won't give up on her.* "Why did she think you could help us?"

"She'd discovered I'd worked with Hermia West at Arkham General Hospital, and that I had an interest in certain types of magic."

"That's kind of a weird combination." I couldn't figure this woman out. Between the dog obsession and the library of medical textbooks lining the wall behind her, I couldn't see any room in her life for ancient gods and spellbooks bound in human skin.

Deborah shrugged. "Not really. Magic has always been discussed in my household. My parents were both occult scholars. Just because I don't have a bubbling cauldron over the stove or crystals around my neck doesn't mean I don't know my way around ancient sigils."

"And what about Ms. West?" Trey asked.

"Hermia is a very dangerous woman. I worked with her in the morgue at Arkham General. It was her job to prepare the bodies for autopsies and for my work — I'm a pathologist, so I would study the patients who died of disease. I started noticing strange things when I went in for my shifts — bodies in strange positions inside the freezer, supplies of certain chemicals and drugs mysteriously depleted, strange marks or puncture wounds on cadavers. I knew something was going on, but I couldn't predict what..." Deborah shuddered.

"What?" I leaned forward, my finger pressing into the burn on my wrist.

Deborah cleared her throat. "I still have trouble believing I saw it. I came in early one night and discovered Hermia had one of the fresh cadavers out of the freezer. I watched from the shadows as she injected him with something, and he sat bolt upright!"

She looked at us as if she expected us to be surprised, but of course, we weren't. Her knuckles were white from gripping her mug as she continued. "This man half-rolled, half-collapsed off the slab and kind of dragged his body around the room. She was talking to him, coaxing him like a child. I was so terrified, I just backed out of the lab and walked around the hospital in a daze until my shift officially started. When I came back, the man was back in the freezer, dead as a doornail, but I knew what I saw."

"Oh, we believe you," Trey said.

Deborah nodded. "I reported Hermia to the hospital's ethics board. Not what I'd seen that morning, because I knew it was too sensational for them to believe, but the theft of the medical supplies, the needle marks on patients, the bodies moved around. I'd kept careful dates and records of everything. They couldn't deny what I showed them – that Hermia was mistreating and experimenting on bodies – but they also couldn't risk it getting into the media, so they asked Hermia if she would resign on the condition they supplied her with neutral references. The whole thing was a farce, and it destroyed my faith in the medical administration. Thanks to the work of the hospital board, Hermia West walked straight out of that job and into the headmistress role at Miskatonic Preparatory."

"How much do you know about what's going on at the school?" I asked.

"I know what Zehra told me, which is that her brother Ayaz, along with 244 other students, died in a fire twenty years ago when it was called Miskatonic Preparatory, but they still reside at the school as the walking dead."

Right, okay. So she knows.

But Deborah wasn't finished. "I also know that the school was reopened after the fire as Derleth Academy, and that every year four students are chosen to enter the school, but none ever return. I know that this is all in aid of a shadowy society of this country's elite who are using the school as a conduit to obtain power from a being not of this world."

"Okay, so basically everything. And you believe it?"

"Zehra was very convincing. And as I said, I'm no stranger to the occult. But no, I don't quite know everything." Deborah set down her cup and flicked her gaze between Trey and me, her slate-grey eyes fixing me with a calculating stare. "What I don't know is who you both are, and how you have come to be in my living room? I assume you have information to share with me."

I glanced over at Trey, who was absorbed in rubbing the old dog's stomach as he lolled on the rug. Uncertainty pinched in my chest. I didn't know anything about this woman apart from her name, and yet here we were. For a woman of science, she seemed far too comfortable discussing my revenant classmates. How did I know she wasn't friends with Ms. West? She could rat us out as soon as we let our guard down.

When I didn't answer, Deborah leaned forward. "Did my perfectly reasonable question unsettle you? Or is it something else?"

"Can we trust you?" I blurted out.

"You must believe you can, otherwise why would you seek me out?"

I hesitated, unsure. I didn't trust anyone by nature. It had taken me all this time to trust the Kings after what they'd done to me, and after what Ayaz pulled, I was more uncertain than ever. If I'd read him so wrong, I could be reading Deborah Pratt completely wrong, too. Hell, why did I even trust Zehra?

But I couldn't help Trey or Quinn or Greg or Andre or any of the other students on my own, especially not as a fugitive from

Dunwich. We needed allies, and if this woman could be one, I had to take that chance. For them.

I ran my fingers over the hard surface of Trey's rock, still hidden in the satchel clutched tight in my hands.

"As I said, my name is Hazel Waite. I'm a scholarship student at Derleth Academy. I escaped before the faculty and alumni could sacrifice me to an ancient god that lives under the school. I tried to smuggle out a copy of the key to Ms. West's laboratory where she conducts her experiments on students, but instead I was captured and sent to the Dunwich Institute."

In halting, jagged sentences, I told her everything – from the day I arrived at Derleth to the bullying and Loretta's strange disappearance and reappearance, to the discovery of the god beneath the school and my admittance to the Eldritch Club. I told her about finding Ms. West's lab, making copies of the key to give to Zehra, and how I'd lost the keys when I was taken to Dunwich. They could be back in the box in the cave, but more than likely they were back in Ms. West's hands. My fingers flew to my wrist, pressing into the scar that was all that remained from my life before.

"Don't worry about the key – the two of you are much more important." Deborah glanced over at Trey as if seeing him for the first time. "If you are as your friend says, then how are you sitting here now? You are supposed to be trapped at the school."

Trey took the satchel from me and flipped back the blanket covering his rock. Deborah traced her fingers over Parris' sigil. To my surprise, a trail of blue flame followed the line of her finger.

I leaned back, startled. The rock rolled off my lap and crashed onto the floor.

Trey scrambled to pick it up. "We've gotta be careful with this. I don't know what will happen to me if it breaks."

"Do you see it too?" I whispered.

"See what?" Trey frowned at the stone.

"The flames?" Deborah fixed me with a strange look. "I see

them."

"Do you know what they mean? I keep seeing them – they were on another sigil I saw back at Derleth."

"Was that sigil also one of Parris'?"

"No, we believe it was placed there by Rebecca Nurse, but we don't know why. Zehra saw it too, but the guys couldn't."

"Interesting." Deborah studied my face, like she was searching for something.

"Is it?" I said, my voice dripping with sarcasm. My head spun. I was tired of all the wondering, tired of not having answers.

"Yes. I don't know what it means, but it means something." Deborah tapped her nails against the spines of the books as she searched through her titles. "What is it you want to do, Hazel Waite?"

"My friends, Greg and Andre, they're still at the school," I said. "I want to save them. I want to stop the Eldritch Club from ever hurting another person."

"And..."

"And..." My nails dug into my wrist. Pain jolted down my arm, stoking the fire within me. "I want to free all the Miskatonic Prep students from whatever spell or curse or crazy voodoo has trapped them as revenants."

"Are you prepared for what that might mean?" Her voice was gentle. "They have died. Their souls have been separated from their earthly bodies. To be free may mean they will pass from this world."

The knot in my stomach tightened. I didn't want to be without the Kings. Trey, Quinn, Ayaz... even Ayaz, because in the deepest recesses of my heart I still clung to the person I thought he was.

And anger, because they had their lives stolen. Trey should have had the chance to be the CEO of a super-important company. I could picture him now in an immaculately-tailored suit, all sharp edges and cruel intellect, going into battle in the boardroom like Caesar subduing the Gauls. Quinn should be in entertainment – a movie producer or talent scout or a comedian if he could ever suffer the idea of being poor, and Ayaz... he should have had the chance to pursue his art, to see where his creative mind might have led him.

I could have had a future with them. With any one of them. With *all* of them.

"That's not fair," I growled, my nails scraping over the stone. "Their lives were stolen. They should get the chance to live them out."

"I agree, but that might not be the way it works." Deborah went to her bookshelf and pulled out a slim leather volume, thumbing through the pages as she returned to her seat. "We're dealing with uncharted territory here. No one has ever done what Hermia has achieved, so even if I had access to her lab there's no way to know what reversing her Dr. Frankenstein work will do. Zehra called them *edimmu* – an ancient Mesopotamian myth that may be the origin of our modern vampire stories. Corpses buried without the proper rites who rose again with insatiable rage."

"Yes."

"From what little I understand about edimmu, there are spells and rites that destroy them, but in all cases, the dead will return to the ground."

No. I wouldn't accept it. I'd lost too many people I loved. I couldn't lose more.

"There's got to be a way. You have one of the edimmu you can test." I pointed to Trey, who nodded.

"That's helpful. However, I've shifted jobs recently. I'm an administrator now. I don't have access to the kind of facilities we'd need to conduct experiments on your friend here. I'd have to get my friend Gail to help us. She's a phlebotomist and could give us access to their lab and diagnostic equipment."

Trey and I exchanged a glance. I didn't like it. Deborah was talking about bringing another person into our circle of trust. I didn't know this Gail from Adam. But what choice did we have? Besides, Zehra trusted Deborah, and I trusted Zehra.

"Fine," I said between gritted teeth.

"Can you also test Hazel?" Trey asked.

"Me? Why would you test me?"

"Oh, I don't know." The corner of Trey's mouth tugged up into a half-smile. "Maybe because you set fire to an entire building using only your mind."

I nearly swallowed my tongue in shock before realizing he was talking about Dunwich Institute. I never told him I set that fire. He'd guessed I was responsible. Of course he had. Trey Bloomberg was nothing if not clever.

Deborah glanced up at me, studying my face. My cheeks burned under the scrutiny. "You never mentioned this before."

"It's not relevant," I muttered.

"It might be very relevant. You can set fires with your mind? How long have you manifested this power?"

"I don't want to talk about it," I growled. My fingers flew to my wrist, where I pressed the scar.

Trey grabbed my arm, prying my fingers away one by one. He circled my wrist, jerking my arm in the air. "Don't do that, Hazel. Don't escape into your head because you're afraid. What if *this* is the key to saving us all?"

"I'm not afraid, and it's not the key." I tried to snap my arm down, but he held firm. Tightness tugged at my chest. I felt cornered, like a rat scrambling to escape a maze with no exit. "We're talking about a cosmic deity that's older than time. I'm not going to hurt it with a little flame."

"That's assuming what you wield is ordinary fire," Deborah muttered as she flicked through another book.

"Hazel." Trey didn't beg. He knew that wouldn't work on me. What he did was fix me with an icy stare that said a hundred things neither he nor I knew how to say.

I swallowed hard. Trey let go of my arm. I dropped it into my lap, my fingers instantly pressing into my scar. A tremor started at the base of my spine and shook my limbs. "I've been able to call up fire ever since I could remember."

"And it's tied to your emotions?" Deborah asked. "How much control do you have?"

I held out my hand. My fingers trembled a little as I summoned a small flame. The orange orb danced on my palm as I moved my hand in a slow arc. Deborah followed the flame with wide eyes.

Trey stepped back, his shoulders rigid. He sunk his hand into Leopold's fur for comfort. *Of course, he's afraid of fire. Fire took his life and the lives of all his friends. He sees this flame and he remembers smoke filling his lungs and pain burrowing into his skin.*

I'd have to be extra careful to keep it in check around him. Luckily, now I had more control.

"I've only recently learned how to do this." I commanded the flame to flare into a column of fire that reached nearly to the ceiling. Deborah's pen clattered to the floor. Leopold whimpered and barreled for the kitchen. The other dog loped after him. Quickly, I commanded the flame to shrink, and I closed my fist, snuffing it out. "I can control the fire when it touches my body, almost as if it's an extension of my skin. I can command a fire to start anywhere, or I can give a fire fuel and direct its power. But I had to teach myself how to do that. Before... I had no control."

That's putting it mildly.

Deborah clutched the edge of her book so hard her knuckles turned white. "It might be nothing. It might be a coincidence."

"What is?"

She shook her head. "It's probably nothing. I'm almost positive I'm wrong, but it's just too much of a coincidence not to explore further. There's so much here for you both to take in. I won't concern you with my theory until I've had the chance to run some tests. Trey might be right, Hazel – you may be the most important piece of this puzzle."

CHAPTER TWELVE

Deborah made up an air mattress for Trey and me in the living room, covering it with more duvets and quilts than was necessary for an arctic winter. She only made up the one bed for both of us, assuming we were a couple. Neither of us corrected her.

What are we? I wondered as I watched Trey peel off his shirt and socks and lay them down in a tidy pile beside the bed. *Are we a couple?*

I'd never spoken aloud what had gone on with the Kings – Quinn and Trey touching me together during the movie night, Ayaz kissing me in the grotto like he needed me to breathe, and then taking my virginity the night he saw his sister again. Everything in my life was so fragile, so easily burned away to ash. I wanted to hold on to the three of them for a little longer. I wanted to live in the delusion that we all had a future together.

It was as though speaking my desires would take everything away again. Because, of course, I couldn't keep all three of them. If Deborah was right, I wouldn't even be able to keep any of them. If I set them free, I'd have to say goodbye three times over, and I'd never even told them how I felt—

I squeezed my eyes shut. No. I wouldn't accept it. They wouldn't die on me.

I opened my eyes, my gaze falling on Trey's face as he punched his pillow. The mattress sank where he lay and I rolled against him.

I bet he's never slept on an air mattress.

Leopold slunk over and claimed a position on Trey's feet, pinning him in place. His sister, Loeb, curled into his armpit. Trey tried to shift Loeb toward her brother, and she responded by covering both of us in slobbery kisses. Despite myself, I laughed. Trey looked so ridiculous with his rich-boy pout as he wiped slobber from his cheeks.

"I always wanted a puppy," he said as he patted Loeb's head and allowed her to settle back into his shoulder. "Dad wouldn't allow it."

Trey rarely offered details about his life. From the way he looked now, like he wanted to claw back the words, I knew this tiny detail had rarely – if ever – escaped before. I took this proffered piece of his heart (I'd say soul, but apparently he didn't have one) and turned it over in my mind, slotting it into place as another puzzle piece in the mystery that was Trey Bloomberg.

"I bet if Wilhem had asked for a puppy, he'd have got it," I ventured.

"Yes, but then he'd have forgotten to feed it, or worse – deliberately starved it. Either way, it would die, and neither he nor my father would shed a tear." Trey's arms tightened around me, and I felt the tug of a boy who had wanted to love and to be loved.

Wasn't that what we all wanted? In Trey's pain, I felt a kinship. I remembered all the nights Dante and I climbed into bed together, warm bodies pressed tight to fight off the chill of freezing Philly winters with no heat. Our breath hung in the air as clouds of mist, my heart rigid and my fingers desperate to explore him. But I was too afraid to destroy our friendship, as if what we had was so fragile that it could be broken with a single kiss.

Turns out, it was.

And that memory made my head fill with images I never wanted to see again. Dante's fingers laced in her hair, his lips brushing her shoulder. Her leg curled around his back. Smoke curling around them as I—

No.

I gulped back the memories. Ever since I'd chosen to embrace the fire at Dunwich and claim for myself what had haunted me my entire life, I'd been walking on eggshells around my old crimes. How long could I be Hazel Waite the firestarter without acknowledging what that had cost?

Trey studied me with those ice eyes of his – as calm and cool as the winter skin of a lake. Through their glassy surface I could see right through to the Trey inside – that brilliant mind that ticked over as he studied me. For the first time, my lips itched to talk about my past. Even though he feared what I could do, I had a feeling that if anyone would understand, it would be Trey Bloomberg.

Fire and ice. Trey and I were opposites, and yet, we were two sides of the same sad story. What was inside us kept us trapped, and when we unleashed the hunger we kept hidden away we learned how destructive we could be. We were monsters created by circumstance and cruelty. He was the bully who'd been raised on indifference and fed with his father's savagery. Trey lashed out because he hungered for everything he'd never had. I was the firestarter cursed with a power I didn't understand, a power that fed on the rage and injustice burning inside me, that never seemed to dim.

In Trey's arms, I felt like maybe being a monster was okay. Maybe even monsters deserved love.

Trey pulled my head into his other shoulder, and my chest did this weird swelling thing where I felt as though I was filled not just with fiery heat, but also light. And that made me think of another time when I'd felt so full and light and loved. Back in my room at Derleth Academy, when Ayaz had held me in his arms and told me I was beautiful.

I bit back the foolish urge to unburden my secrets, and instead begged for his. "You know Ayaz better than anyone. Why did he betray me?"

Trey's fingers dug into my shoulders. He didn't say anything for a long time. I was starting to fade into sleep when he finally said, "From the very day I met him, I wanted to hate Ayaz. When my father brought him to our home, he all but said 'this is the son who will replace you.' He pitted the two of us against each other, and in every instance, Ayaz would come out on top. I should have loathed him. I might have killed him – I had so much hatred inside me burning for release."

"Why didn't you?" I whispered.

"Hatred for my father won out. I realized Ayaz and I were both the same – desperate to please the people who were supposed to love us unconditionally, to be accepted by elders whose morals we never shared. And probably because more than I was angry, I was lonely, and Ayaz made that horrible house tolerable." Trey laughed, his eyes shining as he lost himself in memories. "He had more imagination than I ever did. I only knew about the world inside my prison – my gilded cage – but Ayaz had these wild ideas about life, the universe, everything. He thought I was worldly because I had this big house and lots of toys and my dad was rich and important, but he'd been to places like Damascus that I thought only existed in storybooks. He'd walked in a desert and swam in the Red Sea. He'd stood at the foot of a pyramid and walked in the footsteps of ancient kings. When he spoke Turkish or Arabic to his parents on the phone, I would listen to the musical rise and fall of the words. He was lonely and I was lonely and when we were together we both forgot about that for a while.

"So no, I can't believe it of him. But I believe you, Hazel. If you say Ayaz did those things, then I believe it. But it's the why of it that's killing me as much as it is you. Every atom of me says there's something else going on here, especially considering the way Ayaz has been since you left. He hasn't even talked to me. I think he knows that if he gets too close, I'll see right through him."

I shuddered. "It's what you'll see that I'm afraid of."

Trey traced a line over my breast with his finger. "I don't believe he had a choice. They wanted you out of the way. They wanted to break your mind, and they knew one of us had to do it. They couldn't convince Quinn or I to betray you. So our question should be, what did they do to Ayaz to make him turn against you?"

"You mean like, they tortured him?"

"Oh, I bet they did that." Trey winced. "But they did that to me. Ayaz wouldn't have broken because they hurt him. So it must've been something else. Maybe they've drugged him, somehow? Maybe they used something against him to force him to obey. Or someone."

Zehra.

It was the obvious answer, because she was probably the only person on earth Ayaz truly cared about. But if he knew she was dead, he'd never have given them anything. But if they threatened her life unless he cooperated...

Maybe... maybe she had survived the cave after all.

Trey's words were bleak, but they made a bright flare of hope arc across my chest. I hated the thought that the Eldritch Club and the school might've done something to Zehra and Ayaz, but if Trey was right and Ayaz had been corrupted... then perhaps I could bring him back.

"I won't give up on him," I whispered.

"*We* won't give up on him." Trey's voice cracked, and I felt his love for Ayaz. They might not have been brothers by blood, but they were in every way that mattered.

In the still of the night, in a stranger's house with two dogs snoring on a giant cushion beside us, we explored each other's bodies with silent reverence. Trey's touch was tender, his kisses soft as silk, like he was afraid of breaking me, or of breaking himself.

My dreams that night were ringed in fire. I was back in the cavern beneath the school. I stepped toward the trapdoor. If I opened it again, maybe the god would give me some answers. But as I bent to slide the bolt, voices sounded in the tunnel behind me. Familiar voices that stood my teeth on edge.

I dived for the cover of the alcove just as Vincent Bloomberg and Ms. West walked into the room, arm in arm. They looked the same but different. Instead of her black Morticia Addams dress, Ms. West wore a grey pantsuit and blood-red stilettos, the jacket plunging between her breasts. Vincent wore the kind of clothes movies told me rich people wore on a golf course. Ms. West's eyes caressed the cavern, her head craning to see every angle as if she'd never been there before.

"This is what you wanted to show me?" She faced off against Vincent, her back ramrod straight as she placed her hands on her hips. She looked as if she was about to scold him. "When you said you had a job offer for me, I didn't expect something so... *damp*."

"Indeed." Vincent's graveled voice trembled in the cavernous space. Ms. West shuddered as a wave of the god's hatred escaped the trapdoor and rippled across the room. I leaned against the wall in the alcove, bracing myself until the onslaught was over.

"It's... interesting. What mineral is that – some type of actino-lite?" she pointed to one of the throbbing veins in the wall. "Oh, it's... I can't see..."

"They're impossible to focus on," Vincent said, his tone bored. "You get used to it. And it's not actinolite. We've had it analyzed, and it is not any mineral currently known on earth. We believe this room and some of the tunnel networks are built from rocks that were sent from another galaxy, perhaps as part of the god's ship."

"The god's ship?" Ms. West frowned. "I don't know what

you're talking about, Vincent. I'm a woman of science and an atheist. I don't understand why you've brought me all this way to show me a musty old cave and spout off religious nonsense."

With a start, I realized I was been shown a glimpse of the past. I was side-of-stage while Ms. West had her first personal tour of Miskatonic Prep. She wasn't even a fake teacher yet. She worked in the mortuary at Arkham General Hospital, experimenting on cadavers in her spare time.

"It's not nonsense." Vincent walked over to the trapdoor, picking up a chain between his fingers and unhooking it from the lock. "This is what I wanted to show you."

He slid the bolt free. The trapdoor slammed open, and the wave of noxious hatred rolled out across the room. Ms. West clutched her hand to her chest, pressing against her heart.

"Oh," was all she said. "Oh, my."

My eyes watered as the god's presence wrapped around me, pressing and sliding against my skin, oozing obscenely into my pores. As I struggled for breath, I tasted hatred on my tongue – tart and bitter and strangely enticing. Even in this dream, I experienced the god as if I was right inside that room with him.

"It's been trapped in there for centuries." Vincent's body dripped with tension, his back and shoulders rigid as he stood beside the hole, taking the brunt of the god's oozing aura. "The man who built what is now the school discovered the god while digging his underground tunnels, and he managed to trap it inside this prison."

Ms. West tried to peer into the hole, but Vincent slammed the trapdoor shut, his shoulders visibly relaxing as the vulgar sensation of the god disappeared. "Has the entity been studied?"

"How can a god be studied? We know that if we give him a sacrifice, he will reward us with a share of his power." Vincent gestured to the scaffold above the trapdoor. "However, that surge of power lasts only a short time."

"What does this power do?"

"It's like taking on his essence," Vincent replied. "You felt just now what it is to be in the presence of the god. But when you receive his power, you hold a piece of his godliness within yourself. You appear radiant to those around you. Everyone in a room looks to you for leadership. Whatever you say will become truth."

"That sounds addictive." Ms. West licked her lower lip. "What do you want from me?"

"I want you to find a way to take the god's power and give it to the Eldritch Club. Permanently. We cannot keep the school open much longer. Students are having strange nightmares and complaining to their parents. We've been burying the bodies in the caves under the gym, but now there's a smell... if the school is closed down or authorities investigate, we may lose access to the deity."

"I see. And you believe that I alone could grant what you seek?"

"I read all the eyewitness accounts of your experiments in the mortuary," Vincent fixed her with an intense stare, "including the ones that aren't on public or police record. I read that you raised a cadaver from the dead, that a man who expired in his bed three hours before got up from the slab and walked around the room before collapsing in a messy pile at the feet of a now mentally-impaired pathologist."

Ms. West smiled. "If you've done so much homework on me, you must know that I would approach this in a scientific manner. All this talk of gods and sacrifices muddies the process, makes it okay to cut corners, and that's not how I do things. Tell me, does the entity favor any type of sustenance?"

Vincent frowned. "I don't understand the question."

"Well, must this 'sacrifice,' as you say, be human?"

"Yes. We've tried with many other animals, but the effect is negligible. And the human must be freshly dead – even a body two hours old will not please the god. We now slit their throats right here, above his chamber." Vincent jiggled the chains hanging from the scaffold. "We lower the bodies down and lift them out some time later."

"Intact?"

"For the most part."

"Excellent, then we can already control one of the variables." Ms. West walked slowly around the room, her gaze flickering from the scaffold to the other features of the cavern. "And the sacrifices need to die? Have you tried throwing in a live one?"

Vincent's face turned dark. "We have not."

"Hmmm. Something to ponder. And does the entity respond more favorably to a certain age group? A particular ethnic group? A mental state?"

"The only thing we have noticed is that he seems to prefer them young and when they've lost all hope."

"Young and hopeless? Oh, that's interesting," Ms. West said. "Very interesting indeed. Thank you, Mr. Bloomberg, for your kind job offer. I think I could be very interested. Let us head up to the board room and we can discuss my terms."

I woke in a cold sweat, Ms. West's words like sandpaper on my tongue. Beside me, Trey snored gently, his arm draped over two snoozing poodles.

I hated to wake him, especially when his mouth curled up into such a contented smile as he slept. But this was *big*. It was fucking monumental. Trey would kill me if I casually told him over scrambled eggs in the morning that I'd seen his dad and Ms. West make their deal.

"Trey." I shook his shoulder. "Wake up."

"Mmmmmf." He moaned, rolling over to snuggle even harder into Leopold's fur.

"Trey!" I kicked him.

"Owwwww." He flipped over, hugging his leg to his chest. "What was that for?"

"I had a dream. No, not a dream. The god showed me something from before you died."

Trey bolted upright, grabbing my cheeks, his fingers shaking. "Tell me everything."

I filled him in on as many details as I could remember about the dream, doing my best to recall the exact words used. Trey was a perfectionist – even in this, *especially* in this, he wanted all the details precisely as they had happened.

"This only confirms what we already knew," he said. "Our parents planned this. They knew exactly what they were doing when they enrolled us in Derleth."

"But it sounds as though Ms. West was the one who figured it out. It also sounds as if they were killing people long before she arrived on the scene."

"Honestly, I'm not surprised anymore," Trey said.

"Well, what should we do about it?"

"Nothing." Trey sighed, sinking back into his pillow. "It's in the past. We can't undo it. So just try not to think about it. Go back to sleep."

In minutes he was snoring again, but I couldn't close my eyes. I watched his chest rise, his fingers curl into Loeb's fur as he sought her comfort subconsciously. He looked every bit like an ordinary human boy. A boy with a soul.

Trey breathed. He felt. He hurt. When he was injured, he bled. In every way, he was a living human. Except that he was trapped inside the school's sigils and trapped inside his teenage body. Except that he had crawled out of his own grave and now didn't have a soul.

Whatever that means. What did a soul even give him, anyway? I'd never been one for religious iconography, but I thought a soul was supposed to be your essence – the nebulous life force that made a person who they were. How could Trey be separated from his soul and yet still be vulnerable and *real* and *whole* here with me?

Zombie. Revenant. Edimmu. The students of Miskatonic Prep had given these names to themselves. But there was no word for what they were, for what had been done to them.

They have to be young, and without hope.

I turned this over in my mind, finding no real answer. The sun broke through the trees, and the dogs rose with it. At first, they loped around the room, then they scratched at the kitchen cupboards, making pathetic whimpering noises as though they hadn't been fed in weeks. From the staircase leading up to Deborah's room, the terrier Roger barked and jumped at the door handle.

After a breakfast of Deborah's chocolate chip pancakes, all six of us – me, Trey, Deborah, the two old dogs, and the excitable Roger – piled into Deborah's pickup and headed to a private medical lab in the city. Trey warned me to keep my head down and not to look out in case anyone spotted us, but he couldn't keep his eyes on the road. I watched him staring wistfully at an ice cream parlor and reminded myself that this was Trey's first time outside the walls of Miskatonic Prep in twenty years. He had a lot to catch up on, and I'd be happy to help him start if ice cream was involved.

Deborah's friend Gail – a slim brunette with a kind smile that made me feel slightly less on-edge – let us in at the back entrance to the lab and ushered us into a small utility room.

"Our security cameras don't cover this area," Gail said, wheeling in a tray covered in needles and other medical equipment. "But we need to hurry if I want to get the sampling done before my colleagues arrive for work."

Gail drew five vials of blood from Trey and five from me, all the while keeping a steady stream of chatter with Deborah. They threw around medical terms until my head spun, then in a moment, the conversation would flicker to gossip about a wine and painting evening at their local bar. Watching their easy friendship, I felt a flicker of something... part fascination, part wistful envy of something I'd never had. I'd hoped that maybe Zehra and I could have had the kind of friendship Deborah and Gail shared, but thinking of Zehra just made me feel all twisted up with nerves inside.

But it was part something else, too. In Deborah and Gail, I felt a sense of maybe what my life could be. An interesting career. A circle of friends. A wine and painting evening. A purpose.

Could have been, but would never be. I was still tied to my bargain with Ms. West, and it was highly unlikely I'd survive the year, let alone with any friends or boyfriends intact.

When Gail was done taking my blood, I jumped down from the chair, surprised at the spring in my step. "Can we see the lab?" I asked.

Gail glanced at her watch. "I won't be able to take you inside, because the security camera will be operating and I don't want you to be seen, but you'll be able to look in the window."

We followed Gail down the hall to a door with a narrow window. Inside were rows of white benches and steel shelves, upon which sat various gleaming machines and robotic arms that spun and jerked and beeped. Gail pointed to each machine and explained the diagnostic tests they ran and how the tests could determine if the blood carried certain diseases or matched other samples. Trey strode away, bored and anxious, but my fascination rooted me in place. I wanted to see the machines in action, to prepare samples and watch science reveal answers.

Far too soon, Gail tapped her watch and ushered us back out the service entrance. "I'll call you as soon as I have results."

"How long will that take?" I asked.

"I can't say for certain, sweetie. I'm fitting this around my other work, and the DNA sequencing could take some time."

Deborah drove us back to her house. My head buzzed with questions about the lab and Deborah's job as a pathologist. Trey stared out the window, his mind somewhere else. Deborah had her own inquiries. She wanted to know about Ms. West's lab, the sigils in the cave, and the restrictions placed on the students by their undead status. She was especially curious about Ayaz's translations of Parris' book. When I asked her why she wanted to know this stuff, she shrugged. "It's like loose strings dangling in the wind. I'm certain some of them connect, but I'm not sure which ones yet. I have to pull at them all to find out where they go."

"That's accurate." Right now we had all these questions, all these nameless fears, and no answers.

Deborah pulled into her driveway and idled the engine. "I have to get to my office. Can I leave the two of you here by yourselves? I'll be back around 6PM, and I'll bring home some takeout for dinner. Help yourselves to anything in the fridge, and don't let those dogs take liberties."

"Sure," Trey agreed with more enthusiasm than I'd ever heard him express for anything.

She handed us a key and instructions for the alarm code in case we wanted to leave the house. I narrowed my eyes at her – it was an insane amount of trust to place on two kids she'd literally just met the night before. Trey looked equally skeptical as he climbed out of the car and Deborah showed him how to put the dogs on their leads.

"Why are you doing this?" he demanded, the question coming out as an accusation.

Deborah looked us both straight in the eye. "You've both been let down by people who were supposed to care for you. I don't want you to judge the rest of the human race by their standards. I think you'll find outside the walls of Derleth Academy people like you for who you are, not what you can do for them."

With that, she backed out of the drive and sped away, leaving Trey and I with the keys to her house and three very excited dogs tugging at their leads.

"What do you want to do?" I asked Trey as we watched Deborah's car round the corner of her street. Above our heads, birds sang in the trees like there wasn't a cosmic deity threatening the world.

A sly smile tugged the corners of Trey's cruel mouth. "I've been trapped inside that cursed school for twenty years. I want to party."

It turns out that Trey's version of 'partying' was walking the dogs around the forest trails near Deborah's house. He couldn't keep the smile off his face as he stopped to sniff flowers or admire the birds while a sedate Leopold and Loeb ogled him with wide-eyed adoration. Behind them, I struggled with the overexcited Roger who wanted to chase every leaf that blew in front of his face.

"When you said you wanted to party, I pictured us knocking back shots in a dive bar," I said as I dragged Roger away from a particularly enticing pile of deer crap. "Maybe find cocaine and hookers."

"I did all that stuff at school," Trey said. "Our parents made sure we had any alcohol or drugs we wanted. Anything to keep us distracted so we'd continue to do their dirty work."

"If you could have a future, what would you want to do?"

"My parents would make me go to Harvard to study business, like every other male in my family. Then I'd go to work for my dad and—"

"That wasn't the question. What do *you* want to do?"

"It doesn't matter what I want."

"Again, not the question."

Trey sighed in exasperation. "Fine. I'd study engineering and go into renewable energy and cleantech. The way we burn fossil fuels and generate electricity is inefficient and wasteful. We only do it like that to make a bunch of asshole friends of my dad even richer – remember, Dad only took in Ayaz to get access to his family's oil fortune. But it would be a big scandal in my dad's circle if I went into that field, which is why it was pointless to dream about it even when I thought I could go to college. I try not to think about it. Right now I want air and light and dogs and ice cream and—whoa!"

A squirrel darted across the path in front of us. Leopold's eyes widened, and he galloped after it, yanking Trey along behind him. Trey's feet slid out from under him, and he ended up face down on the muddy path.

For a moment, he lifted his mud-smeared face and his eyes were filled with cold fury, but then he burst out laughing. A wild giggle escaped my throat as I bent down to help him up.

Trey dusted mud from the front of his t-shirt and glared at me. "Don't you tell anyone you saw me like this."

"Don't worry. This is going all over social media." I dug into my pocket for my phone to snap a picture, before remembering that I didn't have a phone. Mine was back in Ms. West's hands again. It was funny how an old habit like that stuck around.

It felt weird to be laughing with Trey about such a mundane thing. It was like hanging out with Dante again, only better because we had dogs, and also because I didn't feel as though there was this power imbalance between Trey and me anymore. I'd been crushing hard on Dante for years, but he either refused to see it or he chose to ignore it for reasons that he took to his grave. Trey might be seven-million social classes above me, but he'd taken a massive risk to defy his father and find me. Even though we hadn't talked about what happened between us, I knew the feelings I had for Trey were at least somewhat mutual.

With his mud-splattered thrifted t-shirt, ill-fitting jeans, and the wide grin he wore as he got the dogs back under control, it was easy to believe Trey was just a normal teenager. I got the feeling that Trey had never felt 'just normal' in his life. And then Roger barreled past them, knocking my arm against the heavy stone inside Trey's backpack, and I remembered that neither of us was normal.

This peace we felt right now – it was an illusion. But it was something I'd had before and Trey had never experienced, so I let him have it.

After another hour or so, Trey decided he wanted to see the town. I thought it was risky since we were still so close to Arkham, but I couldn't refuse Trey anything today. On the main drag, Trey made a beeline for the ice cream parlor we'd seen from the bus window. I stood outside with the dogs while he agonized over flavors. He came out with a big grin and two double cones groaning under the weight of multiple scoops and toppings – nuts, candy, chocolate sprinkles, seven wafers, cookie crumbs... he'd gone crazy.

"Did you leave anything in the store?" I accepted the cone with incredulity.

"A couple of wafers and some flavor called 'rum & raisin' that sounds awful." Trey's eyes closed with bliss as he licked the full length of his cone. Heat pooled between my legs as I thought of other things he'd licked like that.

As I licked a drip of chocolate ice cream off my hand, something occurred to me. "Trey, how did you pay for these ice creams?"

Trey flashed me a black card. "With my money."

"But you don't have money. You've lived locked away in that school for twenty years. That card can't possibly work anymore."

"This is the kind of card that doesn't expire," Trey slipped the card back into his pocket. "There's so much money in this account I could buy a house if I wanted to. It was my expense account from happier times. I checked it in a machine at Arkham and the money's still there. Dad hasn't touched it."

"Your father has access to this account? He could track the purchase to us." I gaped at him. How could he be so stupid?

"Relax. My father has so much money in so many different

accounts, he's not going to notice a tiny ice cream purchase. He has no idea I still have this card. He'll have forgotten all about it. Now, eat your ice cream before it melts. Let's go back to Deborah's place. I bet the dogs could use a rest."

Trey's clipped tone dictated the end of the discussion. I didn't share his certainty about Vincent's lack of interest, but I couldn't do anything about it now. He'd done the damage, now we just had to hope Vincent wouldn't pick up on our location.

Trey better be doing a fuckton of 'hoping,' because I was all out of hopes to give.

CHAPTER THIRTEEN

It was weird hanging out in someone's house while they weren't there, but the fully-stocked kitchen cupboards and the dogs enthusiastic (if slobbery) excitement soon put me at ease. Trey spent the rest of the day playing with the dogs on the deck. It was amazing to watch him come alive as he rubbed bellies and threw balls and sticks for them. I found stacks of medical books on Deborah's shelves and cracked them open, surprising myself by how much I understood just from listening to Gail's descriptions of her lab.

"Why are you reading those?" Trey asked as he came inside for a snack, three happy canines circling his heels.

I set down the book. "I don't know. I guess... I find it interesting. I wonder if I might have been a chemist or a phlebotomist or a pathologist if I had another life. If I'd graduated from a different school."

Trey's ice eyes swept over the text, hardening as they lifted to meet mine. "You could still be those things."

I snorted. "Yeah, right. Even if I do survive my year at Derleth, which is unlikely, then I doubt any respectable college will accept my diploma – if I earned a diploma, which is even more unlikely."

I realized as I spoke I sounded just like Trey did earlier, quashing his dreams of being an engineer before he'd even had a chance to try, all because of shit he felt he had no control over.

Trey must've realized it too. He pounded my book with his fist, his eyes flashing. "Don't sacrifice your future for me, Hazel. I don't want that. You should run as far as you can from me, from Derleth. I could wire you some money. Get yourself into a good school, graduate with honors, live your life the way you were supposed to before we fucked it up for you."

"Yeah, that's not happening." I gripped the spine of the book so hard my knuckles turned white. "I'm staying right here."

"No. I forbid it." Trey's face twisted with rage.

"You can't forbid shit. I'm a fugitive now. A fugitive with no high school diploma and a bargain with a cosmic god hanging over my head. Getting into medical school isn't even on my radar. I'm not leaving you guys to fight this yourselves. I care too fucking much, and even if I didn't, I have to stay and fight because it's my future on the line, too."

Deborah arrived home, diffusing the tension flowing between us with two heaving bags of Chinese takeout. Trey peered into the containers, apprehensively sniffing the contents. "What's this?" he demanded. "I've been to China. This isn't Chinese food."

"Poor little rich boy. He's never had food served from cardboard cartons before," I explained to Deborah as I shoved a heap of sweet and sour pork and moo shu vegetables onto his plate.

Trey gulped down the food like he hadn't eaten a mountain of ice cream, and loaded up his plate with seconds. I leaned over and wiped a smudge of sauce from his cheek. Away from Derleth and all the trappings of wealth he wore so perfectly, Trey was so much more... human.

I liked it. I hated how much I liked it.

Deborah reached under the table and pulled out a thin book.

"I have something to show you both." She set the book on the table and opened the cover.

I recognized the symbols dotting the pages as sigils – a ritual drawing that denoted the names of entities or the patterns of a spell. Between the symbols, delicate watercolor illustrations showed animals playing in the trees or detailed line drawings of plants and flowers. It reminded me a little of Parris' skin-bound grimoire, except prettier.

"This book belonged to one of my ancestors," Deborah explained, turning the page. I peered at the image of a deer wreathed in a border of flowers and herbs. "She was a great magic worker, but she wasn't content to dabble in healing potions and midwifery – the types of 'soft' magic usually reserved for women. She was interested in *power* – especially the power of what we now term a soul. She wanted to know how to obtain power, wield it, and redistribute it from those who had it to those who didn't. A lot of her writings read like proto-feminism – shocking ideas for a time when even being a literate black woman with ideas would likely get you killed. This was her grimoire – written and illustrated in her hand and the hands of her descendants. It's been passed down through the women of my family for generations."

"It's beautiful," I breathed. "Why are you showing it to us?"

"Because my ancestor was Rebecca Nurse. This is her grimoire."

"I know. Zehra had your name on a family tree. But why didn't you think to show us this before?"

Deborah paused. I knew there was something else she wasn't telling us. Unease prickled up my spine. I trusted her, and she was keeping secrets from us. "I needed time to think about whether you require it. I thought it might just be a coincidence – you sought me out because I worked with Hermia, not because of my ancestors."

"Don't you think that seems like an unlikely coincidence?"

"Not necessarily. I grew up in Arkham. Many of the families in the area have been here for centuries. Descendants of Parris' cult still inhabit the area, including my own. Many members of the Eldritch Club, including Trey's father, are descendants of the cult."

"Did you show this to Zehra?"

A shadow passed over Deborah's eyes – a flicker so fast I barely registered it before it was gone. She closed the book and pushed it across the table to me. "I didn't. I knew she would want to take it with her. I tried to take photographs of the pages to send her, but they all come out blank – something magical in the binding doesn't allow it to be copied. This is the most precious thing I own – a record of the magic flowing through my veins. And look," Deborah opened the book and pointed to an entry at the back. "This is my sister's handwriting. She wrote it before she ran away from home. She was fifteen. It's the last thing I have of hers. I didn't want to part with it unless it was absolutely necessary."

I folded my arms and glared across the table at her. "It's necessary."

"I realise that now." Tears pooled in the corners of Deborah's eyes. "I didn't know... how bad things had gotten at the school. I think you need it more than I do."

I reached gingerly for the book. "It's not bound in Rebecca's skin, is it?"

Deborah touched the cover with affection. "Nope, just ordinary leather."

"I like this woman already." I reached out and touched the book. As my fingers brushed the carved leather, a flicker of flame darted between my fingers like an electric shock.

"Just remember, Hazel." Deborah's eyes bore into mine. "The power Rebecca speaks of takes no sides and offers no moral judgment. It's you who must decide how it is used. You seem to have a particular connection to Rebecca's magic, but be careful of the power you wield. It can come back to haunt you."

CHAPTER FOURTEEN

With our test results still in Gail's hands, there was nothing else Deborah could do for us. She begged us to stay with her a final night, where she stuffed us so full of burgers and fries and apple pie and ice cream that I felt sure I'd burst. The next morning she sent us off with brand new cellphones, a supply of snacks, and backpacks stuffed with new clothes.

"Call or message me with any new information," she said. "I will do the same. If you find those keys again, I'll try to find a way to get into Hermia's lab and see what she's been up to. We'll get to the bottom of this. In the meantime, you two look after yourselves."

"We will," Trey promised, embracing her and accepting slobbery kisses from the dogs. I shook Deborah's hand, not yet willing to give over my trust to her. I felt guilty about doubting her after all her generosity, but I didn't like that she'd waited to tell us Rebecca's relationship with her family. She was keeping something from us, and I didn't understand what, or why.

"What do we do now?" Trey asked as we hiked through the forest in the direction of the bus stop in the next town over. I hiked the backpack on my shoulder, the corner of Rebecca's grimoire jabbing into my spine. "California? Hawaii? Budapest? I've always wanted to see Prague…"

"Don't be ridiculous. You know we're not going to Prague. We're heading to the school."

"Be serious, Hazel. We're lying low somewhere until we get the test results—"

"No. We're going back to Derleth Academy."

Trey stopped in his tracks. His fingers circled my wrist, jerking me back. "No way. It's suicide. Dunwich Institute will be shitting themselves over letting you escape. They're going to be looking everywhere for you. My father, too. Remember those assassins he sent after Zehra? I bet he's got them on speed dial."

Once again, Vincent Bloomberg spoiled everything. I jerked my arm from Trey's grasp.

"So? I've told you, I'm not abandoning everyone just because of a little death threat. Besides, they won't expect us to return to school. They don't have enough imagination for that."

"Right. Because that would be stupid." Trey looked exasperated. "And we're not stupid. Although right now you're doing an excellent impression."

I punched his arm. "Maybe you can live with yourself running off to Budapest and carrying a giant hunk of rock around with you for the rest of your life, but I'm not abandoning Greg or Andre, or Quinn either."

"And Ayaz?"

I looked away. "He already abandoned us."

"Maybe not." Trey sighed. He fingers knitted in mine, and he squeezed a little. I looked up at him and dared a smile.

"Of course I want to save him too, as long as he accepts my help. What are you thinking, rich boy?"

"I'm thinking that you're an exasperating, headstrong, stubborn person and that if I wasn't already dead, spending time with you would rapidly make me so."

I grinned. "You're welcome."

Trey sighed again. "So we're going back. Quinn will be pleased. Can we stop at a store? He asked me to bring him back something called a Twinkie. Apparently, they're his favorite food from when he was a kid."

"Quinn's still a kid." I grinned. *And I can't believe you don't know what a Twinkie is.* "Thank you."

"You won't be thanking me when we're staring down into the god's abyss, right before they throw us in." Trey linked his arm with mine. "Fine. I should know better by now than to argue with you. Back to that hellhole we go."

CHAPTER FIFTEEN

Trey and I hitchhiked back to Arkham with a truck driver delivering food to the general store. He kept teasing Trey about wearing his hoodie pulled tight around his face the whole time. "You're Kenny from South Park," he kept saying. It was some cartoon I'd seen on Hulu but never watched, so I didn't get the reference, but Trey seemed to know exactly what the guy was talking about. I guess it must've started back when he entered Miskatonic Prep.

I forgot sometimes that Trey's life had this huge pop-culture black hole. The only shows he remembered were from 20 years ago. He'd never seen *Stranger Things* or *American Horror Story* or even *Supernatural*. I wished we'd had more time so we could have watched movies and TV shows together and I could have introduced him to Netflix. I bet he still thought TV had commercials.

When I freed him, we were going to have some serious fun.

If I freed him.

After waving goodbye to our driver, we peeled off the main road as quickly as we could and entered the woods. My stomach twisted as we began the long climb up the peninsula. We passed by a strange rock formation – a jagged circle of sharp points ejected from the earth beneath like predator's teeth. Trey leaned in between them and deposited his rock in a small gap, hiding it beneath a pile of dead leaves and moss. "I don't need to keep carrying that around now," he said, picking up an old t-shirt wrapped around another object.

"What's that?" I pointed to the damp bundle.

Trey unrolled the edge of the t-shirt, showing me the collection of hammers and chisels wrapped inside. "I stole them from the maintenance shed," he said proudly. "We're going to need them."

After twenty minutes, we both puffed as we clambered over craggy rocks and scrambled through dense forest. Nothing looked familiar, but I guessed I'd only ever traveled this far from Derleth blindfolded, under cover of darkness, or sedated. After what seemed like hours, we mounted a wooded ridge and I could just make out the roof of the dormitory building sticking out above the trees.

The moon was high by the time we reached the edge of the fields. Trey stood behind the row of rose bushes where we hid after tagging the gymnasium wall. I looked over the field – they'd painted the wall a blazing white to cover over our graffiti. A line of charred earth burned through the middle of the field, breaking the symmetry of the space with its cruel irregularity. *That's from the fire in my dream.*

My dream was real. My fire could reach beyond my subconscience and impact the real world.

What.

The.

Actual.

Fuck?

I didn't have time to ponder it in any great depth. Trey turned to me, and the look on his face was unreadable. "What do we do now?"

"We're going to see our friends. Quinn told me there were

three secret passages into the school, and Andre and I found an additional one that leads to Ms. West's lab. The swinging mirror was bricked up, and I don't like our chances with the icehouse. Where are the others?"

"Neither of them will work," Trey said. "One goes into the faculty wing, the other one comes out near the gymnasium, and it's filled with those... shadow things."

I shuddered at the memory of the shadows that attacked me in the gym. "No thanks."

"Agreed. It's why we never use them. Show me the bricks. We're going to have to get through them. Luckily, I'm now a champion at chiseling."

We picked our way back through the woods to the edge of the cliff, where rough stone steps led down to the ancient pleasure garden. At the top of the stairs, Trey thrust out an arm, holding me back.

"What gives? You almost—"

The fierce look in Trey's eyes silenced me. It was then that I heard the voices rising from the garden below. Students laughing. Not just any students. I recognized Courtney's unmistakable purr.

We're not alone.

Unable to stop myself, I laid down the tools and flattened myself against the ground. I drew out Zehra's knife from my boot and gripped it in my hand as I peered over the edge of the cliff down onto the pleasure garden.

"Oh, Ayaz!" Courtney squealed in delight. She stood on the edge of the grotto, her panther-like body clad only in a white bikini. She held up her hands to her face as a figure in the water splashed her playfully. The figure laughed, his voice like velvet.

Ayaz.

The sight of him made heat flame inside me. He looked amazing, his torso glistening with water and painted with tattoos, his dark hair lost against the murky water. He picked up a squealing Courtney, threw her over his shoulders, and dragged her into the water. I leaned out further, twisting my head to see, but they'd gone under the rock shelf and deeper into the grotto.

To the place he had kissed me, when I told him I'd seen Zehra. *How can he be there with her? How—*

A hand grabbed my shoulder, yanked me back into the trees. Trey frowned at me as he clutched me against his chest, sand-wiching my arms in place with his superior strength.

"We should get closer," I whispered, struggling against his iron grip. "We need to hear what they say."

"We can't. They'll see us as soon as we leave the trees."

"Fine. You run around, create a distraction. Then I'll sneak down and—"

"Hazel, right now you don't want to hear what Ayaz is saying."

I sagged in Trey's arms, the knife slipping from my grasp. "You're right."

Trey let me go. I bent to retrieve my knife, needing the reas-suring weight of it against my skin. Even though my whole body prickled with heat in my desperation to run after Ayaz, to shake his gorgeous shoulders and drag answers out of him, I stayed crouched beside Trey, the knife handle hot against my fingers, straining to hear something from below and yet not wanting to hear. After what seemed like hours while my imagination tore wretched images of what they might be doing down there, Ayaz and Courtney and the other monarchs climbed back up the staircase, laughing and joking as they headed back in the direction of the school.

As soon as they disappeared into the trees and we were certain we were alone, Trey and I crept out from our hiding place and headed down the stairs. The garden felt strange now. It had been the location of so many memories of my time at Derleth – some of them horrible, some of them wonderful, but tainted now because Courtney was in the arms of my guy.

He's not my guy.

I've got Trey. And Quinn. It doesn't matter.

He said I was beautiful.

I followed Trey as he picked his way through the weed-choked pathways to the tunnel. He parted the vines we used to disguise the entrance and disappeared inside. "We should have thought to bring a lantern," he called from within as he held out his hand to me. "We could go back and see if there's one in the maintenance shed."

"No need." I opened my palm up and let the warmth spread along my veins until it pooled in my hand. A tiny flame burst from my skin and danced in the air.

Trey's eyes widened. He swallowed hard. "That... that is..."

"I know. It's freaky as fuck. But it's our best option."

"Right. Yes." Trey looked like he was trying hard not to throw up. "Is it safe in this narrow space? It won't burst free and burn us?"

"Nope. I've been practicing." I allowed the flame to dance a little higher. "I can keep it burning for hours. I promise it won't hurt you, unless you ask me about the fire that killed my mother. Then all bets are off. Deal?"

"Deal." We climbed into the tunnel, the tiny light illuminating a circle at our feet. Trey walked stiffly, jumping at every water drip or flickering shadow. The fire made him nervous.

I ran my fingers along the walls, noticing the marks of the tools that had hollowed out this cave. I wondered who the workers were who made this secret route for Parris, and what he did to them once they had finished their clandestine task.

Trey's broad shoulders and athletic frame blocked my view down the tunnel. After a time, he stopped short. I skidded to a halt, flinging my arm in the air before I accidentally set fire to his shirt.

"You might've warned me you were putting the brakes on."

Trey didn't apologize. That wasn't his thing. He shrunk away again, flattening his back against the hunnel wall to be as far from the flame as possible. "I've found the blockage. You weren't kidding."

With Trey cowering against the tunnel, I had a narrow view in front of him. The entire width and height of the space had been blocked by a wall of reddish-brown bricks, each one mortared in place to create a wall. It looked expertly done and solid as stone.

"I don't understand," Trey said. "The only people who know about this tunnel are the four of us. So how was this done?"

"It was maybe an hour after I left your room when I tried to get through here," I asked. "Could it have been done after your father took Ayaz and did whatever he did to corrupt him?"

Trey shook his head. "Even if they did somehow manage to get the tunnel bricked up in that time, which I doubt, the mortar would've been wet and soft when you came through. You could have easily removed the bricks."

"True, and they were already hard when I was here. Then it must've been done earlier. The last time we used the tunnel was the night we saw Zehra. It could have been done any time after that."

"Fuck." Trey rubbed his temple. "How long have they known?"

"Don't know. And right now I don't care. Do you think we can move the bricks?"

"Come closer and shine that light." Trey flattened his back against the wall, but I didn't need to crowd him to help. I directed the flame to leave my hand and float above his head, so that it sat at the highest point of the tunnel, shining its flickering light down on the bricks.

"That's amazing." Trey managed to sound both impressed and horrified.

"Yeah, yeah, I know. It takes a lot of effort to hold it in place, though, and I can only do it with a tiny flame. Anything bigger I lose control once it leaves my body. So work quick, rich boy."

Trey rolled up his sleeves and used the pick to clear as much of the mortar as he could from between the bricks. Red dust swirled around us, stinging my eyes and making it difficult to breathe. Several times we had to run back outside to gulp in fresh lungfuls of air.

I took over from Trey for a bit, driving in the chisel with the hammer, sending chunks of brick and mortar raining down on the floor of the cave. I had to work in pitch black because I couldn't control the fire at the same time. When I couldn't lift my arms any more, Trey took over again, peeling off his shirt to reveal strong muscles that flexed as he attacked the wall with everything he had. His torso soon glowed with a covering of red brick dust.

My throat tightened. We ran outside again. This time, the moon was higher in the sky. Back outside, Trey mopped crimson sweat from his brow with his ruined shirt. "I've never had to work this hard in my life. Even chiseling out that sigil wasn't this difficult."

I squeezed his biceps. "How'd you get these?"

"Lacrosse. Rowing team. Pure genetic good luck." He dared a half-smile. "My dad did give me something useful, after all."

"Remind me to thank him." At the mention of his dad, my veins boiled. Our light flared up, flames licking around the sides of the tunnel. Trey slammed his shirt against the rock, smothering the flame.

"Maybe you'd better keep hold of this one," he muttered as I summoned another flame, his shoulders heaving with silent panic.

Slowly but surely, we chipped out the mortar around one of the bricks. Trey whooped with delight as he wiggled the brick free and tossed it toward the cave entrance. A faint rush of cool air blew through the gap. More bricks followed soon after, and a short time later we had a hole big enough to crawl through.

I went first, sending my flame floating through the hole in front of me before getting down on my hands and knees and climbing through. Cold brick dug into my thighs as I twisted to fit through. I rolled on the tunnel floor and pulled myself to my feet. "Your turn, Bloomberg."

It took Trey some time to fit his broad shoulders through the gap. He had to back out and remove two more bricks in order to make enough room. Finally, he was through, too. We slung along the tunnel, arriving at the short, narrow stairs leading down to the mirror that served as the tunnel's secret entrance.

To my relief when I pushed on the mirror, it swung open unhindered. They must've figured the bricks were enough to deter anyone using the tunnel. I climbed down into the storage room, Trey on my heels. I snuffed out the flame, plunging us into darkness as we crept through the boxes and junk piled around the room. My hand grazed the door handle.

I poked my head into the hall, my breath caught in my throat. Cold, oppressive silence greeted me, broken only by a thump in one of the hot water pipes that stretched along the low ceiling.

I dragged Trey into the hall. It was only ten feet to reach Greg and Andre's room. My gaze fell on the door opposite theirs – the door that had been mine, that I'd shared with Loretta until she'd been taken by the creature and reborn with popularity. So much had happened in that room – stilted conversations with Loretta, midnight schemes to get even with the Kings, Courtney and the monarchs assaulting me, Ayaz telling me I was beautiful...

I turned away from things that were too painful to consider, raised my fist, and rapped lightly on the other door. The sound ricocheted like gunshots down the hollow hall. "Greg, Andre," I whispered. "It's me. Let us in."

The door flew open. Andre's dark skin was barely discernible from the night that crept around him. His eyebrows shot up as he recognized me. Wordlessly, he ushered us inside, closing and locking the door behind him.

As soon as he'd pushed the bolt across, I grabbed him and held him close. He felt just like the Andre I loved – the kind, silent giant with the gardenia and coconut scent. His hands on my back felt like shields against the world.

I pulled away, casting my eyes around the dim room, resting

on the two beds – one rumpled, one empty and perfectly made. "Where's Greg?"

Andre flicked on the light beside his bed and scrambled for his pad and paper. He dashed off a note and handed it to me. His usually neat handwriting was a messy scrawl.

"Three days ago Ms. West took Greg out of class. She said it was for an extracurricular project. I haven't seen him since."

CHAPTER SIXTEEN

Andre pulled me down to sit beside him. The bedsprings creaked under our combined weight. Trey sank into the hard wooden desk chair, his long legs hanging over the side as he clicked on the desk lamp and started riffling through the papers. "What happened?" I demanded. "Tell me everything from the time you last saw me."

Andre reached across the bed and swiped a paper out of Trey's hand. He gestured for Trey to get out of the chair. Trey leaped up and flattened himself against the wall. He still wasn't used to being around Andre. In Trey's world, people like Andre only existed to be ridiculed.

Well, too bad. Andre's awesome and Trey will have to get used to him. He's my friend and he's not going anywhere. I wasn't going to force Andre to act differently just to make Trey comfortable.

Andre slid into the chair and pulled his pad toward him, scribbling frantically. Trey bent over his shoulder, trying to read the words.

"Don't interrupt him." I shoved Trey onto Greg's empty bed, crowding him down the far end. Trey's gaze settling on the ceiling, where the rats circled frantically above our heads. *Scritch-scritch-*

scritch. Trey's fingers gripped my knee so hard pins and needles shot down my leg.

He's scared.

"They're just rats," I said, prying his fingers off my knee.

"You say that like it's a good thing," Trey muttered. "I've never heard anything like it before. It sounds as though the ceiling is about to cave in."

"That's because you have a room on the top floor."

"If you say so," Trey said cryptically. Andre tore off a paper with a flourish and handed it to me. He bent his head to continue writing. I angled his lamp over the paper, my eyes scanning his neat, looped handwriting.

"You didn't show up for exams. We knew something was wrong. None of the teachers would tell us what happened to you. They cleared all your stuff out of your room. I asked Sadie to see if she could find out anything downstairs. She said the groundskeepers saw orderlies placing something wrapped in white into a van. There was a doctor too. They recognized him from Dunwich Institute. A couple of days later, Sadie delivered coffee to Ms. West and overheard her on the phone, discussing your 'treatment.' Greg was convinced that whatever happened to Loretta was about to happen to you."

I waved the paper in Trey's face. "If you were trying to find me, why didn't you just ask Greg and Andre? According to this, they knew where I was well before you did."

Trey bristled. He opened his mouth to speak, then shut it again. I didn't need to hear. I knew what he was going to say.

It never occurred to him because even when someone dear to him was in trouble, people of his status didn't associate with people like Greg and Andre.

Well, that was going to fucking change.

Andre tore off his second paper and handed it to me. "Greg was making plans to leave school and look for you. He found a map of Dunwich in the library. He was stashing food and water in case he had to go the whole way on foot. He was going to leave that night when they took him away. Sadie says she can't find him anywhere, and she's looked in all the dark corners of the school. She even checked Ms. West's 'laboratory,' whatever that means, but she says it's been cleared out. Nothing left."

I shoved Andre's note into Trey's hands and turned to my friend. "I'm here now, and we're going to find him. They can't have sent Greg to Dunwich. That place is toast, literally. So he must still be on the grounds somewhere—"

BANG. THUMP.

I froze as sounds came from the hallway. The door handle rattled.

"Open this door!" A muffled voice commanded.

CHAPTER SEVENTEEN

Trey yelped as I shoved him to the floor. "Shut up," I hissed, crawling under Greg's bed and gesturing at him to get under Andre's. Trey indicated the cold floor, the smudges of filth and unidentified particles – as if he had to worry about sullying his already filthy clothes. I made a slashing motion across my throat. This was no time for his pretty rich boy concerns. He wasn't too good for the floor if it would save his life.

BANG BANG BANG.

The door rattled on its hinges. Trey's eyes widened. He scrambled under the bed, coating himself in even more dirt and grime. I wished I had a camera to capture the moment forever. Andre yanked down the covers on the beds to better hide us from view. Then he flung open the door.

A figure barged past Andre and strode inside like he owned the place. The door slammed shut behind him.

"I heard voices from this room, which means you've either listening to contraband beat poets or you're hiding a lover. Please tell me you're getting some tail, because a guy with your physique is going to waste being celibate."

My heart skipped. *That familiar voice. That jocular tone. That complete disregard for the brevity of the situation. It has to be, but it can't...*

"Quinn?" The word escaped my throat before I could stop it. I clamped a hand over my mouth. I didn't know if Quinn had been turned like Ayaz, if he was still on my side. If he'd ever been on my side to begin with.

In an instant, the figure dropped to his knees and flung back the blankets. The smile that broke out across his face melted my heart. "Hazy, you sly minx. I knew you'd be back to save us all."

Quinn reached under the bed and grabbed my shoulder, dragging me out and wrapping me in his arms. The warmth of his embrace told me everything I needed to know. Quinn Delacorte may not know how to take anything seriously, but he had my back.

After not nearly long enough, Quinn broke the hug, holding me at arm's length and twirling me around as though we were waltzing. "Let me take a look at you. No broken bones, no missing limbs. What about that delicious brain of yours? Still intact?"

I rubbed my head, a smile playing over my lips. "Still intact, but it was a close call."

"What am I, chopped liver?" Trey poked his head out from under the bed. Quinn reached down and gripped Trey's arm, pulling him to his feet.

"Sorry, Bloomberg. I didn't see you down there in the dirt. I was starting to think they'd caught you, too." Quinn said it in his usual jokey manner, but the way he gripped Trey's forearm betrayed how worried he'd been.

"What are you doing down here?" I asked.

"Didn't Trey tell you?" Quinn pointed over his shoulder at the door. "The Kings have fallen. Trey and I have been disowned. Our parents are no longer supporting our fine education, so we can't keep our fancy dorm rooms upstairs. We've been stripped of most of our merit points for helping you escape out the window. We're bunking in your old room, which is a complete rat-infested shit-hole, if you don't mind my saying."

I glanced at Trey in surprise. "You didn't think to mention this?"

He shrugged. A flash of something passed over his features for a moment. Hurt. Even after everything his father had done, there was still that little boy inside Trey who hungered for his dad's approval and who was mortified to fall from favor.

Well, too damn bad. This was about so much fucking more than wounded pride.

"Trey hasn't adjusted well," Quinn said. "That's why he volunteered to go after you. It was the best of our shitty options."

Quinn's voice bounced off the walls. I grabbed Andre's towel off the hanger and stuffed it under the door. "Can you keep it down? I don't want our voices to carry."

"I resent the implication that I'm a loud-mouthed idiot." Quinn flopped down on the bed, stealing all Andre's pillows to place behind his head. "And also, good call."

I sat down on the end of the bed, wanting to be near him, to touch him, to know he was real, but also afraid of what that meant. Quinn had no such qualms. He pulled me into his arms, cradling me against his chest, the way Trey had done back in the RV.

"We found that woman Zehra spoke about, the one who used to work with Ms. West." I tried to explain what we'd discovered about Deborah and her relationship to Rebecca Nurse, but as soon as I tried to talk about magic, my voice froze in my throat. I couldn't speak. Andre handed me a glass of water, but that didn't clear the—

Of course. Andre was here. The bloody agreement was still in place. How could it be when Ms. West broke her end of the bargain? When she'd hurt Greg...

Wait a second.

If our agreement was still in place, that must mean Greg was still alive. He was safe.

For now.

"Hazy?" Quinn raised an eyebrow. "You look surprisingly smug for someone who's snuck into a school filled with people who want to kill you."

"I *am* smug. I just figured something out." I sat up, sending Quinn's arm slamming into the wall. I touched Andre's hand. "Greg's safe. I can't explain how I know that, but you have to trust that I do." Andre nodded. "I don't know for how much longer, though. I need you to get Sadie to keep her ear to the ground. If possible, find out where Ms. West has moved her lab. I can't explain what it is, but just know it's important."

Andre nodded again.

"I also need you to go across to my room and wait for me. I have to speak to Quinn and Trey alone for a sec. I'm sorry for kicking you out of your room, but I promise that it's important and I'll be done soon."

Andre looked like he wanted to argue. I think if it had been me in his situation, I'd have demanded to stay, but Andre wasn't me. He nodded placidly, caught the keys Quinn tossed to him, and slunk out of the room.

I locked the door behind him, replaced the rolled towel and leaned against the door, my eyes darting from Trey on one bed to Quinn on the other. Being in the same room as the two of them gave me flashbacks to what happened between us at the movie night. It was too much testosterone – it made my throat constrict and my stomach to dance in a strange and pleasant way. I swallowed hard.

Quinn looked between Trey and I, and his expression darkened. "You two boned, didn't you?" he demanded.

"That's not important," Trey said. He sounded tired.

"Of course it's important. You boned and Hazy and Ayaz

boned and poor Quinn is just left out here in no-Eskimo sex land."

"It's *edimmu*," Trey corrected without thinking.

Quinn waved a hand. "Whatever. I don't begrudge our girl the chance for a little undead lovin'. I just think Hazy should keep her options open. Once she's gone to bed with me, there's going to be no—"

"*Quinn.*" His name hissed through my teeth, even as my body flared with heat. Because I wanted it. I wanted him, which was ridiculous because I shouldn't even be thinking about sex right now. "Don't you want to hear what we've found out?"

"I want to find out how Hazy reacts when I roll her nipples under my tongue." Quinn licked his upper lip. "What do you say, friend? We could have a repeat of the movie night—"

I pressed my legs together, trying to stop myself from thinking of the two of them with me, touching me, taking me... *No, no, no, not now.*

"As tempting as that is, you're going to want to hear this," Trey said. "Although it's probably going to destroy your hard-on. I was right about the fire. It wasn't an accident. It wasn't faulty wiring. The Eldritch Club knew it would happen. They *chose* us to sacrifice."

Quinn's body froze. His mouth wobbled. He looked completely flustered.

"You don't have a smartass comeback to that?" Trey sounded upset – as if somehow hearing one of Quinn's quips would make what we knew somehow less horrific.

"I really, really don't." Quinn lay back on the pillows, his body rigid. All thought of boning fled from him. "Fuck."

Trey nodded. "Yup."

"But... my mom is in the Eldritch Club." Quinn's mouth wobbled again. "She'd never agree to that."

He sounded like a little kid, so lost, so unable to believe his beloved parent was capable of such evil. I slammed my fingers into the burn on my wrist, which flared with a bright heat.

I believed it.

I knew what someone who claimed to love you more than life itself could do to you for their own selfishness.

"I don't know the details, man," Trey said quickly. "Maybe your mom protested, but you know what Damon is capable of. She might not have had a choice."

Quinn winced and sat up again, his body curling as if he felt the whip across his back once more. He touched a hand to his cheek, his skin pale, his features devoid of his signature mirth. He'd been hurt too many times at the hands of his father, had thrown himself in front of his mother to protect her from worse pain. But even knowing that wasn't enough to take back the hurt she caused him now.

We'd just destroyed a piece of what made Quinn who he was. I hated that I was responsible for breaking his spirit, but I hated his parents more. Damon for being cruel. Elena for being weak, for convincing him that her guilt was true love.

I longed to gather Quinn into my arms, but I had no comfort to give. I couldn't tell him it was okay, because my own guilt would burn him even worse. But I could give a distraction. I pulled out Deborah's book and dumped it in his lap. "This is Rebecca Nurse's grimoire. We know she placed sigils in hidden places around the grounds. We know she protested Parris' raising of the monster. After she left here she went all around the country, publishing occult pamphlets, so we know she survived the Great Old God. There might be something in this book that will help us."

"If only we still had Ataturk," Quinn said, turning the pages. "This is his jam."

"That would be nice, but we don't have Ayaz. It's just us. Luckily, Rebecca doesn't seem to have used as many dead languages as our friend Parris. Most of this book appears to be in

English, albeit an archaic form. Between Trey and I, I think we can make some sense of this."

"You and Trey?" Quinn looked at me in alarm. "You're staying here? At school?"

"Of course. I'm not leaving you guys again, not unless they're dragging my corpse away."

Quinn shuddered. "Don't joke about that, Hazy. That's the reality if you stay here."

I grinned, even though on the inside I was even more terrified than he was. "Coming back is *genius*. Vincent's cronies are probably scouring the country for me. They'd never guess I'd be right under their noses."

Quinn tried to grin back, but it never quite reached his eyes. "Okay, Hazy. What do you need from me?"

"The whole reason the Eldritch Club got away with this in the first place is that they bred you all to believe you're serving some great purpose and that your family's wealth, power, and donor come before everything else, even their own lives. And they used the booze and drugs and the scholarship students to keep you all in line, to keep you from asking questions. I believe the only way we're going to free all the Miskatonic students from whatever spell keeps you here is to shatter this illusion."

"And how do you think you're going to achieve that?"

"I have an idea," I said. "Remember last quarter when I pulled those pranks on Courtney and the monarchs to give them a taste of what they'd done to others?"

"I'll never forget it." There was Quinn's cheeky grin again, a little wobbly at the edges but still enough to melt my heart. "Courtney tearing out her hair after you glued those cat ears to her head! Priceless."

I smiled too, because the memory of pulling one over Courtney Haynes was pretty sweet. "That was fun, but I decided it wasn't enough. I swore that I'd have my revenge in such a way that it would break the cycle of hate and abuse that's defined this school. I had a plan that I hoped would make everyone see why they couldn't just treat people the way they did. I think with a few tweaks, it might be just what we need. But now I don't have access to the school, I'm going to need your help to make it happen."

CHAPTER EIGHTEEN

We let Andre back into his room, and Quinn and Trey and I snuck back across the hall. It was so strange to see Quinn's clothing and Trey's books tossed around the room where I'd spent so many hours. They didn't belong down here in the basement with the exposed pipes and mysterious dripping – they weren't part of this world.

The Kings had fallen.

But it might be the best thing that ever happened to them.

Trey climbed into his bed and fell asleep almost immediately. I borrowed a shirt from Quinn to sleep in. I turned away from him, facing the wall as I pulled my damp hoodie over my head and tugged down the t-shirt. My skin sizzled where Quinn's eyes grazed across it.

I wanted him to want me. Which was crazy, because I was with Trey now, wasn't I? I couldn't have them both.

But you did have them both once before. Remember what they did to you, *together.*

I pressed my thighs together as the memory of it sent a flare of heat through my core. I had to stop. Leading Quinn on and teasing him with my body was something my mother would do, and I wouldn't be like her. I *wouldn't*.

Not in this room that already dripped with Ayaz's memories.

"I'll go back to Andre's room." My voice came out strangled, husky. "He'll let me sleep in Greg's bed."

"Oh, no, you don't." Quinn yanked me back, wrapping his body around me and pulling me into bed beside him.

"I can't," I whispered. "Not here."

"Because of Trey and Ayaz?" Quinn cocked an eyebrow. I nodded.

"Ayaz mostly. I just... if you and I... I don't want it to be tainted by his memory."

"I'm not so keen on that myself." Quinn sighed. "Okay, Hazy. No boning tonight. But you're not going anywhere. Just don't be surprised if my hard-on jabs you in the thigh all night."

He wasn't wrong. My naked thighs pressed against him, and I could feel *everything*. The strain of his muscles as he tried to relax, the sharp intake of breath against my neck as his hand accidentally brushed my breast.

My whole body buzzed with sensation. Every touch sent flares of fire through my nerves. Each breath became an erotic art, each groan of the mattress beneath us a tantalizing promise of what could have been.

No way was I getting any sleep in Quinn's arms.

I was right. By the time the sun peeked in through the window, I was a live wire of hormones and desperation. Quinn must've been suffering just as much, because when I tried to adjust my arm into a more comfortable position, my ass rubbed down his rigid cock and he shuddered.

"Fuck this," he growled, his voice dripping with need.

Before I could say anything. Quinn grabbed my hand and yanked me roughly from the bed. His lips captured mine in a total collapse of willpower, a total abandonment of all sense that left me ragged, breathless, burning for more.

His hands explored my body in the dark, tugging at the flimsy t-shirt, pressing hot skin against skin. His fingers grazed my hardened nipple, and I moaned against his slicing tongue. I was gone. I was his. I kissed him hungrily, not caring about the noises I made, the groans of desperation that Trey might've been able to hear.

As we kissed, Quinn lifted me into his arms, carrying me easily across the room. "Where are we going?" I demanded, breaking the kiss to demand an answer.

"Somewhere we can be alone," he whispered back. I could hear the smile in his voice. "I want to show you what you've been missing."

Quinn grunted as he struggled with the door, but he wouldn't put me down. He finally managed to yank it open. He carried me down the hall, squeezed through the tunnel, then carried me again down to the pleasure garden. With every step we took away from the school, my longing for him burned ever brighter, until I was an inferno, ready to raze down a forest for another taste of him.

The rising sun warmed the air just enough that my naked flesh responded, sizzling with need as Quinn lifted me through the overhanging trees.

I expected him to go to the grotto, but perhaps he'd read from my expression that Ayaz's memory haunted that, too. Instead, he pulled me under the crumbling rotunda. In the center was a metal fire pit, the coals cold and raked over. No one had been here tonight.

Quinn. My back pressed against an ancient column, the cold stone doing little to cool my searing skin. I wrapped my legs around him as he slammed his body against mine, pinning me with his need while he attacked my mouth with his.

Danger lurked in every kiss; every caress was another chance we'd be caught. But that only made it all the more exciting.

Quinn tugged off my t-shirt, his hands palming my breasts, his thumb brushing over my nipples as he sought my mouth. His hips thrust forward, grinding against me, in case I was in any doubt just how much he wanted this. Wanted *me*.

It felt greedy to kiss Quinn like this. He gave me everything I demanded, his body rising to meet mine. I kissed him harder, faster – it was a kiss of the here and now, of the way Quinn lived his life because he'd lost all hope in a future.

For the undead, Quinn's kiss dripped with *life*, with the verve and vivacity and Bacchanalian abandonment that were uniquely his.

He pulled away, panting hard, and dragged a condom from his pocket. "I heard from Ayaz you don't trust us not to give you a zombie baby," he grinned as he tugged down his boxers and rolled it on.

A smile crept across my face. I couldn't find the words to answer, so I grabbed a fistful of his dirty blond hair and pulled Quinn's face to mine. My other hand drifted over his body, enjoying his tight muscles, the tension in my shoulders relaxing as he held me against that pillar and thrust.

He penetrated me in a single deep stroke. My neck bent back and I howled into the dark. No one but Quinn Delacorte could make me abandon all my senses like this.

Hot. Primal. Desperate. Quinn Delacorte drove into me like I was the only thing tethering him to earth. I wrapped my legs around his back, crossing my heels to lock them in place and pulling him deeper inside me. He held me easily, slamming my body into the rotunda with each thrust. Rough stone scraped my back, but it was nothing on the way Quinn fucked.

An orgasm tore through me like a forest fire. I threw my head back, the scream bubbling in my throat. Quinn's hand sought my mouth, cupping his fingers across my teeth as I released my rage and heartache into the night.

"Ayaz also might have mentioned you're a screamer," Quinn whispered. "I like it, Hazy. I like making you scream."

He fucked hard and fast, bringing me back to earth and then pushing me toward the stars again. A second, more intense orgasm ripped through me. I was torn in two as Quinn shuddered through his own release, his body trembling against mine as he finished with another searing kiss.

Quinn released me, setting my feet back on the quiet earth. We knelt on the ground, our bodies razed with heat, our mouths still seeking each other.

"Well now," Quinn helped me to my feet, pulling the t-shirt back over my head. "You've had all the Kings of Miskatonic Prep, Hazy. Which one are you going to choose?"

I slapped him playfully around the ears. "Right now, I can't choose any of you, not while you're still undead and I'm still bound to be the god's next victim."

Quinn didn't demand further conversation, but his words haunted me as we climbed back through the tunnel and slid into bed opposite a snoring Trey. They pulled my heart in three directions, and I didn't see how it could possibly end well for any of us.

Would I have to choose? If so, who would it be?

CHAPTER NINETEEN

Trey and Quinn and Andre went back to classes and pretended everything was normal while we waited for word from Sadie about Greg. Trey had been clever, waiting until he was on senior study leave to look for me. They had a week off classes to prepare for exams, so no one noticed he was missing.

I hid downstairs in their rooms, studying Rebecca's book and eating whatever cold leftovers they could sneak me from the dining hall.

The first third of Rebecca's book was written in her hand, and that was the section I focused on. The remainder of the book appeared to have been added to over the years with diary entries and spells from women descended from Rebecca's line, until the very back where the last entry was dated from the early 2000s. I started with Rebecca's entries, but they mainly repeated history I'd obtained from Zehra's files, with some added occult mumbo-jumbo thrown in for good measure.

I could barely focus on the task I'd set myself because I was so worried about Greg. I would read a couple of pages before my desperation to find Greg would get the better of me. Only I couldn't walk around the grounds looking for him and risk being seen, so I had to sit down and keep reading.

Is he okay? Is he truly safe? Is Zehra with him? How can we find them?

It didn't help that the rats were going nuts. It was like they knew I'd returned and were determined to make themselves known to me, just in case I could've somehow forgotten them. Every time I moved across the hall to Andre's room and back again, they followed me. They circled above my head, their awful scritch-scritching pounding inside my skull.

Being invisible did have its benefits. Even though Ms. West had to know I'd escaped from Dunwich Institute, there were no additional security measures at the school. As far as I could tell, she wasn't concerned with locating me. In fact, from what the guys told me, she was barely attending to her duties as headmistress at all. I suspected I knew where she was – hidden away in her new laboratory location communing in secret with the god or doing something horrible to Greg. Or Zehra.

If we found the laboratory, we found Greg. And I had an inkling of where we first needed to look.

I didn't bother telling the boys what I planned to do. They'd either refuse to let me go or insist on going with me. I couldn't risk either of those outcomes – I wouldn't put them in any more danger to find Greg. Besides, after three days of hiding in Andre's room while they went to classes, I had serious cabin fever.

As soon as they headed up for breakfast, I hid Rebecca's book behind the desk, picked up the hammer and chisel we'd used on the bricks, stole out of my old room and snuck through the secret tunnel.

I emerged into the pleasure garden, keeping low to the ground as I crept along the path toward the rotunda, trying not to let the memory of what Quinn and I had done there distract me from what I had to do.

Trey's reaction to my fire prickled against my skin. I wondered if that's why the students liked to party here, around the grotto. Maybe they felt safe near water. Maybe their brazier was a way for them to try to control their fear, to cage and conquer it – the way Vincent and Ms. West tried to cage me.

I planned to head to the cemetery. That was where the dead Miskatonic students had been brought back to life. They'd had to dig themselves out of their graves. That wasn't an insignificant amount of work to bury so many students. There had to be some clue there that explained how Ms. West did what she did, and maybe where she'd taken Greg. It was worth a shot.

I hoped I'd find answers.

I hoped I wouldn't find a grave with Greg's name on it.

As I picked my way through the narrow path and emerged at the rear of the rotunda, a sound reached my ears that turned my stomach to ash.

Voices.

Students laughed and chatted as they crowded beneath the rotunda. I'd been so absorbed in my thoughts I hadn't seen them until I was practically on top of them. I dove into one of the overgrown garden beds, shielding myself behind a Grecian statue choked with weeds. I lay in the dirt at the bottom of the garden, my fingers grasping for the knife handle sticking out of my boot. I tried to silence my pounding heart as I strained to hear any sign they'd heard me before I dared raised my head.

I tugged the knife free, feeling the reassuring weight of it in my palm. Slowly and silently, I rolled over in the bed, covering my body in the vines, camouflaging myself in the wasteland of a garden that once was. I bent my head toward the edge of the bed and peered over the edge – listening, watching.

Voices talking. Laughing. Kids sprawled around the grotto, passing a liquor bottle and bags of chips between them. I recognized monarchs. Courtney, John, Tillie, Amber. Nancy shifted uncomfortably in her spot sandwiched between Paul and Barclay. And...

Ayaz.

He lounged against a broken pillar, the same one Quinn had braced me against during our wild boning (boning? Urgh, Quinn said the worst things sometimes) the other night. Courtney snuggled under Ayaz's arm, looking like she belonged there. My fingers tightened around the knife, fantasizing about sticking it into Courtney's neck.

With his free hand, Ayaz held a pipe to his lips and took a deep drag before passing it to John. His features transfixed me until I caught the topic of conversation.

"...Mommy says that the entire institution burned down," Courtney drawled, her long red nails clawing at Ayaz's arm as she tried to twist around to kiss his cheek. "Can you believe it? The official story is faulty wiring, but no one believes that. Hazel was so *obviously* deranged, and her mother died in a fire. She could have killed so many people! I don't feel safe knowing she's out there somewhere."

That bitch. She had a part in locking me up, and now she's over there feeding Ayaz more lies. The urge to wrap my fingers around Courtney's throat and squeeze crept all the way up my arms.

"I wouldn't worry about it," Ayaz said in a bored voice. "She probably died in the blaze."

"We'd know about it if she was dead. Aren't you afraid she might come after you?" Courtney twirled her fingers through his hair. "She had all those delusions about being in love with you, remember? She might be coming back to claim you as her own. She'd probably threaten me because I got you now."

"She wouldn't dare," Ayaz growled, and the venom in his voice turned my stomach. No matter what happened now, I knew that Ayaz believed in this version of events. He was lost to me.

"We should get back to class," Tillie punched Ayaz playfully in the arm. "I won't have my salutatorian status ruined because you lot wanted to get high."

Nancy snorted. "I don't know why you guys still care who gets top of class. It's not as if it matters."

"It's a matter of *pride,* Nancy – a concept you obviously don't understand. All the weed in the world won't ruin Ayaz's chances," Courtney rested her head on Ayaz's shoulder and beamed up at him in a way that made me want to gag. "Now that Trey's lost his points, you're miles ahead of everyone. You'll be the first scholarship student to make valedictorian. And they say this school's not progressive."

Of course. With Trey and I out of the picture, Ayaz would be next in line for the top of the class, and Tillie after him. Much good it would do him – there was nowhere to go after he graduated except back to repeat the year over with new scholarship students to torment.

The monarchs packed up their things and disappeared back up the steps. Ayaz wrapped his arm around Courtney's tiny waist, allowing her to lean against him, to brush her lips against his neck in a way that made my blood boil. Halfway up the steps, Ayaz paused, his shoulders tensed. He turned back, casting his dark eyes over the pleasure gardens.

I dropped my head and flattened myself against the bottom of the bed, hoping my covering was enough to hide me from his gaze. I counted my pounding heartbeat in my ears until I reached five hundred. Nothing. Not a sound. I dared to raise my neck just enough to peer over the side of the flower bed. The stairs were empty.

Ayaz was gone.

I was alone again.

I wasted no time in untangling myself from the weeds and racing down to the cemetery. The waves crashed against the cliffs below, shooting a salty spray through the air that razed my skin. I ducked into the protective shade of the trees. Here, the roar of the ocean disguised the crunching of my footsteps through the fallen leaves and vines that choked the ground. I swung the gate open and slipped inside.

I didn't know what I was looking for exactly. All I knew was that these kids had supposedly perished in a fire and then climbed out of their own coffins, alive-but-not-alive. The edimmu. The revenants. The dead who had not been properly buried.

But Ms. West had raised a cadaver to life in the hospital morgue. Deborah had seen her do it. So why bury the bodies? What did that achieve?

Maybe there was some clue here. Maybe I could find the answers we so desperately needed.

I'd only ever been to the cemetery at night before, and it loomed with memories of the guys telling me what they were, what happened to them. In the daylight, the toppling rows of graves appeared less sinister – almost jaunty, like the teeth of the children in my grade school whose parents couldn't afford braces. I dropped to my knees in front of one stone, brushing aside the weeds choking it. My fingers traced the faded lettering.

QUINN DELACORTE

The same boy whose body had seared mine against a pillar died twenty years ago. I still couldn't wrap my head around it. Quinn walked and spoke and smiled like a normal, living person. He felt pain. He desired. He *loved*. How could he not have a soul?

And how could his parents do this to him? Damon was a horrible human being, so I could understand his part. But surely his mother hadn't wanted her son to become undead? How hard did Elena fight it? Was the care she showed for Quinn now only her way of assuaging her guilt?

My fingers scraped the stone beside it, faltering on Trey's name, and then on Ayaz.

It was too painful to stare at their names. My chest cracked open, and out poured my treacherous doubts and my deepest fears. *I might lose them. I might have already lost them.*

No, don't think about it. Focus on what you came to do.

I tore myself away, heading to the next row, pulling back the weeds to reveal more names. There was Courtney, her stone wreathed in carved flowers, and Tillie's name written in gothic script. Beside her lay Nancy, and behind her Barclay and John Hyde-Jones. There were all the monarchs of the school and all their followers – gravestones chosen with great care for kids who were so unwanted their own parents sacrificed them to a god.

In that moment, I felt something I'd never expected to feel for the likes of Courtney and John Hyde-Jones. They attacked me and my friends because we had something they didn't – life and love. I thought they had everything, that they couldn't possibly know what it was like to go hungry or to not know if your mother would come home in a body bag. But for all their riches, they had so much less than I.

I might have been the girl from the wrong side of the tracks, the daughter of a whore, but I had been loved.

And I let that love destroy me.

A tear rolled down my cheek. Surprised, I let it topple off the edge of my chin onto the back of my hand, staring at that tiny, perfect droplet as it reflected the grey light.

Mom.

Memories burned behind my eyes – Mom dancing with me before the club opened, her bright eyes shimmering as she looped a feather boa around my tiny shoulders, Mom counting out the wads of dollar bills she stashed around the house to give me enough money to go on a school field trip, Mom buying me a Big Mac and fries and watching me eat it all with hungry eyes, never taking a single bite even though she hadn't eaten in two days, either.

Mom, crying alone in her bed at night when she thought I couldn't hear. Her proud smile when I topped the class list every year. Hiding her bruised face behind a veil after one of her boyfriends beat her.

If she had the chance to obtain power from the god, to pull herself out of the life she'd been given, she never would have taken it, never in a million years. She would keep dancing on tables because everything she did, she did for me.

The guilt and grief that I'd buried under layers of rage bubbled to the surface, raw and primal. I rocked back on my heels, still staring at that tear as it wobbled on my hand.

I hadn't cried for her. Because crying meant admitting what I'd done.

And if I admitted it, if I owned it, then I probably deserved to be behind the walls of Dunwich. I shouldn't be here, free, trying to save other lives like I was Mother-fucking-Theresa.

"Fuck." I wiped my hand across my dripping nose and damp eyes. This wasn't what I came to do. I was supposed to be looking for answers, not wallowing in self-pity.

These kids deserved answers. They deserved someone who cared.

Overcome by the neglect of the cemetery, by a desperate need to *do* something, I stood up, wiping my hands on my jeans. I moved back to Trey's stone, my hands clawing at the weeds choking it, tearing them from the ground and tossing them away. Dirt burrowed under my fingernails as I scraped at the leaves, uncovering the curve of the stone and the carved border beneath, the ridge where the stone had been set into the earth.

There. That at least looked like someone cared...

Wait a second... what's that?

I knelt in the dirt, bending low and twisting my head around to get a better view. My fingers traced the lines. Yes, it was definitely there. I wasn't imagining it.

I'd never noticed it before because the leaf litter was so deep, but there was a sigil carved into the bottom of Trey's stone.

My heart pounding, I scrambled over to Quinn's grave and

tugged away the weeds. His had the same sigil, carved so low it might never be noticed.

I rushed around the cemetery, my hands raw from pulling up the weeds, my nails breaking from scraping at cold stone. But I had my answer. Every single gravestone included the same crude sigil. I didn't know what it meant, but it had to have something to do with whatever Ms. West had done to them.

I dug around in my pocket for the cellphone Deborah had given me. I snapped a couple of pictures. I didn't have any bars to send it, so I shoved the phone back into my pocket. I'd probably have better luck back at the school.

If the graveyard itself is some kind of ritual space, then maybe there are other signs of the ritual as well. I stood up and stepped toward the fence marking the boundary, then froze.

Hazel.

A voice whispered my name on the wind. The hairs on the back of my neck stood on end.

"Hazel."

No. Not the wind. A person, standing right behind me.

Loretta.

CHAPTER TWENTY

My breath hitched. My hands curled into fists, but there was no point running. Or attacking. Loretta was one of them now, one of the edimmu. I could hurt her, but she'd keep on coming.

I had my fire, but I didn't want to use it on her. Not unless I had to.

So I kept my hands at my sides and turned toward the gate. She stood just inside, one tiny hand clutching the iron post, the other shoved into the pocket of her skirt. I studied her, resplendent in her immaculately-tailored Derleth uniform, her once-unruly frizzy hair now tamed and lacquered into place. I'd never been able to understand her. Even now I didn't know if she was friend or foe.

How is this was going to play out?

"Loretta, hi." I kept my tone light, friendly. "How'd you find me?"

"I was reading in a corner of the garden when I saw you hide in the flower bed. You got up after the others left, but you didn't see me. I followed you here." Her eyes didn't leave mine, not even to flicker over the gravestones of her classmates.

"Did they erect a gravestone for you?" I searched the rows for a newer-looking stone, but it was hard to see in the gloom of the trees. "Or is a permanent marker for Miskatonic Prep students only?"

Loretta folded her arms across her chest. "I heard you were placed in Dunwich Institute. That's a cutting-edge facility – some of the most revolutionary medical procedures for treating mental illness have come from there."

"Oh, yeah. It's a real swell place." My voice dripped with scorn. "You should visit one day. I'm going to make it my vacation spot."

"I heard you burned it to the ground." I wasn't sure if she was accusing me or congratulating me.

"Probably an exaggeration, but I haven't been back to check." I sucked in a breath. If there was one person at this school that could help me, it would be her. "Loretta, I don't know if you've noticed, but Greg's missing."

"Of course I noticed." Her voice took on an edge I didn't like.

"I think Ms. West might have him. She used to have a laboratory in the old icehouse. She might have taken you there when she..." I wasn't sure how to say it. "Changed you. But it's not there now. Do you have any idea where she might have moved it?"

"If I knew, do you think I'd be standing here talking to you about it?"

I bit back a mean response. The truth was, Loretta never wanted to take action, not even when Greg was the one being bullied. "If you hear or see anything, can you let Andre know? That way you don't even have to talk to me. I just want to find Greg before she..."

Loretta's eyes blazed. "You made a deal, didn't you? So she can't hurt him."

"If I know anything from my time in Dunwich, it's that Hermia West knows how to loophole her way to getting exactly what she wants. I don't know how you know about my bargain, unless she told you. Unless you're working with her. Are you going to tell your pal Courtney I'm back? Or Ms. West?"

Loretta didn't answer. Instead, she stepped toward me. "I haven't decided. It all depends on why you came back."

"I know you don't like me, but I want to help you. To help everyone." I gestured to the graves. "I think there might be a way to reverse all this, to give them all back their lives. But what I really, really want *right now* is to find Greg."

"Why don't I like you?" The faintest hint of a smile played on her lips. Ice crept down my back. I didn't think I'd ever seen Loretta smile.

"Huh?"

"Tell me why I don't like you, since you're such an expert on my feelings."

"I don't see what that has to do with anything, but okay, sure. You don't like me because you think I made things worse for you. I drew attention to myself, and you suffered for it. You don't like me because I always tried to stand up for myself and for others, but you just rolled over and took their cruelty. You wanted to be more like me. You were jealous."

Loretta snorted. I was beginning to hate that sound. "Of course you'd think that."

"Fine. You tell me why you didn't like me." I shrugged. *Why has she surprised me just to talk about this?* "Or not. I really couldn't care less."

"But that's not true. You *do* care. That's your problem. You pretend you're so above everyone, you've had such a hard life that nothing could possibly affect you. But everything you do is about getting attention and making people see you." Loretta mocked me in a high-pitched voice. 'I'm amazing Hazel! Notice me! Love me!'"

I sighed. "That's why you don't like me, then?"

"I never liked you because you don't learn anything. You think you can get what you want because you stamp your feet and you scream the loudest."

"It's better than doing nothing." I swept my arm across the tombstones. "How can I just pretend this didn't happen? How can I wait for them to hurt Greg and Andre? I'm trying to give all our classmates back their futures. *Your* future."

"By sneaking around school and poking at their graves?" Loretta sneered. "I bet they sure are glad Amazing Hazel is on the case."

"Fine. Then help me. Work with me. Tell me about the ceremony Ms. West used to give your soul to the god and bring you back from the dead. Tell me what happened!"

"You're Hazel Waite. You know everything," Loretta shot back. "You tell *me* what happened."

"I don't *know*." My hands balled into fists again. "I don't know anything, and that's the whole problem. I know that all the students are trapped on the school grounds, but I don't know what that *means*. I don't know why you seem to be different, why you were allowed back into class. All I know is that it was supposed to be me they took away, but instead, you disappeared and you returned the next day, but you were changed."

"Was I changed?" Loretta asked. "Or did you just never bother to get to know me?"

"I..." I didn't know how to answer that.

"Was I in fact *exactly* the person I'd always been, except that I had a new haircut and better fitting clothes and different friends? Was it in fact that you know so little about me that you couldn't even tell?"

My mouth opened and closed. I couldn't comprehend what Loretta was saying. It sounded like she was saying that she hadn't been turned by the god. But then why did she go away and come back? Why did she suddenly become friends with Courtney? Why...

Fuck.

"You're not an edimmu?" I managed to choke out.

Loretta smiled without mirth. "I'm still alive, just like you. No thanks to you, either, since it was your boyfriends who tried to have me sacrificed when it should have been *you*."

They hadn't been my boyfriends then, and I wasn't even sure they were my boyfriends now. But I wasn't going to split hairs with Loretta over that. Trey had given me his points so that I wouldn't be sacrificed, but that had put Loretta next on the soul-stealing block. Only it turned out her soul was intact. "But *why* would the god spare you?"

"Because you and I are the same. The god doesn't want to drain us of our life. He wants to study us. We fascinate him."

"We do?"

"Of course. He wants to understand us. Because we're the murderers. The only ones he's ever met."

"Loretta, what the fuck—" But I couldn't ask her any more questions.

She had vanished. *Again*.

CHAPTER TWENTY-ONE

Because we're the murderers.

What did she mean by that? Loretta wasn't a murderer. She was a super-intense orphaned Southern Baptist girl with severe depression and suicidal thoughts.

Who wasn't dead.

Loretta wasn't dead.

And it sounded to me as she was keeping it a secret.

I longed to ask her exactly what happened in that cavern beneath the gym, but she'd never tell me, so I had to guess. They lowered her into the god's prison, into that void of infinite blackness, and he was supposed to drink from her tortured soul until she was dead, and then Ms. West was supposed to bring her back to the frozen life of the edimmu. But if the god didn't kill her...

That meant Ms. West knew Loretta was alive. She knew something was wrong with the god, and she hadn't told the Eldritch Club. Interesting. I remembered my dream from the other day and the conversation I'd overheard in her office where she'd complained about not being rewarded for her work. I wondered if perhaps Ms. West and Vincent Bloomberg were no longer working toward the same purpose.

What interested me the most was the god's decision. If the god spared Loretta, then it meant he acted of his own free will, if such a concept as free will existed for a cosmic deity. It meant that Ms. West didn't control him. Vincent Bloomberg didn't control him.

I could use that. I didn't know how, but I could use it.

I shuffled around the perimeter of the graveyard in a half daze, searching for other signs of a ritual. But the trees were so dense, vines twisted through the metal fence and weeds choking the roots, that I had no hope of finding anything in there. Besides, maybe I had a much easier way of figuring this out.

Maybe I could just ask the god.

He showed me things in my dreams. Sometimes those things were true – like when he sent Trey to me. Sometimes they were things other people wanted me to see. But I had a feeling the communication went both ways. When he'd shown me Ms. West and Dr. Atwood when I was on the bus, that hadn't come from them. The god *meant* for me to know.

And he'd tried to speak to me. He'd tried to have a conversation even though neither of us could comprehend the other. Loretta was right – he *was* curious.

Maybe there was a way I could get the god to reveal more of his secrets.

CHAPTER TWENTY-TWO

"Here!" I jabbed my finger at the page in Rebecca's book.

"Read it out," Quinn demanded, slouching over the bed. Trey leaned against the wall, frowning at the book.

I held up the page and exalted in my best Shakespearean accent. "The Nurse sigils cannot be used to summon spirits or beings from other planes of existence. We do not believe in dragging others between the realms against their will. Instead, these sigils allow open communication through the veil by way of dreams, where the magician's mind is most open and receptive, and where the spirit has access to the full spectrum of weird imaginings with which to find a common ken. The magician's earthly form and worldly concerns will not hinder communion—"

"Sounds like a load of magical twaddle to me," Quinn said. "So what you're suggesting is..."

"We draw one of these sigils on the wall," I said. "And then I go to sleep and talk to the entity in my dreams. And I get him to tell me where Greg is."

"No." Trey frowned.

I glared back at him, ticking off points on my fingers. "A. You're not in charge here, so I don't have to listen to you. B. It's not dangerous. I'm not actually going to talk to the god. I'm just dreaming and you'll be here to wake me up if anything seems wrong, and C. If this is going to help us find Greg, then we have to try it."

"We don't have to do anything," Trey growled. "Besides, how do you know you're a magician?"

I touched my hand to my scar. Trey's frown only deepened – a fact that should have been physically impossible given the sheer amount he was *already* frowning.

I sighed. "Look, I know you guys don't give two fucks about Greg, but I do. And I'm not—"

"We care about Greg," Quinn piped up.

"No, you don't." My hands balled into fists. I was done with this. Done with sitting in this room while my friend was out there having cosmic-god-knows-what being done to him by Ms. West. Done with the Kings not understanding why it was important. Tired of them not giving Greg or Andre the respect and friendship I knew they were capable of. "You barely even remember his name."

"Barely remembering is still remembering." Quinn pointed out. "Besides, why do you think the god would even know where Greg is?"

"Because the god knows much more than he's been given credit for." I set down the book and picked up my chalk. "I'm doing this, with or without your help."

I stepped across the room toward my old bed, Loretta's damning words echoing in my head. *Because we're the murderers.* I had to find out.

Trey moved in front of me, pressing his body against the wall. "No."

I grabbed his shoulder and shoved him aside. "Maybe the rest of the world bows down when you issue a command, but I don't."

I knelt on the bed, trying to control the shaking in my hand as I drew a large circle. It was slightly lopsided, but I wasn't an artist like Ayaz. I glanced down at the diagram, following the instructions for the order in which to draw the lines.

Behind me, Trey tapped his foot against the floor. Quinn sucked in his breath. As I drew, heat flared along my arm. Out of the corner of my eye, I noticed a flicker of blue flame arcing down the lines.

I resisted the urge to pull back, to push the fire back down inside me. Back in the cave with Zehra, I'd seen flames like this around Rebecca's sigil. And then again when Trey set the boundary sigil on the table in the RV. Maybe the fire was a sign it was working.

My hand buzzed with heat. An invisible force gripped my fingers, dragging my hand over the wall, dipping and swooping and forming beautiful, perfect lines.

With a final flourish, my hand flew off the wall. The chalk sailed across the room, hit the other wall, and broke into two pieces that fell on Quinn's head.

"*Voila!*" I struck a pose. Trey shook his head. Quinn picked up the broken chalk and pretended to draw a penis in the air.

I didn't ask them if they could see the fire. If Trey knew it was there, his face would have given it away. He'd make a big deal about it, and I couldn't deal with any more tantrums tonight. I needed to get this done, for Greg.

I lay back on the bed, kicking off my socks and diving under the covers. I downed the glass of milk Andre had snuck down for me. I'd warmed it over the radiator so it went down easily. Above my head, the rats circled with renewed vigor, their tiny feet scratching and scrabbling in their haste.

"Goodnight, boys." I waved at the Kings from beneath the covers, then reached out to flick off the light.

"This is a bad idea," Trey muttered from the darkness.

"I don't know how you even sleep with that racket in the ceiling," Quinn added.

"I find them comforting," I said. "I can't explain it. When I came here I was so lonely. Not even Loretta would talk to me, and when I lost Dante's journal... I lay on this bed and stared at the ceiling, and the rats were doing their thing. They're always *there*. I like that."

Quinn wrinkled his nose. "Nope, doesn't make sense to me."

"It doesn't have to." My head hit the pillow. I closed my eyes, willing sleep to come. But I was too wound up with worry over Greg and with unspent energy from being cooped up inside all day. Quinn fidgeted and Trey coughed, and I threw the covers off in annoyance.

"This isn't going to work," I muttered. "I need sleeping pills or something."

"Let me help." The bed creaked as Quinn sat down. He lifted the corner of the blanket. "May I?"

"Sure."

Quinn climbed under the covers with me, wrapping his arms around me, pressing his whole body against mine on the narrow bed.

This was a guy who didn't do true affection because affection meant admitting some deeper connection that terrified him. And I couldn't blame him — I knew what it was like to hold back, to put my trust in one person in the world who was supposed to love me and to have that ripped away. I used anger and Quinn used humor to push people away, but they were two sides of the same fucked-up coin.

This embrace was Quinn starting to let his guard down, to drop the facade he'd so carefully crafted. And the boy beneath that mask was more fragile and more beautiful than I'd ever imagined.

He snuggled against me and nuzzled my neck, his breath hot against my skin. And without realizing it, I relaxed into his body. My eyelids drooped, the comfort of his affection cradled me...

My eyes flew open.

Bitter-cold wind tore at my skin, ripping me from the safety of Quinn's embrace. I was alone. And freezing my ass off.

Even before my eyes adjusted to the gloom I knew where I was – in the cavern, facing the scaffold once again, staring down the trapdoor beneath which the cosmic god slumbered in its prison.

This time, I didn't hesitate. Greg's life was at stake. I kicked out the bolt and flung open the trapdoor, bracing myself against the onslaught of vile darkness.

The god's touch was like being caressed by hatred. It was as if every dark thought in the world had form and mass. It wrapped around me, its shadow blocking out the light until I swam in its bleak embrace.

You found me. Its thoughts appeared inside my head, not words but made of a tangled web of screams – a nightmarish mockery of our language.

"How do you do that?" I whispered, digging my nails into my scar in a desperate effort not to slam my hands over my ears.

I have listened. It is nothing to me to learn your primitive tongue. The voices of my sustenance provide the vocalizations. You have returned to me.

I choked back a scream of my own. The voice I heard was made of the screams of all those sacrifices. "Y...y...yes. I was hoping you could answer a few questions. Did you... have you had a sacrifice recently?"

I have not consumed for some time. I starve alone in my prison, for I must wait for the one I crave.

Relief washed over me. I'd guessed correctly. Greg was safe. For now. My agreement with Ms. West was still binding. But knowing that only brought up more questions. "Am I the one you crave?"

Yessss.

The way he said it, like teeth crunching against bone, made me realize that something about me *was* different to him.

"Do you want to consume me?" I asked.

I want to understand you.

I didn't know what that meant, but I'd take it. "Ms. West told me that when I am hurt, you hurt, too. Why is that?"

I am heavy with the weight of my greed. You are heavy, too. You have gorged yourself on the life of others. We have an affinity.

"Because you think I murdered someone?" I asked. I pressed my fingers to the scar on my wrist. "You think we're the same because you devour souls and I... I..."

The darkness and the hatred stole the words that staggered to the edge of my tongue. The words I hadn't been able to utter since the fire.

Luckily for me, the god didn't seem to expect an answer. The screams crashed against my skull. *You want to ask me about a particular soul. My servants have seen him alive and intact. Would you like them to show you?*

"Yes." My heart leaped with hope. "Very much."

The darkness closed around me, squeezing me, pulling me backwards until I stumbled and toppled over. Instead of slamming into the floor of the cave, the god caught me in his dark embrace. Before my eyes, the darkness resolved itself into a pack of the shadow creatures that chased me in the gym. They drew back snarling lips to reveal teeth made of midnight. Tenebrous claws sliced the air, cleaving holes in the world from which more of their vile number spilled. They surrounded me, leaping on top of me, tugging my clothes and squeezing the air from my chest.

As one, they tossed their heads back and howled. The sound wasn't of wolves, but of a great maelstrom battering the prow of a flimsy ship. From their mouths burst forth a net of oily strands that crossed and stretched out in all directions. They quivered and twanged against each other, and some even emitted a low hum – as if they were violin strings pulled taut.

A string wobbled in front of my face. Heat flared in my palms, and I didn't know how I knew to do it, but I reached out and grabbed it. The string coiled around me, wiping the repulsive oil all over me as it swung me forward, dragging me through a maze of darkness until a shape resolved itself in front of me.

Greg.

His head slumped against his shoulder. His hands had been tied behind him, and one leg was pulled to his chest. Marks along his arm glowed red in the god's vision – precision cuts, and small puncture wounds that looked like blood draws. Blood streaked his pale skin, and his blue eyes swam with pain and defeat.

My heart snapped in two. Greg came to this school for a second chance. He was kind and fun and wonderful and funny. He might be alive, but he was in great pain, and he didn't deserve any of it.

"Greg?" I called out, thrashing against the oily threads. "Can you hear me?"

Greg turned toward my voice, but his eyes couldn't focus. I tried to discern something about his location that could help me find him, but all I could make out was that he was tied to some kind of metal frame before a dark shadow moved in front of him, its doglike limbs long and lithe as it leaped toward my head.

I screamed and yanked myself back. Malevolent claws scraped against my arm, raising goosebumps against my skin. Teeth made of darkness snapped at my face. I screamed again, throwing up my arms. The threads around my torso tightened, dragging me back into the gloom.

I flew back through the web of strings until I came to face the god's trapdoor. The shadow creatures disappeared, leaving me slumped on cold stone. I tried to stand, but my legs wouldn't cooperate. I knelt on the edge of the platform, clutching the trapdoor.

You cannot reach him through his dreams. He is fragile. You will damage his soul.

"Where is he?" I demanded. "Is he still here on campus?"

My servants watch over him.

"Your servants?" I realized he meant the shadows – the foul beasts of darkness that spat those oily strings. "What about the Eldritch Club? The faculty? I thought they were your servants."

They are my wardens. Nothing more.

A shudder ran through my body – part horror, part hope. I never thought I'd say this, but the god and I had something in common. We'd both had our freedom stripped away. We'd both been experimented on without our consent. He was as much a prisoner of Derleth as I was – more so, for he had been trapped here for hundreds of years.

"Why do you give your wardens your power?" I asked. "They only keep you trapped here because you give them what they want."

If I do what they want, they will set me free.

I laughed. "Yeah, right. That's not going to happen. If they set you free, they don't get to keep drawing your powers. Sorry to be the bearer of bad news, but they never had any intention of setting you free."

I don't understand.

"They lied to you." My stomach heaved as the god shifted in the prison, agitated. The screams in my head increased in volume, in agony.

What is lied?

I remembered then that I was addressing a being from beyond space and time. It might have no concept of deception. I couldn't think how to explain lying in a way that would make him understand.

Instead, I pressed my hands to my head and called up the memories I'd hidden down deep, the secret shame that I'd kept to myself. The lies I'd told the authorities, the school, the Kings. The lies I told myself. The rage that grew and grew inside me like a cancer I could never cut out.

And I gave it to him.

"*That's* lying," I said through gritted teeth as I pushed the truth into his screams.

The god's pain came in a silent wave, his screams so loud they had no sound at all. I dropped like a stone as the screams tore the strength from my limbs. It was the scream of a universe burning, of a million souls that had never known peace, of all the agonies of past, present, and future rushing at me all at once.

I didn't know how long I lived inside the god's torment, but it was too fucking long. Finally, finally, his pain rolled over me, and I was able to surface.

I don't know, he cried with the screams of his victims.

"What don't you know?" I demanded, struggling for breath. "I have told you the truth. You have been lied to. What will you do with that?"

I don't know. The darkness shifted uneasily. The god was confused. It had no experience to frame this feeling.

"I'll tell you what you do." I scooted forward on my knees so I leaned right over the trapdoor and stared down into that lightless abyss. It made bile rise in my throat, but it was the closest I could get to looking the god in the eye. "You do exactly what I tell you, and we all get what we want."

I will listen.

"First, your servants will protect Greg," I said. "Because he's not a part of this. He never lied to you. And then, you will stop. Stop everything. Stop giving them power. Stop taking souls. Stop it all."

Without sustenance, I am weakening. I do not want to return to my death-slumber. I wish to be free, as you wish to be free.

"I can respect that. Can you go back to your own universe?"

I am too weak. Too changed. I will not survive there.

"What do you mean by too changed?"

I have become... not what I once was. The sustenance here makes me different. I have... feelingsss.

He hissed the word, testing it on his screaming tongues. He didn't understand it, and yet he knew that he felt. *Of course! When he eats a soul they become part of him, and he experiences all their emotions and memories.* Whatever he used to consume in his previous universe, it didn't have this same effect. "What if I found a way to take away the feelings? It might make you weaker, but you would be yourself again."

I would be... happy.

Again, it tested the word, unsure what it truly meant. "And then maybe you could go home?"

I do not know. It is possible.

"You have taken the souls of some of my friends. They're people I care about. You know this feeling?" I drew up from within me images and sensations of Trey and Quinn and Ayaz – their kisses, their secret smiles, their broken hearts. The god groaned as I drew him into my head through my dreams and showed him the depth of what I felt for the guys.

I know it. Their souls were given to me some time ago – but there was little for me to enjoy. They didn't know pain like the others that came later. When you show me your feelingsss, I have a... feeling of my own. It's not pleasant. I don't want it.

"I don't want you to have it, either. Because you took their souls, my friends are prisoners, too. I want them to be free. Can you give their souls back?"

I do not have that ability. But my wardens... they are masters of the energy that sustains me. They can manipulate and make new what has been destroyed. They woke me from my death-sleep. They may have that answer.

"I believe you." I balled my hands into fists. "If I find a way, will you help me? It might hurt you, but then we could all be free."

I will. I will free your... friends, if you tell me how. My servants will remain with you. They will do your bidding. They will keep you safe while you search. On one condition.

"Whatever you want."

You will join with me. Your soul would be my companion.

Fuck.

Um, what?

I opened my mouth to reply, to tell the god thanks but no thanks, but the darkness grabbed me, dragging me backward. I fell through the ground, toppling over myself until I slammed into something hard.

Fuck. Fuck. Fuck.

Did I just agree to that?

Did I just agree to spend eternity with a cosmic soul-eating deity?

"Hazy!" Quinn's voice was frantic, his eyes wild with fear as he shook me like a near-empty ketchup bottle. My head wrenched, slamming into the stone and sending a jolt of pain through me. "What happened? Are you okay?"

I rubbed the back of my head where it had hit the wall. It was nothing on the screams of the god. "Of course."

My gaze flicked between the two of them – Trey's cruel mouth twisted in concern, Quinn's eyes so wide and innocent.

Innocent.

They were innocent. Not like me.

I knew when I entered Derleth there was a timer ticking down on my freedom. I'd known all along that when I left this school I'd likely replace one prison with another. I'd allowed my feelings for them to take over my practical side, and I'd indulged in dreams of what the future might be. I'd even told Trey I might become a scientist like Deborah.

It was just that – a dream. A career, a family, a life – that wasn't in my future.

But it could be in theirs.

In that moment, I made a pact with myself. I wouldn't reveal the deal I made with the god. I'd promised myself that I would free the Kings of Miskatonic Prep at whatever cost. That was my pact, my mission – I would give back what was taken. If that meant I had to hang with the god for the rest of existence, then so be it.

"You were crying," Trey said. "And mumbling these strangling sounds. They weren't words, just random guttural noises. It was *horrible*. What happened?"

"I spoke to the god," I said, sitting up. Quinn's grip tightened. I placed my hand over his, noticing that I didn't tremble. I wasn't afraid. I knew what I had to do. "It's okay. He's actually kind of a cool dude. He's going to help us."

CHAPTER TWENTY-THREE

The god could give me everything I wanted.

The students... free. Check.

The Eldritch Club stripped of its power. Check.

The god no longer a threat to humanity. Check, check, and motherfucking check.

Provided I found a way to reverse what Ms. West had done. Provided I stayed with him and became part of him. All I had to do was dive into that dark hole in the ground and allow the god to catch me.

It wasn't even a question. Of course I would do it. For Trey and Quinn and Ayaz to have their chance to grow up. For Greg and Andre to go to college and change the world. Even for Courtney Haynes to get her modeling deal.

As I lay in Trey's arms, knowing that sleep wouldn't claim me, I thought about what that meant. What would happen to me in the darkness?

Would I become a soul-eater, just like him?

I'd never see Trey or Quinn or Ayaz again.

But I had to do it.

There was no other way.

The god was right – he and I were two peas in a pod. I too bore the weight of innocent souls. When compared to my sins, the Kings of Miskatonic were downright angels. I didn't deserve to share the future with them.

I tried to put it out of my mind. I needed all my focus to enact our plan. The date of the school production loomed, and it was the perfect time to test our plan. If it worked the way I hoped, it might induce the other students to help us.

Or make them all hate me. But what else was new?

It would help if we knew something from the samples we gave to Deborah. As soon as the guys left for class the next morning, I whipped out my phone and texted her. "Any update on lab results?"

I only had to wait a few moments for a reply. "Gail sent them to me late last night. Both your blood and Trey's blood are completely normal. No bloodborne diseases. No cellular death."

"That tells us nothing!" Frustration licked along my spine. My fingers mashed the keys so hard I ended up with a string of gibberish and had to rewrite.

A long message came back. "It tells us that there's nothing physical that defines Trey as dead – that is something. It tells us there's nothing physiological that explains why he won't age or why his wounds heal so quickly. It gives us hope, Hazel. I'm waiting on some more results and for your DNA test, but that shouldn't be long. How are you? Have you read Rebecca's book?"

"Parts of it. Want to know something crazy? I tried a spell and it worked. I drew a sigil on the wall and it allowed me to speak to the god through my dreams."

"That's not crazy at all," Deborah wrote back. "Be careful. I will text you if I have any news."

"Ditto. Hug the dogs for me." I paused, then added, "And for Trey."

That done, I cracked open Rebecca's book and continued my studies, half-waiting for Ms. West to break down the door and drag me away. But she never came. Loretta never told and the god never revealed my return.

My life followed the same pattern for the rest of the week. I read Rebecca's book. Deborah and I texted back and forth – I told her everything the god showed me, and she sent me a video of Leopold with his head stuck in a kibble container that Trey watched on repeat for a whole hour. She also asked me for the names of my immediate family members. Apparently, she believed I might've had some magical lineage. I gave her my mother's name – Laura Waite – but I couldn't tell her anything else. Mum never spoke about her family, and if she knew who my father was, she'd never told me.

Quinn and Andre would return to the room with more supplies for our plan. We stayed up late fashioning all the props we needed until Trey returned from late-night rehearsals. He might have been disowned, but he still carried the Bloomberg name and was expected to dance like a trained monkey for his father's amusement.

"It says here that your friend Helen would cut pictures of the deceased from photographs and glue them onto dolls or old bits of cloth," Quinn read from the library book on Helen Duncan's faked ectoplasm.

I pointed to the stack of magazines he'd stolen from Courtney's locker, for which he still had the combination. "That's why we've got these."

"But they're all celebrities. It won't work as well as if it were actual faces."

"Agreed, but I don't see how we're going to get all actual faces. I've got a couple of pictures I took from the noticeboards for the main event," I pushed Courtney's photograph across the floor. "But I think everyone will get suspicious if they all go missing. You've got the projection – that should be enough."

"We could use the photocopies we have from the student

files," Trey piped up. "They're not students, but people will recognize them."

I tapped my chin, remembering the day I discovered Parris' skin book under the sink in Ayaz's dorm. As the leaders of the student chapter of the Eldritch Club, the Kings had been given copies of the files of all the scholarship students – photographs of each of us with intimate details of our lives to make their torment more personal. Those photographs would still be there, and all the Miskatonic students would recognize those faces.

"That's perfect. As long as they agree to having their photographs used." I leaned forward, my mind spinning as I thought about everything else that was in that book. "And speaking of Parris, while Ayaz was translating the book, he would tell me about some of the spells and rituals, just in case we could connect them with something in the other books that might help. He had lists of pages that might potentially help us recover your souls."

"Do you remember any of them?" Quinn asked.

I shook my head. "Memorizing spells didn't seem relevant, and besides, all this magic stuff is gobbledegook to me. But Ayaz translated the instructions."

"So all we have to do is ask our old buddy the betrayer if he'd mind spilling the beans on how we can fuck over our parents, who he is probably helping?" Quinn twirled a strand of blond hair around his fingers. "Great plan, Hazy."

"We don't have to tell him," I shot back. "Ayaz kept all his notes and translations hidden inside Parris' skin book, and you'd better believe it'll be more useful to us than it is to Ayaz right now. I know we can't take photographs of the pages – they just come out blank. So all we have to do is sneak into his room and steal it." I stood up, but Quinn grabbed my arm.

"That's not going to be as easy as you think. Ayaz is in Trey's room now. Vincent gave it to him."

My heart sank. Whereas Ayaz's old room was down a corridor

without too many other students, Trey's old room was on the top floor of the dormitories. We'd have to walk through practically the entire dorm to get there... without being seen by a single student. "We don't even know if the book is still there," Trey added. "He could have given it to Ms. West, or back to my father."

My hands balled into fists. *I'm doing this for them. They don't have to fight this so much. If they knew what I agreed to—*

"We have to try," I said through gritted teeth.

Trey and Quinn exchanged a look that said there was no use arguing with me. Which was true. I was doing this, with or without them.

"I'm always down for a suicide mission," Quinn grinned. "When do you want to pull this ridiculous stunt?"

I turned to Trey. "Next play rehearsal is tomorrow night?" He nodded. "Good. Make sure Ayaz doesn't leave early. Do whatever you can to keep him there as long as possible without it looking fake. Quinn and I will sneak up to his room and find the book."

Trey shook his head. "That's a terrible idea. Students are going to be back and forth at that time of night. If anyone sees you upstairs, they'll march you straight to Ms. West, and we'll lose you again."

I glowered at him. "I'm going. Help or don't help, I don't care."

"She's not kidding, mate." Quinn grinned at Trey. "Hey, if you don't help, that means it's my job to distract Ayaz. Do you think if I put MC Hammer's 'can't touch this' on repeat during his monologue, that would do the trick?"

Trey sighed. "Fine. I'll help. Only because Quinn will turn this into a disaster. But I want it on record that I'm not happy about it."

"Right. Because you're usually Mr. Chuckles." Quinn punched him in the arm. Trey grabbed him around the neck and pretended to do some kind of wrestling move that looked vaguely homoerotic. The boys fell onto the bed laughing. The sound was like an arrow through my heart.

I'd fallen for the Kings of Miskatonic Prep. Totally and utterly. I needed Trey's possessive protection, Quinn's boisterous enthusiasm. And Ayaz... my whole being ached for him to be mine again.

In order to save them, I had to leave them forever.

It was tough waiting a whole night and day before we could sneak into Ayaz's room. I hated standing still when I knew there was something nearby that could help us. I paced the room, tapping my pen against the desk and bouncing my foot on the edge of the bed while I waited for Quinn and Trey to return from their classes. Above my head, the rats mirrored my jitters.

Finally, the clock ticked over to 4PM and Quinn dashed back into the room, shrugging off his satchel and running his hands through his rumpled surfer hair. Andre followed soon after. He dropped a key in my hand along with one of his handwritten notes. It read, "The staff agree you can use their pictures. I hope you know what you're doing."

I hope so too, Andre.

Trey went straight to rehearsal after class. The production was now in dress rehearsals, which meant Ayaz would be occupied until at least 10PM. Theoretically, the dormitory was supposed to be lights out by nine, and teachers would occasionally come through the dormitories in some half-hearted attempt to enforce the rules, but few students obeyed. This was a problem for us because if I was seen in the halls, the whole plan would be ruined.

Which was why Trey had pilfered a couple of black robes from the drama department costume room. Mine had a stiff Dracula collar sewn in, but after ripping that out and adding a hood torn from one of Greg's old hoodies, it looked identical to the robes the teachers wore. If anyone saw us in the hall, they'd hopefully scamper before stopping to look too closely at our faces.

Quinn went up the stairs first, then called down to me. "It's clear."

I threw the robe over my shoulder, tugging the hood low so it covered as much of my face as possible, and flew up the stairs after him.

Quinn and I dashed down the hall, past the dorms to the grand staircase that led to the top story, where the richest students had their private suites. As we passed the dorms, I flicked my gaze to the noticeboards hanging outside the students' doors, where they'd pinned the pictures and notes that offered clues to their past lives, their lives when they thought they had families and futures.

We ascended the staircase. I was just about to step out into the hallway when the sound of a door opening and voices talking reached my ears. Quinn shoved me against the wall, his chest pressed against mine, our hearts pounding together as we strained to listen.

A door slammed. The voices disappeared. Quinn grabbed my hand and yanked me down the hall.

Trey's suite was the grandest of them all, located right at the end of the hall to take full advantages of the high stained glass windows on both sides. I slid Sadie's skeleton key into the lock and turned. It clicked easily. I shoved the door open and Quinn and I stumbled inside, pushing the door closed behind us.

Quinn fumbled for the light, but I flicked it off again. "If Ayaz steps out the stage door, he could notice the light on. We don't want to give away that someone's in here," I said, feeling my way along the wall until I reached the bathroom door. Ayaz used to hide the book in his bathroom cabinet. He said when the cleaners wiped down the bathrooms they never looked in the cabinets. I tugged open all the drawers in Trey's bathroom, trying to ignore Ayaz's distinctive scent rising off every surface.

The book wasn't there.

"Shit," I breathed.

"What?"

"It's not here."

"Don't panic, Hazy. It's got to be around here somewhere. He wouldn't let that book fall into anyone else's hands." Quinn opened a kitchen cupboard and squinted inside. "Not in here, although I see Ayaz has been cooking. There's a container of lokma. Have you had his lokma? They're like tiny Turkish dough-nuts except they're chewy and amazing and coated in sugar syrup, which trust me is delectable when poured on naked flesh and then licked off. We should try that sometime. I bet Ayaz won't notice if a few tiny pieces go missing..."

"Put those back." I scrambled across the room, trying to ignore the way Quinn's suggestive tone made the fire inside me leap and dance. I tore the room apart – hunting behind the furni-ture, pulling up the beanbags and peering behind the curtains. Quinn moved to the kitchen and riffled through the drawers, one hand stuffing sticky lokma balls into his mouth.

"You can tell Ayaz has moved in," he wrinkled his nose between bites. "This whole place reeks of weird spices."

I thought it smelled amazing. "At least Ayaz can cook, so he's not as completely useless as you are. Shut up and keep looking. And don't get your sticky fingers over everything. We've got to get out of here quick—" Something scratched at the ceiling. I looked up but realized it was the rats circling above my head. *Scritch-scritch. Scritch-scritch.*

Interesting. They're not usually up here.

Except for that time they were.

It had been the night I learned about the god's existence. I'd fallen asleep in Trey's bed. Quinn came in and we started talking and I'd been so afraid, so unsure, and before I knew it we were kissing away our pain and his fingers brushed my nipple and I wanted him for the first time – wanted his body and his heart.

But then the rats scritched in the walls and I'd snapped out of it.

Almost like they were trying to protect me from the Kings.

"They're going mad." Quinn stopped searching. He frowned at the ceiling.

"They always do this," I said, but it wasn't true. Not here. I remembered last semester I'd heard a few rats in the upper levels of the school a couple of times as well. Even in Trey's room, it had just been the scritch of a couple of rodents. This was *hundreds* of tiny feet and claws circling, scratching, and scrambling over each other as they completed their frantic circular dance right above my head.

I took a step toward the living room. The rats followed, their feet beating a circle around my body as they scurried faster, faster.

I walked toward the window, but the rats stayed where they were, slowing their steps. When I started back toward the living area, they picked up their pace. Almost as if...

No. It can't be. That's nuts. No way do the rats...

I did it again, and once more the rats churned up a storm when I turned back toward them. They were so excited I wondered if they might tear through the ceiling and drop down on us.

I fucking *hoped* I never met these rats, especially after the way they seem to be drawn to me...

"Hmmm."

"Hazy—" Quinn started, but I held out a hand. He shut his mouth, a rare and welcome occurrence. I stepped around the empty coffee table and moved toward the bedroom. The feet above my head scurried ahead of me.

Warmer.

I peered into the bedroom. Last time I'd been in here, it had belonged to Trey – his trophies and ribbons hung from every shelf, documenting how he'd distracted himself from the horror of his life by stacking up achievements like a game of Jenga. Now,

Ayaz's clothes were tossed in a hamper in the corner, his school-books stacked beside the bed. His honey and rose scent clung to every surface, torturing me with memories that belonged to another time. The shelf was empty apart from a scattering of books. I went over and picked one up, knowing from the way the rats stopped moving that I'd made a wrong turn.

My throat constricted as I recognized the title. They were Ayaz's art books. My fingers caressed the pages as I flipped through plates of Impressionists, Cubists, and Renaissance masters. There was a book on Monet that stole my breath with the vibrant color and almost spiritual devotion within such simple scenes.

Beneath the art books was a sketchbook in a battered leather case. Unable to help myself, I picked it up and flicked through the pages.

My breath caught in my throat as I drank in the details. I'd only seen Ayaz's drawings on our history project and the sketch map he'd made of the school. These were a window into his mind, his heart.

They were beautiful. They were terrifying.

Voluptuous, naked renaissance women reclined on couches while inky black tentacles crept up their legs. Gardens of luscious flowers bloomed with human skulls that had teeth for eyes. A flying scorpion with a humanoid head. A pastel rendering of Monet's garden being devoured by rats.

I knew what Ayaz was doing – recording the dreams the god showed him with pen and ink. Everyone in Derleth had the dreams, and they were more vivid the closer one got to the god. Ayaz was closer and more sensitive than most.

I flipped another page and nearly dropped the book in shock.

My hands trembled as I beheld a page of figures, the lines so fine and perfect, I couldn't believe they'd been drawn by the same hand.

They were drawings of *me*.

In one, I bent over a textbook in class, my dreadlocks covering my face like a curtain. He must've drawn that when I'd first arrived at school, before Trey and Courtney put tar in my locs so I had to cut them off.

In another, I reached across a table toward the viewer. There were papers strewn around me, and it looked like one of the tables in the library where Ayaz and I worked on our history project. My lip curled back in a scowl, but he'd drawn my eyes with these bright sparks so it was clear I wasn't entirely serious.

In another, I had my head tossed back, my short hair feathering my face as I laughed from deep in my belly. I wondered with a pang if I was laughing at something Quinn said.

In still another, I stared out at the viewer, my eyes cruel. Fire wreathed my head, licking against my skin without burning me.

I flipped the page and nearly dropped the folder again. There I was, lying down on my stomach, my chin propped up with my palm. Ayaz had lavished attention on my face. In all of his other pictures, my gaze was intense, packed with the rage and venom that lurked just below the surface. Here, I was soft.

I was also completely *naked*.

"My my," Quinn whistled from over my shoulder.

I slammed the sketchbook shut and shoved it back into the stack. "This isn't the book we're looking for." Heat flared on my cheeks.

Quinn sniggered. I turned my head to the ceiling. The rats circled in front of the door to the closet.

I threw open the door. *Bingo*. The book lay open on the floor, notes strewn in all directions. I grabbed it up in my arms, stuffing loose papers into the pages. "Thank you, rats. Let's go."

"Not so fast." A dark voice said from behind me. "That book belongs to me."

CHAPTER TWENTY-FOUR

I froze. Ayaz stood in the doorway, his jaw tight and eyes blazing.

"Is this why Bloomberg kept harassing me about my cues?" he murmured as he flicked his dark eyes between me and Quinn. Tension crackled between us like lightning. "To give you two time to sneak in here and take my property?"

Quinn stepped in front of me, shielding my body with his. "Listen, mate, I know this looks bad, but we can explain."

"You're right – it does look bad. It looks like you're trying to steal from me."

"You've been working on the translations." I hugged the book to my chest, searching his eyes for some sign of the Ayaz I knew, the one who drew those amazing pictures, the one who had held me and told me I was beautiful. "Some of these are new. Have you found—"

"That's none of your business. Give that to me." Ayaz crossed the room in two strides. Quinn tried to block him, but Ayaz shoved him aside. He grabbed a corner of the book and tugged. I staggered back, and his hand flew off.

Ayaz raised his hand to lunge at me again, but something

made him freeze. "It's you," he whispered, his eyes sweeping over me.

"You've been studying the book," I pressed him. "What have you found? Do you know how she made you? If we find the ritual, we can reverse it—"

My words caught in my throat as Ayaz stepped forward, his fingers grazing my cheek. My heart hammered against my ribs as his touch seared me.

"They sent you away," Ayaz murmured, his fingers floating over my hair like he wasn't sure if he was allowed to touch it.

"Why did you tell those lies about me?" I demanded. "Why did you want me to believe I imagined everything between us?"

"You did imagine it. I don't know you." But his hand remained fixed over my hair.

"You *do* know me." I was practically shouting now. "Don't you remember that night in my room, the things you said, the way we made each other feel? What about the grotto? We kissed under the waterfall, and you..."

"I don't know you," Ayaz murmured, but he sounded less sure of himself.

"Of course you know me. You spent the first quarter of this year torturing me because you believed you might be able to save me. You became my friend. You became so much more than that. We worked on the history project about the Salem Witch Trials, and I know that you love to draw, that you're an amazing cook, that you hate anything licorice-flavored. I know you had a sister named Zehra who wanted to free you from this hell—"

At the mention of Zehra's name, Ayaz staggered back, his eyes wide. Quinn swooped in on him, but Ayaz shoved him so hard, Quinn hit the wall.

"Had?" Ayaz managed to get out. "What do you mean, I 'had' a sister? Is she dead? She can't be dead. They promised—"

"Ayaz, honey!" Courtney's voice called from the hall. The

doorknob jiggled. "Open up. I thought we could do a little late-night studying."

The flirtatious tone in her voice turned my stomach. Ayaz must've seen something in my eyes. He stared from me to the door, and for the first time since I'd met him, he looked utterly flustered. He didn't know who to trust, what to believe.

He held my life in his hands.

Ayaz took a step toward the door. Quinn scrambled to his feet. "Don't tell on us, mate," he whispered. "Hazel knows stuff that could help us be free."

Ayaz's dark eyes bore into mine. I nodded. "It's true. We think we have a way to bring you back to life, but if the teachers or the Eldritch Club find out, they'll destroy any chance we have."

Ayaz whirled away. My heart sank. He was going to open the door, and Courtney would sound the alarm that would bring the wrath of the entire school and Eldritch Club down on me. But instead of opening the door, he crossed to the window and shoved it open.

"Get the fuck out of here," he growled, gesturing to the tree outside. "Before I change my mind. And I need that book back before the night of the school production or else I'm dead."

"I promise." With a trembling hand, I bent down and helped Quinn to his feet.

"See you, Ataturk." Quinn swung his long legs out the window and disappeared into the tree. The branches brushed against the brick as Quinn's bulk bent them.

"Ayaz, I know you're in there! C'mon, let me in! You've been so weird lately. I just want to hang out with my boyfriend!"

From the flicker of disgust that curled Ayaz's lip, I could sense that hanging with Courtney was the last thing he wanted. Hope bloomed in my chest. He didn't want to be with her. So why was he? And before, when he nearly touched me, he seemed so confused about me.

Glimmers of hope lit up inside me like fireflies.

"I didn't do this for you," Ayaz hissed as I swung my body over the sill. I tossed the book down to Quinn and wrapped both hands around the branch to steady myself.

"Good." I leaned forward, so my lips just grazed the side of his mouth. Sparks shot through my body. "You should do it for yourself."

CHAPTER TWENTY-FIVE

I scrambled down the tree and jumped from the lowest branch. As soon as my feet touched the grass, Quinn and I bolted for the forest before anyone saw us.

My chest burned and my breath came out in ragged gasps by the time we reached the steps leading to the pleasure garden. But we had the book safely tucked under Quinn's arm. And I had something even better – I had Ayaz.

Something about the way Ayaz's body reacted when my lips brushed his told me everything I needed to know. He hadn't recoiled. Heat surged up from inside him and rushed across his skin, drawing me to him. Deep down inside, Ayaz remembered me, even if he didn't know why he remembered me.

He'd had something done to him, probably by Ms. West. She'd once said she could alter memories. She tampered with Ayaz's mind so he believed himself when he said he didn't know me, and yet some part of him recognized the connection we shared.

What had he started to say about Zehra? Had they used her against him in some way?

That tiny flame of hope inside me flared bright and bold. Quinn handed me the book and went down into the garden first to check if anyone was around. After a few moments he called up to me, and I followed him to the tunnel. He had a torch, so I didn't use my fire. I hadn't shown Quinn yet – I didn't want to see him afraid.

As we clambered through into the darkness, he wrapped his arms around me.

"We did it, Hazy." Quinn's lips grazed my cheek, sending a charge of heat through my body.

"Yeah." I buried my face in his shoulder. My chest heaved from the running and the fear. My fingers rubbed against the leather cover before I shrunk away. *I'm touching Parris' skin. That's never going to not be gross.*

"You okay?" Quinn's hands tightened on my back. "I know Ayaz—"

"He saw *me*," I whispered into Quinn's collar. "I think his memory has been altered, and that's why he's acting like he is. But something inside him recognized me. He's still in there, Quinn. We just have to make him realize it."

Quinn tapped the spine of the book. "Maybe there's something in this skin sack that'll bring back the real Ataturk."

"Maybe." We walked in silence until we came to the end of the tunnel. I pushed open the mirror and we ducked out. I knocked on my old door. Trey flung it open and ushered us inside.

"Got it." I spread out the book on Trey's bed, flicking through Ayaz's pages of notes and translations.

Trey yanked the pages from my hands. He tossed them on the bed in a messy pile and smushed his body against mine, his kiss dragging up the darkness from inside me and smothering it with his own. The flame inside me danced at his possessive touch, even as I tried to wriggle out of his embrace.

"Fuck, I hate this shit," Trey muttered into my neck as he crushed me under the weight of his fear. "I was worried."

"Yeah, well, we were fine." I managed to extract myself and grabbed the book. I flipped open the cover and spread the rest of

Ayaz's notes out in a fan across the bedspread. "Now we've got work to do."

"What's this?" Quinn asked, bouncing on his bed. He lifted the blankets to reveal a roll of clothes stuffed underneath.

"The teachers came by to check we were in our beds, so I made it look like you were asleep," Trey said.

"You need to improve your sculptural skills. I'm not this fat." Quinn yanked out rolled-up slacks and socks and tossed them at Trey. A pair of his boxers hit Trey in the face. Quinn fell on the bed laughing. Trey pounced, putting Quinn in a headlock until Quinn slapped the wall and begged for mercy.

I rolled my eyes, even though seeing them joking around together like normal teenagers made me happier than I ever could have expressed. *They'll look after each other once I'm gone.* "If you're all done being idiots, we can get to work."

Trey wiped dark hair from his brow and scrambled across to help me, while Quinn went back to tossing his clothes around the room.

In a rare display of thoughtfulness, Trey had snuck down some cocoa from the dining hall. He warmed it on the radiator and passed it around while we turned each page carefully, searching for something, anything, that would help us.

I noticed now that Ayaz had added notes and circled things that hadn't been marked before. His notations seemed confused, erratic – like he was trying to figure out some puzzle between the pages. Whatever they'd done to his memory must've messed him up real bad.

I swear that you won't have to wait much longer for answers, Ayaz. I swear that I will give you back what was taken from you.

The next day was a Saturday, so Trey and Quinn didn't have class. Apart from meals and lacrosse practice, Trey stayed inside with me the whole day, poring over Parris' book. Quinn paced around the room annoying us until Trey threw a book at him.

Quinn rolled his eyes as he pulled a leather jacked over his school blazer. "I'm going for a walk."

"You shouldn't run off," Trey glowered from the desk. "We've got work to do here – you could be helpful."

"I am being helpful." Quinn slammed the door behind him.

I worried about him all afternoon while Trey fumed beside me. He returned long after dark, sweat slicking down his brow and wet leaves clinging to the hem of his slacks.

"You dropped this, Hazy." He tossed something on the bed.

I picked up the object. It was the molds we'd made of Ms. West's lab keys. Most of the soap had dissolved, but the metal keys were still perfectly intact. "Where did you get this?"

"In the lockbox in the cave," Quinn slumped down on his bed with a self-satisfied grin. "I can't believe you never thought to go see if they were still there. I went down to see the cave-in for myself. There's a sigil on one of the stones – I think it's the type that's designed to call those gross shadow creatures that were in the gym and that Courts used to attack Hazy in the cave."

The god's servants. "I bet that was how the Eldritch Club got to Zehra so fast – they sent those shadows after her. But the god said they will obey me now, so hopefully we don't have to worry about them." I reached for my phone to text Deborah. "I can't believe they were still there. You're right, we should have checked immediately. This key is just what we need to get Deborah into Ms. West's lab, if we could find it. Sadie said Ms. West moved her lab from the icehouse."

"Confirmed," Quinn grinned. "I checked the icehouse myself as soon as I found these. No lock on any of the doors anymore. Apart from a couple of old freezers, it's completely cleared out."

I whomped him across the head with a pillow. "You shouldn't have done that alone! But yes, thank you for finding the key."

"See." Quinn gave Trey a pointed look. "I was being *helpful*."

"For once in your life," Trey muttered.

I rubbed soap off the key with the edge of my hoodie as I texted the news to Deborah. "Do you think this will work in the new lab?"

"She probably changed the lock," Trey said.

"With what?" Quinn shot back. "It's not as if anyone at this place can just drive down to the hardware store."

"Don't be stupid. We get deliveries here all the time. Otherwise, we wouldn't get fresh food and new pencils and shit."

"Can we maybe stop bickering about it and get back to searching for something that'll help...something like this." I jabbed the page in excitement.

Most witches or magicians favor the cat as a familiar, due to their superior intelligence and predatory nature. Other animals such as bats, crows, and lizards are also common. The familiar carries the secrets of the witch and may even be used as a conduit for their power. Some witches have even, upon death, passed their souls into their familiars.

A powerful magician may choose for their familiar not one creature but many – a herd of malleable minds akin to those of the humans they seek to control. The rat, therefore, makes the perfect such familiar, as they think and act in a form of hivemind reminiscent of the human sheep who have not yet woken up to our true position in the cosmic hierarchy. Rats make the perfect spies, the ideal servants, and the most loyal soldiers. However, one must be careful to remain on their good side, for they have been known to consume the flesh of a magician who treats them unfairly and asks of them more than they are willing to perform.

"That sounds like it was written by a conspiracy theorist," Quinn said. He hiked his pants up to his nipples and cried in a high-pitched voice, "'The rats are the army of a cosmic god. Wake up, sheeple!'"

I glanced up at the ceiling. The rats circled above my head, and my mind circled with them.

It's ridiculous. They're just rats.

But they led me to the book. They knew what I wanted, and they knew where it was located.

I thought of all the times I'd heard the rats, about how their feet seemed to respond to my moods and save me from bad decisions. How they could have attacked me when I was in the various secret tunnels and passages around the school, but they stayed away. How the scritching of their feet in the walls had become almost a comfort to me.

How they were doing that same frantic circling now that they'd used to lead me to the book. They knew where something was I wanted to find.

The rats know. They know where we can find Greg!

I stood up, slamming the book shut. "I need to get into the walls."

"What? Why? Yesterday you only just made it out of Ayaz's dorm without being reported. We can't do anything else that will risk—"

"Because the rats know where Ms. West is keeping Greg, which means we'd have the location of her current lab. They've been trying to tell us this whole time. I'm going to follow them."

Trey rolled his eyes at the ceiling. "You get that's insane, right?"

"Oh sure, there's a cosmic deity trapped in a prison of darkness under the gymnasium and that's just business-as-usual, but super-intelligent rats are a stretch."

"You just read that rats are ruled by a powerful magician," Trey shot back. "Have you asked yourself who's controlling these rats?"

"Someone who is trying to help me, which is more than you're doing right now." I waved a finger at Trey. "Before you pull your macho bullshit and say I can't go, I'm going. Don't try and stop me, but you can come with me if you want to."

"I'll go." Quinn stood up, shoving the book toward Trey and grabbing his cloak. "I'm helpful like that. You stay here, keep reading through this. See what you can find."

Trey looked set to argue, but honestly, Quinn had a point. Trey was book smart, but Quinn could weasel his way out of any disaster, and that was exactly the kind of person I needed if we were going hunting for Greg, for answers.

Quinn and I donned our black cloaks again and stepped out the door. The rats scritched along the ceiling, leading us toward the staircase that went up into the dorms. We followed, crouching low. Quinn poked his head up to see if the coast is clear.

"The teachers are checking the rooms again," he said. "They're all dressed in their robes. I bet they're going to the gym."

The rats scrambled up the wall, following the teachers as they made their way through the dorm. They wanted us to follow them.

Quinn and I pulled our hoods low over our eyes and crept up the stairs, hiding behind the corner of the hall near Courtney's and Loretta's rooms. As soon as the teachers went past, we ducked out and joined the back of their line as they exited the dormitories and made their way across the bridge into the classroom wing.

I kept my head down as I fell into step behind them. If anyone noticed us, we'd be in trouble, but no one turned around. Down, down, down, we traveled – past the locked classrooms and deserted lockers, down the darkened staircase to the gymnasium. The rotten stench grabbed my stomach and squeezed. Now I knew what caused the smell – the bodies of sacrifices prior to the fire – it was even more horrible. I choked back a sob as I fought for breath. Even Quinn, whose revenant body had a diminished sense of smell, also struggled not to vomit.

None of the other teachers seemed fazed by the smell. They must've been used to it by now. I gulped as we entered the low, black hallway. We needed to keep our cover, which meant I had to pretend things were perfectly normal even as my lungs begged for air.

At the front of the crowd, Ms. West handed off her torch to Dr. Atwood and rolled back the door. Teachers staggered back as a fresh wave of the foul smell rolled into the hall. That was too much even for them. Dr. Halsey broke down in a coughing fit, and Mr. Dexter made a strangled sound.

"Silence!" Ms. West snapped, ushering them inside. I squeezed Quinn's hand as we filed in after them. As soon as we'd all entered, Ms. West slammed the doors shut, sliding the inside bolts shut so no student could enter.

The gym looked exactly as I remembered it, aka terrifying. Empty bleachers sagging with damp and age lined three walls. Everything was coated in a layer of dust and soot. A single shaft of moonlight illuminated a square of the court. Shadows lurked in every corner, their presence dripping with balefulness.

These weren't ordinary shadows. I had to remind myself they were on my side.

Forty-two teachers filed into the lower bleachers, huddling in small groups. Quinn and I took seats in the third row, far enough away from the others so we could whisper without them hearing us. I sat on my hands so no one noticed them trembling. My heart knocked against my ribcage.

This was by far the most insane thing we've done.

But it wasn't the most insane thing I *planned* to do.

Ms. West stepped onto the court, standing under the moonlight. She shrugged off her hood, allowing the pale shaft to cast her face in eerie shadow. The stark light made her cheekbones appear shrunken – as if her skin ate away at her face. "Thank you for coming to this meeting. I've called you here because our situation has become dire," she said.

"Why aren't we meeting in the faculty lounge?" Dr. Halsey called out.

"Because we're concerned with what went on in this very room twenty years ago, and because I don't trust that the maintenance staff isn't accepting bribes to report on us. The Eldritch Club have ears everywhere. I know I can trust you all."

"You sound disturbed, Hermia," Professor Atwood called out.

"Do I? If you knew the things I knew, you'd think me not disturbed enough." Ms. West paced along the center of the court, her hands wringing behind her back. Where she walked, symbols and lines appeared beneath her feet, lit up with blue flame. No one else acknowledged them – perhaps I was the only one who could see them. "All this time, the Eldritch Club has kept the power of the god to themselves. They made us promises – that we would have comfortable lives, that we had liberty to indulge our darkest proclivities free from the eyes of authorities, that we might possess any material good our hearts desired. All these things to make up for the great sacrifice we made. Many of us left families, friends, promising careers to forfeit our lives to babysit their bratty re-animated children. And what do we have to show for it?"

"Nothing!" Mr. Dexter called from the front row. I heard a few grumbles of agreement.

"Exactly." Ms. West's lips curled back into a wicked smile. "For what good are material possessions if we cannot show them off? What good is comfort without challenge and stimulation for the brain? After twenty years trapped inside this school, even indulging my desires has become stale. And then Hazel Waite arrives and things are exciting once more. She is connected to the god in a way I do not understand. Her pain causes him pain and weakens the Eldritch Club's power.

"This year's trouble has shown us that the god's power is waning, and with it, the Club's authority and influence. They have become so glutted with their power that they no longer acknowledge where it came from. Few of them ever visit the god. They know nothing of the rites or the history that gave them their blessings. They refuse to listen to us, we who spend our days in worship to the god. Their incompetence allowed Hazel Waite to escape. They are no longer worthy of our sacrifice. If we are to have what we deserve, then we must act now."

"What are you proposing?" Dr. Halsey asked.

Ms. West raised the torch in her hand and walked backward toward the center of the court. The light punctuated the darkness, illuminating the faded paint and the fainter, flame-tinged lines of the sigils. Around her feet, the five-pointed star glowed bright – in the same sickly color as the veins of strange stone in the caves below.

"I have told Vincent numerous times that our current system is no longer sustainable, but he will not see it. They have grown careless – no, they have always been careless. I discovered recently the student who escaped ten years ago was Ayaz Demir's sister. How could she have been allowed to enter the school? Another mistake like that and Derleth is done for. What will become of us?"

All around us, teachers murmured to each other as they took in this information. My heart hammered against my chest. *That means either Ayaz told her or she got her hands on Zehra and got those answers from her. Either way, that means there's no hope Zehra is still alive.*

Beside me, Quinn squeezed my knee. He'd figured that out, as well.

Zehra, I'm so sorry. I wish more than anything I could have saved you.

I forced my grief-stricken mind to focus on Ms. West's words. "—Vincent refuses to listen to reason. He wants to take more power from the god, not less. He will not entertain the idea of giving us our due while his own power deteriorates. But he has forgotten one important fact – every one of us in this room has immortality. We do not need the god's power to keep us young and strong. As the Eldritch Club wane, we have the power here."

Several teachers cheered.

"What are you proposing we do with that power, Hermia?" Dr. Halsey called out.

"I want to leave the school. Let the Eldritch Club find new babysitters for their brats, or let the whole place burn to the ground, I don't care. But I'm done wasting all *this*—" she indicated her lithe body. "And *this*—" she tapped her brain "—trapped inside these four walls. When we return to the world, our families will have moved on. Our friends will have forgotten us. Our careers will be non-existent. We can view it as our curse, or as an opportunity. The Eldritch Club owes us – I say that it's time to take what we are due."

"Vincent will never agree to let us go," Atwood argued. "And we need the Eldritch Club to break the sigils to allow us to leave. They have abandoned their old ways, but they are still the descendants of a long line of powerful magicians – and only their magic could undo the boundaries. Why would they do that when it would free their children, as well?"

"They will find a way to make it work," Ms. West said. "I don't intend to give them an option to refuse. The school production looms closer. All the club members will descend upon us. There will be the usual chaos and disorganization and parties till all hours of the night. It will be the perfect time for us to kidnap Gloria Haynes."

I glanced at Quinn. *Kidnap Courtney's mother? Why?*

From the rumbling in the bleachers, at least some of the teachers agreed with us. "What will that achieve?" asked Mr. Dexter.

"Leverage," Ms. West replied. "If they want her back in one piece, they will break the sigils for us."

"How do we know they'll agree to that?" asked Dr. Halsey,

who seemed willing to entertain the idea. "They might just leave Gloria to our mercy."

"If you paid attention to the politics at play here, you'd understand that they'd have no choice but to agree. Many of the Eldritch Club families – including the Bloombergs – are running low on funds. It's hard to keep the kind of secrets they keep and continue in the manner they've become accustomed to without burning through your fortune. The god can give power, but it doesn't understand how money plays into that world. They need the Hayes fortune to fund their campaigns and activities. They need Gloria to pay their bribes and grease the wheels of their machine. She's their meal ticket, and they know it."

"But they have the power of the god behind them!" cried Dexter. "We'd be going up against a cosmic deity!"

"They may wield the god's power, but we're the ones who feed him. If he's loyal to anyone, it's us. Their power is already weakened because of Hazel's disappearance and the deception we pulled with Greg Lambert." My ears perked up at Greg's name. *He really, truly is alive.* "They know nothing of the old spells or rituals, and they cannot get into the cavern to see the god without coming through us. If we cut off their access to the god, they won't have any advantage over us. Remember, they can't kill us, but we can kill them."

Quinn's fingers tightened around my thigh. I turned to him, noticing the brightness in his eyes from the shadow of his hood. We both leaned forward in unison, clinging to Ms. West's every word.

All around me, the teachers chatted, their voices tight with excitement. Ms. West clapped to get their attention. "I'll have a show of hands. If we're all in agreement, we must make arrangements before—"

Her words cut off. She swirled her head up, her piercing eyes searching the bleachers. My heart pummeled against my chest. My whole body froze.

She's seen us. She—

But she was looking behind us, up toward the roof of the gym, to the area shrouded in deepest shadows. "What's that?" she demanded.

In the silence, I caught the sound she'd heard – a faint scratching. A tingle of anticipation ran down my arms. Ms. West leaned forward, attempting to divine the source of the scritches and scratches that grew louder and more urgent.

Something wicked this way comes.

"What is that?" cried Dr. Atwood, throwing off his hood as he leaped to his feet. The wooden bleachers groaned and trembled as some force landed on them, shaking the rotting planks at it rolled down toward us.

The sound grew louder – thunder clapped in the enclosed gym. The walls bounced it back so it came from everywhere at once, surrounding us, closing in.

Scritch-scritch. Scritch-scritch. Scritchscritchscritchscritchscritch-SCRITCH.

Dr. Halsey shrieked. "It sounds like... rats!"

The scritching circled beneath me. I lifted my feet just in time – a stampede of large, furry bodies skittered across the bleachers, tiny tails flickering through the air like whips as they descended upon Ms. West and the faculty.

Teachers leaped off their seats and barreled for the exit. Rats poured from the bleachers, spilling on the court in a waterfall of grey fur and sharp things – a thousand tiny teeth gnawing and gnashing in anticipation of a meal.

Where the rats led, other things followed. Tiny dark shadows chased them across the court, snarling and snapping from the gloom. My chest tightened as they leaped onto the bleachers and hurtled toward us. Quinn grabbed my hand and dragged me to my feet, so we stood together above the tide while the servants of the god rained down upon us.

Dr. Halsey flung her cape away as a rat clung tenaciously to the hem. Professor Atwood spun his arms like windmills as rodents leaped onto his bell sleeves, using them as funnels to burrow inside. Ms. West's haughty expression crumpled into confusion and then fear as she caught sight of the rodent army descending upon her.

"Run!" Ms. West yelled, propelling herself toward the doors.

She didn't have to tell anyone twice. Teachers shoved each other in their haste to escape. Dr. Atwood threw open the heavy door and tumbled into the hall. The rats followed him, crawling over his body and up the legs of his slacks. He screamed, the sound wild and inhuman. The other teachers backed away as he thrashed wildly, trying to extract rodents from inside his robes.

More and more rats poured under my feet. At any moment they could swarm up the bleachers and crawl over me and Quinn, but for now, they seemed preoccupied with the teachers. Quinn grabbed my hand and dragged me up. We stood together on the bench seat, watching the avalanche of rodents descend and the shadows creeping after them, cold and menacing.

"We should make a run for the door on the other side." Quinn leaped onto the next bench, holding out his hand to help me across. We hopped down to the floor. My shoulders shuddered as the door slammed. Ms. West had shut us in.

Rats swarmed along the edge of the court, flinging their bodies against the locked door, clawing at the old wood, scraping away soot and paint in their hunger to devour the teachers. I could just make out the faint outline of the doors on the other side – the ones Quinn carried me through when he saved me from the shadows. The rats were so focused on the teachers we had a mostly clear path if we went *right now*.

We have to run for it.

"Three, two, one..." Quinn counted down. We leaped as far as we could over the rats, our feet slapping against the court. My heel caught the tail of a rat. It twisted and struggled, screeching at the top of its lungs. I lifted my foot. It scurried away before I could kick.

Quinn dragged me across the court toward the other side. My heart burned as I poured on speed to keep up with him. *Scritch-scritchscritchscritchscritchSCRITCHSCRITCH.* Rodents snapped and scratched at my heels, the avalanche rolling behind us as they sensed fresh meat.

The doors led to a short hallway and a staircase up to a steel door that entered the library. If we could get there, the steel would keep the rats at bay. For now.

If we can get there in one piece...

Rats streamed toward us, bringing with them that sickly sweet smell of decay and the dark presence of the shadows that lurked behind them. Quinn pressed himself against me, burying his head in my shoulder as he urged us onward. My lungs burned, and the burn Courtney gave me on my leg tugged and twinged, but I didn't stop running.

Claws scraped across the court as the rats overtook us. Hundreds of grey bodies streamed beside us, rolling around to surround us and block our exit.

Quinn's breath shuddered as he skidded to a stop, throwing his arms around me. Even through the warmth of his touch, I could sense the approaching ice of the shadows. Cold pressed against my throat, silencing my screams as rats circled my ankles and their wild cacophony filled my head.

I closed my eyes, waiting for the first sting of teeth sinking into my flesh.

CHAPTER TWENTY-SIX

I'm sorry, Quinn. I'm sorry it ends like this. I wanted so much to save you.

I squeezed Quinn's hard body, forcing my eyes shut. I might die being eaten alive by rats, but I didn't have to watch it happen. My mother's face flashed before my eyes. Wreathed in light and smiling her beautiful smile, she reached out of the darkness for me. *I won't see you soon, because you're an angel and I'm going to a very different place. But I love you, Mom. I'm sorry. I—*

I waited for the first bite. I waited for the shadows to take me. But it didn't come.

I cracked open one eye, daring a look. The rats still surged down from the bleachers, filling their court with their ranks. But instead of swarming over us they flowed around us, leaving a five-foot circle at our feet. We stood in the center of the court, where the glowing five-pointed star I'd seen last time now lit up our feet.

"Quinn." I shook his shoulder, bringing him back to me. "Look."

Quinn opened his eyes and jumped as he noticed the rats, the star, the cold shadows lurking behind us. "What the fuck is this?"

A single rat stepped out from the army and scurried toward us, stopping at my feet and standing up on its hind legs. A tiny nose twitched.

Silence fell. As one, every single rat in the gym stopped moving. The scritches stopped. The shadows remained mute. My heart pounded in my ears.

What the fuck is going on?

I knelt. "You're the rats in the walls?" I asked.

The rat nodded.

"You understand English?"

Another nod.

"And you stop the shadows from coming closer?" I pointed behind me.

More vigorous nodding. The rats scraped their claws against the wood. *Scritch-scritch-scritch*. It was an answer.

Quinn's fingers dug into my shoulder. "No way."

The rat turned its tiny nose to Quinn, and nodded slowly, as if to say, *keep up*.

"If you're on Hazy's side, why did you attack her last time she was in the gym?"

The rat shook his head. He made a little "tsch-tsch" noise with his teeth as he threw his tiny paws in the air. He seemed to be saying, *you've got it all wrong*.

"Maybe they weren't trying to attack me," I said. "I think they were trying to show me what was beneath the gym. I know this is insane, but I think they've been looking out for me the whole time."

Quinn nodded. "Okay, sure, the rats are our friends. I'm not going to question it with all these sharp teeth around."

I nodded to the head rat. "Thank you so much for looking out for me. I'm only sorry it's taken me this long for me to understand. Can you help me now? I'm trying to find my friend Greg. Do you know where they're keeping him?"

The head rat turned its head and made that "tsch-tsch" noise again. Feet skittered across the floor as the rats parted like I was Moses commanding the Red Sea. They dived and scrambled over each other to line up in perfect rows, leaving us a straight path across the gym into the darkness.

Quinn gripped my hand so tight pain shot up my arm. We stepped onto the path. Thousands of beady rat eyes watched us, unblinking, as we followed the path. I held up my hand and made a flame on my palm.

The rat path led to a small alcove with a roller door. The words 'Weight Room' were scrawled on a faded sign. A length of rusted chain secured the roller door to a ring in the floor, and it was locked with a shiny padlock.

A brand new padlock for a gym no one uses? Not fucking likely.

Quinn pulled out the key mold we'd taken, but of course, it was useless. Ms. West had got her hands on a new padlock. This one was stainless steel – it would take ages to burn through. But the chain was much older. More malleable.

"You might want to turn away," I told Quinn.

He didn't, because he was Quinn and if you told him not to do something it only made him want to do it more. I gripped the chain in my hands and drew up the spark inside me, stoking the fire with my rage and fear until my palms glowed with heat. Quinn leaped back as if I'd burned him, his eyes wide as saucers in the gloom.

"You... you..." Quinn stammered, collapsing in on himself, curling up into a ball like a porcupine.

"Yes. I can summon fire." The chain burned hot, then turned to liquid, which dribbled through my fingers to form a molten puddle on the floor.

One chain destroyed. One Quinn reduced to a mess in the corner.

I went to him, cupping his cheeks in my hands even as he tried to jerk away. "Quinn, listen to me. I swear to you, I don't know why I have this power. I've had it my whole life. But I taught myself to control it. I promise I will never, ever hurt you."

Quinn grabbed my wrists, turning my hands over. His whole body trembled. "What the fuck, Hazy? How'd you not burn yourself?"

"Because I'm awesome." I cocked an eyebrow at him.

Quinn whistled through his teeth and dropped my hands. "You're something else."

"Damn right." *I just wish I knew what that something else* was. "I know this is hard for you, but can you hold on to your sanity a little longer? We need to see what's inside."

"Yeah. Okay." The lack of a witty retort showed just how rattled Quinn was. He pulled himself to his feet and shoved up the roller door. Behind us, the rats skittered and squeaked amongst themselves. Behind the door was another vast room, and I had to send up a flame from my palm to penetrate the darkness. Quinn let out a strangled cry, but he didn't leave my side.

It was an old weight room, but it had a new purpose. Dusty workout equipment had been pushed against the walls to make way for a long stainless steel table littered with lab equipment. I recognized some of the machines from Gail's laboratory. Racks of test tubes lined a rack that once held hand weights, and power cables snaked across the floor. Dry ice curled from beneath a door labeled 'sauna.'

We found Ms. West's lab.

In the corner, chained to a squat rack, was a slumped, shadowy figure. A flash of dirty-blond hair peeked out from a torn and bloody face.

"Greg!" I raced over and dropped to my knees, grabbing his chin and pulling his head into the light. It was him. His eyes lolled in his head, and his tongue hung out the side of his mouth. Blood caked under his fingers, and his usually bright hair was streaked with dirt and clinging to his face in matted clumps.

"Greg, can you hear me?" I slapped his cheeks, but all that elicited was a low groan.

"Hazy, look." Quinn knelt on the other side of the squat rack, cradling something in his hands. I held the flame closer to him and realized it was another body. He turned the head toward me, and a curtain of dark hair fell away to reveal another familiar face.

Zehra.

CHAPTER TWENTY-SEVEN

"Shit." My eyes met Quinn's – my fear reflected in his blue orbs. He tried to shake Zehra awake, but she was even more out-of-it than Greg.

Zehra's here! But is she alive? Please let them both be alive.

"How come she's here?" he whispered. "I thought you said she was dead."

I shook my head. "I never saw her body. I just assumed because of the cave-in and she never showed up to meet me, and the Eldritch Club got hold of my phone... but now that I know she's here, it makes me think that cave-in wasn't an accident. When they saw my text, they would know exactly where she was meeting me. I think they made the god's shadow servants move the rocks so it would collapse the cave on her so that I couldn't tell her what I knew. Then they dragged her out through the god's cavern and brought her here."

I didn't have to ask why. I knew. They needed Ayaz to lie to me, they needed him to complete the illusion so I believed I was crazy. They drugged him to erase his memory of me, but even that wasn't enough to make him agree to it, so they used his sister as leverage.

So much of this didn't make sense. From what Ms. West was saying in the gym, she hadn't wanted to send me away, but then why did she cooperate with Vincent's plan? I didn't have time to consider it further, because Greg groaned and opened one eye.

"Haze..." he murmured.

"Greg, hey." I cupped his face in my hands. His skin felt cold, clammy. Both he and Zehra's chains had been loosely tied so they could move their arms and legs, even stand up, but they couldn't step more than a foot in any direction. Dog bowls beside him held water and some kind of dried food. *This is sick.* "We're going to get you out of here, okay? I won't let Ms. West hurt you anymore."

Greg lifted his chin. "The rats... you have to know..."

"It's a long story, but don't worry about them. They're sort of our friends."

"I know," Greg whispered. His chains clanged as he pointed a shaking finger across the room, where the rats lined up along the wall and started jumping in unison. "They... visit me. Good... company. But that's not what I meant... look."

I followed his finger. The rats lined up along the wall, standing on their hind legs and scraping their claws against the wood, leaving thin marks. They must've done it a hundred times before, because there was already a line of scratches running along the edge of the wall...

Wait a second...

I dropped Greg's arm and crawled toward the wall. The rats parted ways, scampering under the gym equipment to give me a view of the scratches. I ran my hand over the wall, feeling the deep cuts where the rats had dug in with their claws.

These weren't just random claw marks.

They scratched *words* into the wall.

No, not words. *Names.*

Bridget Bishop. Sarah Good. Susannah Martin. Sarah Wildes. Elizabeth Howe...

Someone dropped down beside me. Quinn. His hand dropped onto my shoulder, warm and steadying. Not even he could stop the cold leaking into my heart as I registered the significance of the names.

"That rats wrote these," he said. It wasn't a question. "Is it like some rat version of a dating website?"

"I recognize these names." I touched the edge of 'Alice Parker.' "I've read them in my research about the Salem witch trials. These are the names of the victims. The women who were burned as witches. I think, somehow, but I don't understand it, they *are* the rats."

A voice from behind us coughed. "Four men, too."

I whirled around to see Zehra raise her head and wipe a strand of tangled hair from her eyes. In the flickering candlelight, her dark features blended into the gloom, but I could never mistake those vivid eyes or the warmth and defiance in that voice for one of the shadows.

"You're alive!" I rushed over to her and wrapped her in a hug. She clung to me, coughing, her body brittle and far too thin.

"I'm sorry I didn't make our meeting," she croaked.

"Ssssh, don't talk." I squeezed her. "I'm just so glad you're here to correct my history failings."

"Indeed – get it right. Four men were killed as witches, too. Giles Covey was pressed to death." She coughed again. "Rebecca Nurse was supposedly executed, but then she showed up at Parris' home a few years later."

"That's fascinating, but not relevant right now." I turned to Greg. "Did you see the rats write on the walls?"

He shook his head. "I think that was already here when they tied me up, but the rats were determined we notice it. Do you think it has something to do with the god eating people's souls?"

I stared at him in shock. *He's not supposed to know about the god—*

"Greg and I have had plenty of time to talk," Zehra said. "I told him everything. Honestly, I don't understand why you didn't, especially after he was nearly sacrificed himself."

"I'll explain later." I tugged at the bindings around her wrists.

"How did you find us?" Greg asked.

"The rats led me here. I think they wanted us to know what the teachers were discussing tonight." Above our heads, the scritching started again. King Rat leaped down from the rafters and stood on my shoulder. Zehra jumped, but to her credit, she didn't scream.

I reached up to give King Rat a scratch behind the ears, but he turned his head toward me and bared his teeth in a maniacal grin, and I couldn't quite bring myself to touch him. "I think they've been helping me all along. We've got a lot to catch up on. First, let's get you out of here."

"There's no point." Zehra pulled herself up, hugging her knees to her chest. "If everything you told me is true, you lose your one advantage by taking us with you. Right now you can sneak around anywhere because you're a ghost. But if I'm gone, Ms. West will search the school and find us both."

"Then we'll all go," I said. "We'll sneak through the forest and head for a large foreign city where we can get lost. Trey and I did it before. He cut a sigil out of the rock and took it with him, and he could walk outside the boundary. We could all run to safety."

I didn't intend to leave school. I *couldn't*. But they didn't need to know that.

"If you leave Derleth, you can't come back." Zehra's chest heaved from the effort of crossing her arms and glaring at me in defiance. "You might be outside the walls, but you won't be free, because they'll never stop chasing you. Do that if you want, but I'm not going with you. I'm staying right here. This is our one chance to save my brother, and I'm not letting you waste it."

I glanced over at Greg, and he nodded. "Go. Pretend you never came here. West has made it clear we're more valuable to her alive right now."

"But why? What has she done to you?"

Greg shook his head. "There's too much to tell, and you need to go. Zehra and I will look after each other."

"I can't leave you here to rot."

"We'll be fine – we're being fed and watered." Greg held up a battered paperback titled *At The Mountains of Madness*. "West has even provided entertainment of a sort."

Zehra rolled her eyes. "That author can't write for shit. So many incomprehensible words. So much racism. What I wouldn't give for a copy of *Vogue*."

The rats chittered. The Rat King advanced, standing on his hind legs and tugging on my sleeve.

Zehra coughed. "I think that's your cue to get out of here."

"I can't leave you." Not when her skin on mine was so cold and clammy.

"You have to," Zehra croaked. "But before you go, there's one last thing..."

"Yeah?"

"On that bench over there... there's something you should see."

I followed Zehra's finger to the end of Ms. West's lab table. In a plastic tray sat a stack of newspaper articles. I started to flip through them and realized where they'd come from.

"I overheard a conversation between West and another teacher, Atwood," Zehra said. "They found those articles I left for you in the room of a student named Loretta."

Loretta took the articles. I'd gone to show Ayaz what I'd discovered about Miskatonic Prep, and in my haste, I hadn't picked up the rest. When I came back to the storage room, they were gone. I'd never found out who took them or why. *Loretta.* If the teachers found them in Loretta's room, that means it was probably from her that they learned about the secret passage.

Bitch.

I picked up the stack of articles. I'd never finished looking through them. The first few were about the Miskatonic Prep fire, then there were some about problems at the Arkham General Hospital morgue, although it never spoke about Ms. West by name. If I'd known all this sooner, it might've saved us some time.

Zehra coughed. "Find the article about Loretta."

I flipped through the stack, scanning the tiny print for Loretta's name. It didn't make sense that she'd be in here. These were all articles from decades ago—

I stopped short, my breath catching in my throat.

Loretta's face stared back at me from a small image. She wore a blue dress with a white lace collar. A Sunday School dress.

The headline read, '14-YEAR-OLD GIRL SUSPECTED OF MURDERING HER FATHER.'

CHAPTER TWENTY-EIGHT

I scanned the article. It talked about her mother's suicide, and how Loretta had been given to her father to raise after her death. The reporter in Loretta's local town seemed to believe it wasn't fair that Loretta's father – who'd never wanted her – had a child thrust on him. An unstable child who ran him through with a pitchfork. Police found Loretta standing over the body of her dead father, silent and covered in blood. Her prints were on the pitchfork handle. The reporter made no secret of the fact she believed Loretta wasn't just guilty, but evil.

A pitchfork. My eyes bugged out. *That's brutal.*

Loretta was tiny. How did she even have the strength to lift a pitchfork, let alone drive it through someone's ribcage?

Another article explained details from the court case. The defense argued that Loretta couldn't have committed the crime because of her size and the amount of power and brutality required. They pointed out that a distraught Loretta, upon finding the body, tried to pull the handle free and ended up with blood all over her, and her fingerprints on the murder weapon. They added witnesses who stated her father was a brutal man who had several ongoing disputes with neighbors and with a local shopkeeper. Loretta had been found not guilty, and her grandparents become her guardians.

Because we're the murderers.

With shaking hands, I tidied the stack of articles and replaced them in the tray. Zehra watched me, her eyes swimming with pain. "Ms. West is interested in this girl," she said. "You should talk to her."

"Oh, I plan on it." I hugged them both.

It felt like a betrayal to lock Zehra and Greg back in that room, to find another length of chain and wrap it through the padlock, to turn our backs on our friends and follow the rats out of the gym, but that was exactly what we did. I hated every moment of it. At the bottom of the staircase, the urge overcame me and I turned back. Quinn stopped me by grabbing my arms and turning me around again.

"The only way to save them is to keep going with the plan," he whispered into my hair.

"I know." I buried my face into his chest. "But it sucks."

"Yeah, it does." Quinn rubbed my back. "Greg's pretty brave. I don't know if I'd opt to stay in a rat-infested shithole just to help you save some ungrateful rich assholes."

I smiled. *Ungrateful rich assholes* was a pretty accurate description of the student body. "I told you he was special."

We made our way back to the basement without being seen. Trey was at the door as soon as we turned the handle. "What happened?" he demanded, dragging me into the bed with him. His fresh herb and cypress scent hit my nose, allowing me to shrug off some of the horrors that clung to me like weeds. "You've been gone for hours."

Quinn and I filled him in on everything that happened. Between the teachers plotting to kidnap Courtney's mother, the rats, the discovery of Greg and Zehra in Ms. West's lab, and Loretta's articles, it was a lot to take in.

"What are we doing about the kidnapping?" Quinn asked.

"We leave the faculty to it," I said. "We're continuing with our plan. As far as I'm concerned, any advantage they gain over the Eldritch Club will work in our favor."

"But do you think we should tell Courtney?" Quinn's voice wavered. I had to remind myself that until recently Courtney had been his girlfriend. Even though she was a stone-cold bitch, Quinn cared about her on some level.

"And risk her warning them? Not going to happen. Remember, Courtney doesn't know what we know about what her parents did."

"Not yet," Trey added.

I leaned back against Quinn's shoulder in a way I hoped was comforting, but I didn't know anymore. Comfort wasn't exactly my strong point. "Stop worrying. The god's on our side. We've got this."

Trey refused to let me go, so I slept curled against his shoulder while he snored gently. Quinn tossed and turned for ages before he too fell asleep. I couldn't close my eyes until I heard his gentle breathing interspersed with Trey's snores. My two fallen Kings – we were one step closer to giving them freedom.

I now had a god on my side... sort of. And a rat army at my disposal. That was... interesting. But why help me? Why not the other scholarship students?

How did they understand me?

Why did they write those names on the walls?

Were the names theirs?

Most importantly, what did everything have to do with me? And Loretta? Ms. West seemed to believe Loretta was important, and she knew everything in those articles. It was impossible to think Loretta with her wide, frightened eyes could kill someone, and yet... her last words to me repeated over and over in my head. I wasn't looking forward to trying to talk to her again. Our last conversation had given more questions than answers.

These questions swirled around in my head until sleep

dragged me under. I had no time to enjoy the bliss of oblivion before the god called me back to the cavern. This time, the teachers encircled the scaffold, chanting in their haunting tongue. The sound resonated through the high dome, so the very air itself reverberated with its power.

Ms. West appeared at the tunnel entrance, dragging Loretta's prone body. "Oh, god of the infinite abyss, we come tonight to celebrate your benevolence and to bask in your glory. Tonight, after your long months of starvation, you will be able to feed."

She stepped through her fellow worshippers and threw open the trapdoor. Even though I braced myself, I couldn't stop the bile rising to my throat as the god's essence was revealed once more and its cold hatred stroked my skin.

"We offer up this sacrifice for your enjoyment. Her mind has been broken so that she might please you." Ms. West snapped her fingers. Two of the robed figures moved forward and strapped Loretta into the scaffold, tying the ropes tight around her skinny arms and legs. Her head rolled over. She was awake, although probably drugged. She made no move to fight.

"Begin!" Ms. West commanded. One of the robed figures turned a handle, and the chains clanked, lowering Loretta into the mouth of the god's prison. The chanting rose with pitch and fervor as Loretta was lowered into the hole. The god's hunger rose up from beneath, like a wet tongue licking her body in anticipation of the feast. I surged forward, but the sheer vileness of the god's hunger sent me reeling.

Loretta disappeared into the black void. The chanting rose to a crescendo, reverberating off the polished stone walls until the whole room hummed and constricted like an enormous stomach digesting us all. Green veins flickered on the edges of my vision, completing the horror.

The chanting broke off abruptly as the room pitched. Teachers dropped to their knees, covering their heads as rock and dust rained down on them. The room continued to pulse and shake. It balanced on the edge of tension, ready to tear apart at any time. Teachers staggered across the pitching ground, cowering beneath the alcove where I too hid. I figured they couldn't see me the way I could see them.

The god howled with pain. In the haze of darkness, I *felt* rather than saw its power retracting, the sticky spiderweb of bonds that stretched from the god out into the world snapping and unraveling. Dust and stone rained from the roof, obscuring my view of the room. From deeper in the cave, a great *BOOM* sounded as another cave-in shook the ancient structure.

"What's happening?" Dr. Atwood tore off his hood and glanced at Ms. West.

"This doesn't make sense," Ms. West cried, steadying herself against the wall as the world jerked violently. "There was nothing different about her. She was even more broken than the others."

With a groan, the scaffold bent double. The ropes stretched taut, then pinged back, sending a lump flying from within the prison and skidding across the ground. Loretta's face – pale and frozen – stared with glassy eyes.

Ms. West bent down and dragged Loretta up by the hair. "What is the meaning of this? What have you done to our god?"

Loretta's eyes rolled back. She made no move to respond.

Ms. West shook her, her voice rising as panic settled in. "What did you do?"

With a final spurt of agony and the *snap snap snap* of oily strands breaking, the god slumped back into its prison. A foul wind roared through the cave. I pressed my back against the wall as it fought to tear me away. The teachers clung to each other, their robes whipping around their bodies. With a *BANG*, the trapdoor slammed shut, and the room fell silent and still.

"What do we do now?" Atwood demanded. "The god is even weaker than before, and they already blame us. Now it will not eat. When Bloomberg gets here, he'll have our heads for this."

Ms. West nudged Loretta's prone body with her spiked heel.

STEFFANIE HOLMES

"The Eldritch Club already know about Ms. Waite's effect on the god. We tell them that tonight was a result of Hazel's presence. They don't need to know another scholarship student also has this effect."

"They'll know we haven't sacrificed a student," Dr. Halsey pointed out.

"Will they?" Ms. West brushed rock dust off her sleeves. "Of course it will be clear in a few years when this girl starts to age, but for now our deception will be invisible. She doesn't know what happened to her, and she has no friends to confide in, so how will she reveal the truth?"

"We're not cutting out her tongue like the others?"

Ms. West shook her head. "Courtney Haynes has specially requested she remains in the student body as part of Hazel Waite's torture."

"If Courtney wants it, we must obey," Dr. Atwood whispered to another robed figure, his voice dripping with sarcasm.

"That's exactly true, Derek. And you'd do best not to forget it." Ms. West dropped Loretta's head. Her skull made a loud thump as it hit the concrete. The headmistress stepped over Loretta and made her way toward the tunnel connecting the cavern with the gymnasium. The rest of the faculty followed. At the doorway, Atwood looked back on Loretta, his face twisting.

"You think you've escaped death," he snarled. "You know *nothing*."

Atwood ducked his head, disappearing into the tunnel. Goosebumps rocketed up my arms. I longed to rush to Loretta's side, but when I tried to move my feet, they were glued to the ground. The god didn't want me interfering with this dream – he wanted me to *see* it.

After what seemed like forever holding my breath, Loretta stirred. She curled her knees into her chest, gripping her temples. A strangled groan escaped her throat.

Loretta lay still a while longer before slowly, achingly slowly, pulling herself to her feet. She spun in a slow circle, eyes wide as she took in every detail of the cavern with its dressed stone, creepy veins, and torches flickering from sconces carved in the walls, of the dust and debris coating the ground, of the scaffold and trapdoor. Loretta brushed dust off her Derleth skirt and frowned at her now-soiled cuffs.

"Well," she said to the empty room, to the crawling chaos that lurked beneath. "Fuck you."

I bolted up in bed, my heart pounding. Trey threw his arm around me, dragging me against his chest.

"Another visit from everyone's favorite cosmic deity?" He murmured against my ear.

I nodded. Trey gripped me tighter. He didn't ask about the dream, but waited until I was ready to speak. *Who's this attentive guy, and what's he done with Trey the bully?*

"The god showed me something else from the past. It was the night Loretta was sacrificed. Or rather, *wasn't* sacrificed."

"I thought you didn't believe her."

"I didn't. But the god just showed me that it's true. The teachers strung her up on the scaffold, lowered her into the god's prison, and he spat her back out again. Ms. West decided to put Loretta back into the school. She told the faculty to blame the god's waning power on me so the Eldritch Club wouldn't figure it out."

"That's... interesting." Trey wiped strands of hair from my face, his touch warming me through the fog of my horror. "I wonder why the god wanted you to see it."

I rubbed my eyes. "I think he's trying to help me figure out what's different about Loretta and I. I think that's the key to figuring out how we can free the rest of you."

"Any idea what it could be?"

Because we're the murderers. Loretta's words danced on the tip of my tongue. I knew now that was the one similarity that united us – we fascinated the god because we had taken life, as he had.

I itched to tell Trey what Loretta had said. If I did, I also knew what his next question would be. *Are you a murderer, Hazel?*

And I didn't know how to answer that. I *couldn't*.

Instead, I held the secret to my chest and curled back into Trey's arms. In the bed across from us, Quinn snored. I watched the sun rising through the tiny high window. I hated myself until my loathing burned through my skin and I went numb all over.

I have to talk to Loretta. Alone.

The next morning, while Quinn and Trey argued over whose turn it was to use the shower first and therefore get the one single dribble of hot water, I snuck across the hall into Andre's room and let myself in. "Hey, I hope I didn't wake you. I—"

Andre sat up in bed, his face swallowed by guilt. Behind him, wrapped in the sheets, Sadie glared at me.

"Sorry. You did give me a key." I held it up in my hand. "Can I borrow your pad?"

Andre grabbed it from the nightstand and handed it to me. Sadie burrowed under the covers. I scribbled a message for Loretta, telling her that if she wanted to save Greg she had to meet me in the cemetery this afternoon. I tore off the page, folded it, and handed it and the pad back to Andre.

"Can you give this to Loretta? Don't let any teacher or student see it."

Andre nodded. Sadie pointed at the door. I backed away, hands in the air. I knew when I wasn't wanted.

"Why did you take the newspaper clippings?" I demanded before Loretta had even shut the gate behind her.

"Good afternoon to you, too." The hinges creaked as Loretta swung the gate shut. She leaned against the stone post, her eyes gazing up into the trees. Courtney had been experimenting with her hair again – it was tied in several small pigtails. It might've been a fashionable style on a hip hop singer, but it made Loretta look like a porcupine. "I noticed Mr. Dexter had bite marks up his arm, and Ms. Halsey's head is all bandaged up. Your doing, I suppose?"

"Don't change the subject. Ms. West has the articles now, did you know that?" I balled my hands into fists. When I thought about it, it made me so angry. "Does she know you got them from me?"

Loretta shrugged.

"I read them," I blurted out, trying to shake her out of her indifference. "You told me your dad was never in your life, but that's a lie. I know you killed him."

"Then you know why I took them," Loretta's voice was hard. "They already knew my mother killed herself because she was gay. What do you think would have happened to me if the monarchs found out about my father?"

I fought to keep my anger under control. She was right, of course. The monarchs had one job at this school – to make our lives as miserable as possible. If they'd had that detail of Loretta's life, they would have twisted it and exploited it and made her even more miserable.

Instead, Loretta kept it close, allowing it to twist up inside her and poison everything that had been good about her life. I knew all too much about keeping secrets.

"Someone went to a great deal of trouble to get those articles to me," I managed to say, trying to find another way to convey my anger. "If I'd read them all sooner, I might have been able to stop some of this from happening."

Loretta shook her head. "Of course you think that. I didn't come to talk about the past. You found Greg?"

I nodded. "Ms. West has him locked up in her new laboratory. She needs the students and staff to believe he's been sacrificed, but she won't give him to the god because she's trying to weaken the Eldritch Club. Theoretically, the oath I made still protects him from being hurt. But I don't know for how much longer."

"It sounds as if you have everything figured out," Loretta said in a bored voice. "I don't see what you need me for."

"I need to know about when you were thrown into the god's prison. What happened? What did you see?"

"Everything," Loretta wore her secret smile like a mask. "And nothing."

"Did he speak to you? Do you know why he can't or won't take our souls?"

"I told you why." She frowned at me. "You just refuse to listen."

"I am listening. Please, Loretta?" I clasped my hands together, my voice cracking. The rage inside me threatened to snap at any moment, transforming my pleading into my hands wrapped around her throat. She had answers that could help us all, but she refused to cooperate. "I don't care about what you did. I'm the last fucking person to judge. I just need to know if there's some way I can give the others back their souls."

Loretta cast her eyes upward, focusing on something in the trees I couldn't see. "Do you know what a pitchfork sounds like when it slides through flesh?" she said. "That's what I hear every time I close my eyes. It's a wet *squelch*, like sinking your feet into fresh mud."

Fuck. I rubbed my temple. White-hot flames danced behind my eyes. *I'm not sure I'm up to hearing this.*

But Loretta needed to tell her story. She *needed* me to know.

"He raped my mother when she was just sixteen years old," Loretta said. "He was her youth leader at their church. She came to him for advice because she realized she was gay. He thought he would fuck the gayness out of her. She was a good Christian girl, a virgin saving herself for marriage. He was supposed to be a good Christian, too, but he just took what he wanted. Afterward, she was too scared to tell anyone, too scared to go to a doctor. She felt the baby growing inside her – a baby she loved and hated with equal measure until it tore her heart in two. She had to tell her parents. They wouldn't allow her to get an abortion, so she had to give birth to a child who'd been violently placed inside her."

Loretta closed her eyes. "I think she tried to love me. My grandmother showed me photographs of me when I was a baby. I'm in my mother's arms, and she's crying and smiling as she holds me. But his shadow loomed over everything – he stared back at her from my crib. I don't remember much about her now, except a vague feeling of unease. In her suicide note, she said she tried so hard but as much as she loved me she couldn't be my mother.

"After she died, the authorities said I had to live with my next-of-kin – the man who raped my mother. My grandparents knew what he'd done to their daughter, but as far as they were concerned, she'd made the whole thing up because she was sick. She thought she was gay. She was mentally disturbed, and he was a Godly Man – a church leader, a pillar of the community. They thought he'd be just the person to make sure I grew up 'right.' So off I went to live with a rapist. The first time he came into my room, I was just six years old." Her hand tightened around the gate. "He told me I was beautiful, a good girl. He said God loved me for being with him. He was the only one who ever said those sweet things to me. I wanted to make him happy."

Fuck. Fuck. Fuck. Loretta, I'm so sorry.

"As I got older, I tried to fight back, to tell him I didn't want to do anything. I felt ashamed – a wretched secret that no one wanted. He was ashamed, too, I think – he took to the bottle and he became violent. Not just to me – he would fly into a rage at the slightest provocation. Everyone in the church was afraid of him.

Every day I hoped he'd drink so much he'd pass out – if he didn't drink enough, then he didn't care who heard my screams.

"That day, he went out to the barn to talk to a neighbor, and he took a gallon of moonshine with him. Two hours later he bellowed for me. I knew if I didn't come he would come inside to find me, crashing through the house, destroying our possessions and then blaming it on me. I walked out to him, every step heavy as lead.

"I entered the barn and found him leaning against the haystack. He had that glint in his eye, shit from mucking out the pigs smeared on his hands. Something inside me snapped. He lunged at me, and I ran into the haystack. My hands closed around the shaft of the pitchfork. He laughed, and the laughter was all the wrongs he'd done me. I swung. The fork went in easily, like testing a fresh-baked cake with a skewer to see if it was cooked. He might have screamed, but I didn't hear. Everything felt far away, like I was watching a movie on mute. But maybe he screamed, because the neighbor came running, and he called the police."

I could never imagine what Loretta had been through. Home had always been my safety net, the place I ran to when the outside world was dangerous. She didn't know the meaning of 'home,' or 'safety.' Her home had been a place of terror, where her abuser took advantage of her body and where the other adults in her life had looked the other way because their god said she was broken.

In three strides I closed the chasm between us and wrapped my arms around Loretta's shoulders, encasing her in a hug. Loretta stiffened at my touch, but I flexed my muscles and refused to move, to relent. We were locked together in a battle of wills – she determined to keep her walls up, me desperate to smash them down.

Finally, Loretta's shoulders sagged, and she collapsed against my shoulder, tension fleeing her body as she relaxed into my embrace. She didn't cry. I suspected her tears had dried a long time ago.

"I'm sorry for what happened to you," I said. "I'm sorry that I didn't know before, that I wasn't a good friend."

"It's not your job," Loretta said.

"Maybe not, but I want it. I want to be your friend. Honestly, you deserve someone better than me, but I'm here if you want me."

She sniffed, wriggling away. "Greg was my friend... until Courtney said I couldn't be seen with him."

"You can help me to help him, and then you can be friends again. All I need to know is what happened when you were sacrificed—"

Loretta's eyes fluttered closed as she remembered. "During last period, Ms. West requested I meet in her office to discuss pulling up my low merit points. She had her secretary make tea for us. I guess my cup was laced with drugs, because the next thing I remember was waking up in the dark with my wrists bound." Loretta clutched me, her fingers digging into my shoulders like claws. "I floated in and out of consciousness, and there was this... presence inside my head. It sounded like a hundred children screaming."

"That's the god's voice."

"Yeah." Loretta sniffed again. "He called and called to me and after a while, I longed to join him. Because it had to be better than this school, these people, then living with my memories. They strung me up and lowered me into the hole. I couldn't see anything, but it felt heavy, like the darkness was already full. Something wet and sticky slid over my skin. It wrapped around my legs, tightening, cutting off circulation. I closed my eyes. I pushed aside the fear, because this was what I wanted. The creature asked me to join him, and I said I would."

Loretta hiccuped.

"And then the screaming inside my head erupted. It hurt more than anything I ever felt before. 'You are not the one. You do not carry the flame.' Over and over and over those words pounded against my skull. The next thing I know, I'm flung out of the hole and I hit the cave floor. I lose consciousness again. I wake up in the cave, and I managed to find my way to the gym, where Ms. West and Courtney found me. They took me upstairs to a new bedroom. Courtney gave me a makeover. She told me I was her friend now, but if I spoke to any of the scholarship students again, they would kill all of you.

"So you see." Bitterness soured Loretta's voice. "I'm such a failure, I couldn't even die. No one wants me, not even the creature. He only wants *you*."

Her nails dug into my back.

"I'm not going to give you platitudes about everything turning out for the best and blah blah blah." I chose words as carefully as I knew how. "You and I have both been through enough; we know that's not true. But you've been through too much to let this stupid fucking school beat you. That's the only way I survive – out of sheer spite. And I can tell you that—"

Something rustled in the bushes beside us. Loretta and I snapped our heads around, searching for what made the noise.

We didn't have to look for long. Andre stepped out of the bushes, his jaw set tight. One look into his eyes and I knew he'd heard everything.

Shit. Shit. He's heard everything we just talked about. He knows there's a god under the school and that he was planned as a sacrifice.

That meant I'd officially broken my oath to the god. Greg and Andre were no longer protected.

CHAPTER TWENTY-NINE

Andre yanked out his pad and pen, but his hand trembled when he tried to write. While he scratched his pen across the page, he glared from me to Loretta, daring us to speak.

He didn't need to write. His questions and accusations etched themselves across his expressive face. He finished his page and thrust it at me.

'WHY DID YOU KEEP THIS A SECRET?' was etched in angry letters, the pen pressing so hard it had torn through the paper.

I glanced at Loretta, but she was in no state right now to answer. "Andre, I wanted to tell you, but it was complicated. Ms. West was going to sacrifice Greg. To save his life I made a deal with her that I would offer myself up at the end of the year, but she couldn't hurt either of you. She agreed, but only if I didn't tell you about the god."

He shook his head, scrawling furious words across the page.

"You should have told us. Greg and I had a right to know," I read aloud for Loretta's benefit. My chest tightened at how angry his words were. "You think you're the only one who wants to stop what's happening at this school? My girlfriend had her tongue mutilated. We both deserved the chance to right our wrongs. You don't have a monopoly on pain or secrets. You two think you're the only ones who know anything about murder?"

I opened my mouth to speak, but Loretta squeezed my hand. Andre tore a fresh page and continued writing.

"My father was high up in a gang. He owned a lucrative drug operation. I spent a lot of time surrounded by other gang members, hanging out at the abandoned house where they cooked. There was this one guy – my dad's best meth cook. He made such good shit and he was so cheap that he'd risen quickly in the business, but he thought that made him a god. Dad trusted this guy, so he would leave me in his care while he was out. This guy tormented me, called me names, sent me to do jobs that required talking so he could laugh at my inability to speak.

"One day, he told me to order pizza. He was playing around – they wouldn't order pizza to the house. But he wouldn't let up until even the other guys weren't laughing anymore. He didn't know that my dad came back early and had heard everything. Dad flew into a rage. He whipped out a gun and shot the guy in the chest, right there in the backyard. A neighbor saw and called the police. My dad went away for twenty years. He'll probably die in jail, and it's my fault."

Fuck. So much pain. So many broken families. Too many kids who'd seen far too much. Wordlessly, Loretta and I went to Andre, wrapping our arms around our gentle giant.

"It's not your fault," I whispered.

"You can say the words, but you can't make me believe them. I know all about murder. I know how it twists you up inside." Andre tapped his pen on the spine of his pad, thinking about his next words. "I know that it leaves a mark on a person's soul. It makes sense that if you were a creature that devoured souls, you'd find that murderers tasted different. Brussels sprouts instead of chocolate."

Loretta laughed as she read the words over his shoulder. I

hadn't heard that sound... ever. Her laugh twinkled with mirth and melody – sweet and lifting. Too soon, she reined it back in, drawing into herself and wiping her features clean of mirth. "I like Brussels sprouts," she said stubbornly.

"Gross." I wrinkled my nose. "You're weird."

On the corner of his pad, Andre doodled a monster with seven eyes poking its tongue out at a plate of Brussels sprouts. I shifted a laugh. "If only it was that easy to be rid of the god's influence."

"What will?" Andre asked.

"It's complicated. I'll explain everything to you. To *both* of you." *Everything except the fact that Loretta's right – the god wants me, and I'm going with him in exchange for your freedom.* "Our first step is to make sure every student knows exactly what's going on and exactly who's behind it. Then, we need to get Ms. West to tell us how to reverse what's been done to them, and somehow make sure the Eldritch Club doesn't come after us and the god doesn't eat any more souls. It shouldn't be a problem. Easy peasy."

Andre scribbled, "Whatever you need me to do to help you to break this, count me the fuck in."

CHAPTER THIRTY

"There's an Eldritch Club meeting immediately before the performance," Trey announced as he slipped in that night.

I looked up from the circle on the floor, where Quinn, Andre, Loretta, and I were putting the finishing touches on our decorations. "How do you know? I thought you weren't part of the club any longer."

"I overheard Tillie and Courtney whispering about it. Senior members only. No students allowed—hey, what are you doing in here?" Trey narrowed his eyes at Andre. "Hazel, you know he can't be here in case he learns too much and the pact—"

"He already knows. He found out the secrets of Miskatonic Prep today," I said. "Not my doing. I had to talk to Loretta about something, and he snooped on our conversation."

Trey lunged forward, grabbing Andre's collar and yanking him to his feet. "Do you know what you've done?" he growled in Andre's face, an impressive feat considering Andre was at least half a head taller than he was.

"Trey, stop it!" I grabbed his wrist, twisting until Trey was forced to let go. "It's not Andre's fault. Even if he hadn't overheard us, he'd put most of it together from things Sadie told him and what we said. There didn't seem any point keeping the rest from him."

"Now you've lost your protections, and it's open season on all the scholarship students," Quinn sighed.

"We've survived worse." I glanced at Loretta and Andre, who both nodded. "If we stick together, we'll survive this."

"What was this conversation you two were having, anyway?" Trey narrowed his gaze at Loretta. "I thought you were Court-ney's new BFF? What changed?"

Because we're the murderers. I smiled at Loretta, who gave me a shaky smile back. "We realized we both want the same thing. Now we have Andre and Loretta on our side, so I call that a win. We can stop worrying about it and focus on the production." I hoped Trey wouldn't fixate on the fact I avoided his questions. "Will Ms. West be at the Eldritch Club meeting?"

Trey shook his head. "No teachers are ever invited. The Eldritch Club wouldn't allow plebs to be privy to their secrets, even if the teachers of this school did sacrifice their lives for the club's ends. There was enough of an uproar when Gloria Haynes wanted to become a member."

Andre scribbled on his pad and handed it to Trey. "I don't understand the old money/new money thing. All money is the same."

"It's not," Trey said, with a hint of bitterness. "Gloria could buy and sell this school and everyone in it. But she lacks some-thing money can't buy. Respect. A family name. Power. What good is money if you can't do anything with it? If she wants power and influence, she needs to have people like my father and Quinn's parents on her side."

Which is exactly why the teachers chose her as their kidnappee.

"That's the whole reason I was dating her daughter," Quinn shrugged. "Daddy said so."

"But why?" I asked Quinn. "It's not like you'll ever grow up and get married."

"Because our parents have always treated Miskatonic Prep like a chessboard, using us as pawns in their own game." I'd never heard Quinn sound so bitter. "That didn't stop just because we died."

"If there's drama here, it's reflected in their machinations out there," Trey added. "And vice versa. That's why us shagging you was such a big deal."

"What about Loretta?" I threw my arm around my new friend. "Surely Courtney befriending her counted as major drama."

"Oh, it was. But right now everyone wants a piece of Courtney's mother's fortune, and they thought allowing Loretta back into the student body would further weaken you, so they had to let it slide. Not that any of it has helped. From what I've heard whispered around the school, my dad isn't the only one losing his youthful good looks and power."

"This meeting is probably about you, since they think you're responsible," Trey glowered at me. "And now you've escaped and they can't find you... you're not the club's favorite person."

I held up my hands and flashed an innocent smile. "I'm just over here, innocently trying to help my friends. If they happen to be suffering because of it, that's no problem of mine."

Quinn tipped his head to the side. "You want to be at this meeting, don't you?"

"Damn right." Behind me, Trey groaned. "Do we know where it's being held? In the cavern, I suppose."

Quinn shook his head. "Hell no. The Eldritch Club don't want to see the god if they can help it. They don't like to face the reality of what they've done. The meeting will be in the reading room of the faculty wing."

"There's no way you can get to it," Trey added, slapping the floor for good measure.

I turned to Trey. "Didn't you say there was a passage that led from outside the school into the faculty wing?"

"Yes, but—"

"Great. We'll use that. Problem solved." I held up an image of Sadie's face we'd cut from her file. All around our feet were craft supplies – ribbons, sequins, washi tapes and pinking sheers we'd stolen from the art department. "Now, everyone get busy. I want four lines of cheesecloth with these faces stuck on."

"I can't see how this craft project is going to scare everyone," Trey grumbled.

"Of course you can't. It looks like trash. But it tricked hundreds of people for decades. Add a little low light, some smoke machine, and a room full of gullible people who already believe in the supernatural, and you've got mass hysteria... I hope. Even after Helen Duncan was utterly proven to be a fraud, there are still people *today* who believe she was a real psychic."

Trey sighed. "Very well. Pass me the squiggly scissors. I want my cheesecloth to look extra classy."

CHAPTER THIRTY-ONE

The day of the school production arrived. Trey went off to have his makeup done and costume fitted with Parris' book wrapped up under his arm to return to Ayaz. I wish we knew why he needed it back so bad, but I didn't want to break my promise.

Andre and Loretta left shortly after to get certain things set up. Quinn and I were just about to head out when my phone vibrated. A text from Deborah. "You haven't left for the production yet? Call me."

I lifted the phone to my ear, whispering. "It's me. We're just on our way to crash an Eldritch Club meeting." As quickly and quietly as I could, I filled her in on our new plan.

"Be careful, Hazel. I'm worried about you." Even though it was dangerous to speak like this, my heart lifted at her voice. The line was bad, but we were lucky to get anything at all. Reception at Derleth was practically non-existant. A dog barked in the background. "That's Leopold. He's excited about a road trip."

"Road trip?"

"Yes. I've got the DNA tests for you and Trey back from Gail today. There's nothing wrong, but I think we need to discuss them in person."

"In person? You're coming here?"

Quinn's eyebrow lifted as he listened to my end of the conversation.

"Yes. I'll be there in a couple of hours. I figure with all the cars arriving for the production it'll be easy for me to sneak up without Hermia recognizing me—"

"No. Bad idea," I growled into the phone. "I don't know exactly how it's all going to go down tonight, but it could be dangerous. Trey would kill me if one of the dogs got hurt. You need to stay away. Get a room at the Arkham Grand. I'll come and see you as soon as I can. When it's safe."

Deborah didn't like it, but she agreed. I hung up the phone and immediately forgot about the DNA tests. Whatever she wanted to discuss would keep until after we got through tonight. If it was life or death, she would have told me.

Quinn took my hand. We went through the tunnel out to the pleasure garden then picked our way through the forest to the north until we came to a row of tiny cabins.

"These are the cabins you used when you pretend to be with your families." I admired the modern fiberglass pods, so unlike what I imagined when Trey had told me about them. Each cabin had one wall completely made of glass oriented to give views out over the forest. They looked like something you might see on an architecture blog.

"Yeah. They installed these in the first year of 'Derleth Academy'." Quinn used air-quotes around the school's name. "Ayaz drew the design and an architect friend of Vincent Bloomberg II made them a reality. Ataturk got a ton of extra merit points for it. Trey was so pissed."

"I can imagine." I smiled. "They look so peaceful. Did you like coming out here?"

Quinn shrugged. "It was kind of like a vacation. We didn't have to pretend we had a future. We could completely live in the moment, so you bet I fucking loved it. It was a non-stop party.

They gave us this as a reward for hurting the scholarship students. They'd ship in crates of the finest Champagne, all the A-class drugs you could imagine and some you can't, all courtesy of the Eldritch Club. They made it very clear that they weren't supervising us out here – that as long as we toed the line we could be as wild as we liked."

From the way he bit his lip I knew he'd taken full advantage of that free pass. Just imagining his hands on Courtney's body made my skin crawl.

"Sounds fun," I said dryly. I didn't want to hear about it anymore.

"Don't judge – we were teenagers. Technically, we're *still* teenagers. Fuck, I don't know what we are." Quinn rubbed his head. "Hazy, I'm not... I'm not sure how to deal with this, with what you found out about our families. I can understand my dad doing that, but Mom..."

"Yeah," I whispered. "I know."

"I hope things go the way you plan tonight. I think everyone has the right to know about this."

"Me too."

I moved to embrace Quinn, but it was too much emotion for him right now. He shoved his hands in his pockets and took off along the line of cabins. I followed him to the cabin on the end, which was the largest and most lavish. "The King's suite," he sighed as he pulled a key from his pocket and slid open the door. "Trey, Ayaz, and I had this pod every year. No one else was allowed inside unless they..."

"...unless they were a girl who put out," I finished. "I get it. You were playboys. Whatever. No judgment."

"Right." Quinn cleared his throat. "You should be thanking us for our playboy ways. Us hogging the cabin meant we're the only ones who know about *this*."

With a flourish, Quinn shoved aside one of the beds, revealing the bare floorboards beneath. He got down on his knees and started to lift the boards one-by-one. "Ayaz discovered this in the old cabin. When he made the designs he made sure we still had access to it."

Quinn lifted another board, revealing a large, dark hole. Stone steps led down into the darkness. On the wall of the staircase was carved a large, familiar sigil. Another of Parris' tunnels, leading down into fuck-knows-where.

I held out my hand. A flame danced on my fingers, ready to light the way. Quinn recoiled from it for a moment, his eyes wide. That old fear still flowed through him.

I descended the steps with Quinn behind me. After a time, the tunnel flattened out. We were walking under the forest, back toward the school. Like the other tunnel, this one appeared to have no other deviations – it only went in one direction. I hoped like hell it was back into the school and not somewhere—

Something pinched my ass. I leaped forward, choking back a scream. Behind me, Quinn sniggered.

"Not funny," I muttered, rubbing the spot where he'd pinched me.

"Totally funny," Quinn retorted with that irresistible smile in his voice. That angry, bitter guy from earlier had vanished again, and I was stuck with the old, irresponsible Quinn. I wasn't sure which was worse.

After what felt like hours, the architecture of the tunnel changed. We went up a short flight of stairs, and instead of bare rock walls, we now walked between dressed stone. *We're inside the school.*

The tunnel took a right angle and descended up a sharp staircase. One wall remained cold, worked stone while the other became wood panels. On the other side, I could make out voices, too faint to hear what they were saying.

"Keep going," Quinn whispered behind me. "We have another floor to go."

My thighs burned from the circuitous walk. The stairs grew

steep and uneven, and I tripped over my feet every few steps. We took another right-angle turn and found ourselves in a low tunnel – dressed stone on both sides, with a small drainage ditch running along the middle of the ground.

At the end of the tunnel, we climbed another set of narrow steps and entered a low passage running at a ninety-degree angle to the last. I placed my hand on the worked stone, steadying myself as we stepped over discarded bricks and construction debris until we came to a slightly-wider space with wood paneling and what looked like a spring mechanism rusted over with age.

I knelt and pressed my ear to the panel, flicking out the light. I might've imagined it, but I swear I heard Quinn sigh with relief. Faint murmurs were all I could discern from the other side. Many voices, all talking over each other, but far too low for me to hear through the wall.

Quinn squeezed in beside me. "I can't hear anything," I whispered.

"We'll fix that." Quinn reached up and with a click that reverberated down the silent passage like a gunshot, he cracked open the panel.

My heart hammered in my chest. Now the panel swung out into the room beyond, gifting us with an inch-wide crack of light. I mouthed "shut the door" to Quinn. He grinned and shook his head, shuffling a foot backward so I could see into the room.

I peered out of the crack. From what I could make out, the panel we sat behind was low in the corner of the room. A potted plant or hanging basket of some description stood in front of it. Through the foliage, I could make out features of a large space paneled in dark wood. A fire roared at the hearth. Men and women sat or stood around the space, talking in small groups while they guzzled booze from long-stemmed crystal wine glasses or whisky tumblers. Gold and diamond jewelry glittered from the necks and ears of the women, and the men wore dark tailored suits that looked like they'd been designed by Courtney's mother, which of course they probably were.

Leaning against the mantelpiece, sipping from a glass and scrutinizing the room like Mufasa surveying his domain, was Vincent Bloomberg.

He looked even older than last time I saw him, despite the fact he'd tried to hide it by dying his greying hair jet black. Skin puckered around his mouth, and lines crisscrossed the corners of his eyes. His hand clutching the glass was dotted with liver spots.

"We should call this meeting to order," he said in a bored voice. "We have a lot to discuss and only limited time before the performance."

"Why do we need to sit through another one of these amateur productions?" Nancy's father, Donald, said with a yawn. "I think I might stay behind, peruse the liquor cabinet…"

"You'll do no such thing." Vincent swiped the glass from Donald's hand and tossed it into the fire. "You're going to sit in that freezing auditorium with the rest of us and be bored out of your skull for three hours, because we need our offspring to toe the line. If we don't pretend to take an interest in their pointless activities, they may decide to make friends with the sacrifices instead."

"Friends, indeed. We all know whose children are responsible for the mess we're in," a female voice tsked. It took me a moment to identify Gloria Haynes, for she wore a thick black veil over her face. "Falling in love with a sacrifice. It's never happened in all the years of Derleth Academy—"

"Hazel Waite was an issue before my idiot son was involved," Vincent said. "I dealt with her."

"She set fire to Dunwich and escaped!" Damon Delacorte leaped to his feet. Beside me, Quinn stiffened as his father's angry voice filled the room. "You call that dealing with her?"

"Calm down, Damon. Don't give the girl more credit than she's due – the fire was a freak accident caused by the Dunwich facility's ancient wiring. She simply took advantage of the opportunity. I'm confident we'll soon recapture her, and in the meantime, she's no longer at the school affecting the god and disrupting our plans."

That's what you think, Vinnie boy.

Quinn squeezed my arm.

"I'm telling you Hazel Waite has been neutralized," Vincent was saying. "She's gone to ground somewhere, which means she won't bother us. And if you can make it through tonight without fucking things up for us further, I have some news that will cheer you all greatly. Smiles on, and let's pretend we give a shit."

"How can I smile and pretend everything's okay when I look like *this?*" Gloria wailed. She whipped off her black veil to reveal a face ravaged by aging. The skin around her eyes sagged and her lips pulled back, so when she smiled she looked like a rabid animal baring its teeth. "What's happening to us, Vincent?"

Murmurs of assent echoed around the room. I noticed there was a significantly higher proportion of silver hair and sagging jowls than any previous alumni visit. The god was as good as his word. He'd completely stopped feeding the Eldritch Club his power, and their youthful good looks were reverting to their true form.

"It's become obvious that the power of the god has waned," Vincent said. He paused to take a sip from his glass. "We've waited patiently for years for Hermia to figure out how to make this arrangement permanent, but I see now she was the wrong choice for headmistress. She's made preposterous demands for the faculty when she has not delivered what she promised. And now, our chance is slipping away. We're losing our grip on the world. You've all seen these attacks on our leadership. If you think the freaks and the snowflakes aren't coming for us and everything we have earned by our birthright, then you are mistaken."

You're a disgusting human.

I appeared to be the only one who thought so, because

everyone in the room sat forward, staring at Vincent with admiring eyes. A few even applauded, like Vincent had said something profound and not the most terrifying thing I'd ever heard.

He wanted to keep the world white, and straight, and male – at any cost. *This is why he sacrificed his own son? Because he's so utterly terrified of what women like me could do to him if we had an ounce of his power? Of how people like Andre and Greg and Loretta might change the world?*

Of people like his son stepping aside to give them the chance?

Rage boiled inside me, the hot flickers of it burning against my flesh. *You think you're invincible, but I see how small and afraid you are. And I've got news for you, Vinnie boy. You were right to be afraid. You're about to find out just what it feels like to have your power stripped away.*

"We need to maintain the righteous order of things," Vincent said. "And it's time to take matters into our own hands. The only way to do that is to release the god from its prison."

That caused a stir. People gasped or yelled out. A glass dropped, shattering glittering shards across the floor.

"You sure about that, Bloomberg?" Senator Hyde-Jones demanded.

"I'm deadly certain," Vincent said.

"The whole reason Parris imprisoned it in the first place is that it could... and correct me if I'm wrong here... destroy the world?" Donald kept his eyes fixed on Vincent, phrasing what was a reasonable statement as a question.

"Parris didn't have the power we have. He was a second-rate magician haunted by the ghosts of his father's deeds. Look around this room – we are congressmen, lawyers, senators. We are the most powerful business owners in the world. We have the political elite, the Wall Street investors, and the entertainment industry wrapped around our collective little finger. We have already built the perfect system – all it needs is the god to complete it."

"But how do we know the god will listen to us?" asked a woman I didn't recognize.

"Of course it will listen to us. It wants the same thing we want. Otherwise, why would it have been feeding us power for twenty years? Why would it have kept us young and given us the influence to put all this in place?" Vincent turned to Gloria Haynes. "Do you want to continue to look like *that*?"

Gloria shuddered as she regarded her reflection. She swiped a strand of lank silver hair from her face. "I can't go out in public like this. I didn't attend London Fashion Week, and it's been months since I even snapped a selfie. People in the industry are starting to talk."

"Exactly. The god is fading because after twenty years of fighting against its prison, it's tired. It's sick of being tugged in two directions and being starved of souls thanks to the meddling faculty. If we give it what it's craved all along – freedom – then all of the world will be forced to bow to it, to us. All the detractors, the critics, the snowflakes will be cowed and crushed underfoot. And the god will feast upon all the broken souls he could ever desire."

Vincent's entire speech was so completely ridiculous, so utterly maniacal, that I expected the room to burst into laughter and congratulate him on a great practical joke. And yet, not a single Eldritch Club member opposed him. I could even see Gloria Haynes nodding her head.

World domination, for fuck's sake. What a fucking cartoon supervillain cliche.

"Are we agreed this is the right course of action?" Senator Hyde-Jones poured himself another drink and raised it to his lips. "I call a vote."

He thrust his free hand in the air, not stopping to take a breath as he finished his glass in one swig. All around the room, hands shot in the air. I couldn't see if anyone's remained down, but it didn't matter.

The Eldritch Club agreed. Of course they did. World domination was in their blood.

"Very well." Senator Hyde-Jones started on his next drink. "Vincent, we agree with this plan. How can we free the god without losing control of it? Parris tried for years and never succeeded, and he was a skilled magician."

"Skilled, yes, but not powerful. For twenty years the god has been giving over power to us. Our power may be waning now, but the god has waned more. Even without occult knowledge, we're still more powerful than Parris' coven. And we have a secret weapon. Allow me to introduce my son."

Trey? My heart lurched. Beside me, Quinn squirmed.

What's Trey doing here?

Is Vincent going to hurt him to prove a point in front of the club?

Fire pressed against my palms, ready to escape and wreak havoc if I needed. My eyes glued to the door.

Vincent rapped on the wall a couple of times. After a moment, the door opened, and a figure strode across the floor to stand beside Vincent. The flames wreathed his body, outlining a familiar silhouette.

Not Trey.

Ayaz.

CHAPTER THIRTY-TWO

He can't be here for any good reason.

Ayaz glided into the room like a figure-skater, his dark hair picking out shadows from the flickering fire. In his hands, he held Parris' book. His eyes flicked nervously from face to face, distress etching into his features as he took in their aging bodies.

The club members leaned forward hungrily, desperate to lap up whatever Vincent laid down.

Are they going to hurt Ayaz? My fingers itched, longing to draw out the flames. One flick of my wrist and I could devour them all in fire.

One inferno and this would all be over.

But Ayaz was in the room. There was no way I could burn them all and save him. I didn't know what happened to an edimmu if their body was burned, but I wasn't about to find out.

Besides, I rationalized to myself, trying to force down the rage, these people had answers. If Vincent knew how to raise the power needed to free the god, then he might have what we needed to bring the students back.

Ayaz set the book on the table. *So this is why he needed it back so badly.*

Elena Delacorte whimpered with disgust as she spied the leather cover. "That thing is disgusting."

"Shut your mouth, you ungrateful whore," Damon spat. "Vincent has given you everything, thanks to that book. Show a little reverence."

The answers are in that book.

Quinn's whole body tensed. I glanced over at him. In the gloom, all I could make out was the outline of his face, his jaw tight, his usually sparkling eyes narrowed and cold. Even knowing what his mother had done to him, that old protective streak in him still ran strong.

Elena sat back, her mouth pressed shut against Damon's attack.

"I'd like to start by thanking Vincent for the opportunity to speak to you. It's an honor to be in your presence today. As you know, Vincent placed this book in my care. He had me keep it safe here at Derleth Academy, so that it could never fall into the hands of one of his political enemies. Twenty years ago, much of the book was untranslated." Ayaz cracked the spine and opened the book. Everyone in the room leaned forward to see. "I'm proud to say I have not wasted my fine education. I have taught myself many ancient languages and have nearly finished a complete decoding of Parris' book."

"Spit it out, rag-head," Damon snapped.

My body stiffened at the insult, but Ayaz showed no signs that it registered. He thumbed through the pages, stopping on a particular illustration to smooth out the edges and spread out his pages of notes. I longed to see what page they stared at. I sat up on my knees to get a higher vantage, but Quinn's hand on my shoulder shoved me back down again.

He was right. If we made any noise, we'd be dead.

"As the new student leader of the Eldritch Club, I take my role seriously." Ayaz flashed his intact tattoo to the elders, and they nodded. "At the start of the third quarter, Vincent charged me with a task – to figure out how Parris made the god's prison so that we could continue to strengthen it."

No, Ayaz, you beautiful idiot. Of course Vincent lied to you. How could you not see that?

"We always believed Parris accidentally unleashed the god from slumber when he dug his tunnels into the bedrock, and that he hurriedly created the prison while he tried to figure out how to harness the god's powers for himself. I've recently cracked one of the most difficult translations in the book – he wrote it in a cuneiform cipher – and discovered that according to his very words, this isn't true.

"Smugglers have long used the natural caves in the cliffs to hide their contraband. Of course, when Parris was in Salem with his father the Reverend, he heard stories about something that attacked the smugglers. Sailors called it the 'soul eater' and told tales of how evil things lived in the darkness of the caves, of how men would go missing only to be found later – not dead exactly but their bodies numb, their minds and spirits utterly broken. Parris came to Arkham specifically to seek out what was inside the caves."

"Please, be thorough with your explanation," Vincent prodded Ayaz, as several of the parents glanced at each other in confusion. "Many members of the Club are not as familiar with our founder's history as you or I."

Ayaz nodded. "Thomas Parris' father, the Reverend Parris, played a pivotal role in the Salem Witch trials. He was personally responsible for the convictions and subsequent deaths of several witches. For his remaining years, he believed he was haunted by the spirits of those witches he'd condemned. When he died, the spirits didn't rest, but moved on to his son, dogging his every step and whispering to him that he would pay for what his father did. They grew in power until they could move objects and scratch the faces of people who visited the Parris home.

"Originally, Parris made his study of mysticism and the occult to try and exorcise his father of these spirits. He redoubled his efforts when his own mind became plagued by their malevolent presence. When he heard these rumors about the soul-eater, he wondered if a creature who devoured souls might be able to take from him the souls that haunted him, while leaving his own life intact.

"He purchased the land for next to nothing and set about constructing the house and tunnel system around the principles of sacred geometry." Ayaz jabbed his finger on the page. "According to Parris' account, the entire house and grounds act as the god's cage. I'm not sure how it works exactly, but let's say that in the caves deep beneath the school, deeper even then we've ever tried to explore, is a doorway or portal or rift or whatever from our universe into the god's homeland. And maybe there was a guardian on the other side of that door who took the soul of anyone who came too close – the 'soul-eater' of the smugglers' legend. Instead of going down to meet the guardian, Parris used himself as bait to lure the god up into the trap he created."

My heart hammered against my chest. Ayaz had figured it all out, everything we'd been trying to understand. My beautiful, clever boy had all the answers. But he was telling the wrong people.

"Parris fed the god on the spirits that haunted him. He figured out that ghosts and souls are all the same thing, so there's something for a pop quiz." Ayaz smiled at Vincent. When no one else in the room smiled back, he continued. "So, anyway... the god devoured Parris' spirits, but kept him alive to bring him more. This part is quite hard to understand, but it seems as if Parris started feeding the god with human sacrifices. The god grew fat and gluttonous, and it could no longer break free from Parris' trap. Perhaps it didn't want to. With each sacrifice, Parris' coven grew in power, and—"

"We already know this," Damon snapped.

"Right." Ayaz's eyes fell to the page. "You know all this

because it's similar to what happened to us after the fire. I don't understand why we didn't die and why we didn't end up as hollowed-out shells like the smugglers, but it's the same thing. There's an alignment between the god's prison and the gym, so when the fire tore through, it..." here Ayaz paused. "Yes, sorry. This isn't about what happened to me. What I'm trying to say is that feeding the god *is* its true prison. It has everything it wants and needs right here. As long as it keeps feeding, you can leave the door open and it won't leave."

Oh.

Shit.

Shit, shit, shit.

That means, if you stop *feeding it, or say, if you make a bargain with it to force it to stop feeding, you take away its excuse for staying in its cage.*

Exactly the thing I'd just done.

"And there was something else, son?" Vincent prodded.

"Yes." Ayaz lowered his gaze. "Ms. West told you sacrifices continued as normal this year despite Hazel's disruption, but I don't believe that's true. One of them, Loretta Putnam, was released to be a friend to Courtney, who is now my girlfriend. I've seen Loretta slipping food into her pockets in the dining hall. She goes to the pleasure garden sometimes to read, and I've noticed empty candy bar wrappers and potato chip bags hidden in the weeds. She's hiding the fact she requires food to survive. She's not one of us. She's still alive."

"Thank you, son." Vincent patted Ayaz on the shoulder. "You may go."

"Take that disgusting book with you," Gloria sniffed from beneath her veil.

Ayaz picked up the book and his notes and sauntered out of the room. He didn't look back.

I let out a breath I didn't realize I'd been holding. Quinn's vise-like grip on my thigh loosened off ever so slightly. Vincent moved to stand beside the fireplace again.

For several moments, no one in the room spoke. Senator Hyde-Jones broke the silence. "That Turk has presented us with a compelling plan. If we agree that freeing the god is the right course of action, it appears we're heading in that direction anyway. Perhaps the god itself has realized this, and that is why it's stopped feeding us power? What concerns me now is that if we trust the boy about everything he's said, then it brings to light an ugly truth – for I distinctly remember being told a very different story by our headmistress."

"Precisely the issue for which we are gathered," Vincent said. "When Ayaz brought this revelation to me, I saw we had a bigger issue on our hands than we initially realized. Hermia made it clear that order for the club to have a steady flow of power, we needed this large sacrifice. Then, she claimed the god wouldn't accept our children because they were too spoiled, too rich, too laden with promise and opportunity. And so the scholarship program was born. We were promised that as the god grew stronger, we would be able to access more of its power. And yet, the exact opposite has happened. And now we learn that we have been lied to once more and actively sabotaged. We could have unleashed the god ourselves without any of this nonsense."

"I don't appreciate being tricked," Gloria spat. She flung off her veil. "Especially when it's cost me my face."

Damon nodded, his jaw tight. "I don't appreciate it, either. *You* brought her in, Vincent. This is on *your* head—"

BANG.

Vincent's fist slammed against the mantle. A ceramic dog rattled off and smashed on the floor. No one in the room moved a muscle.

"I'm *aware*, Damon. She manipulated me from the start." He flexed his fingers, wincing as a drop of blood appeared on his knuckles. His aging skin wasn't as thick as it once was. "Hermia wants to keep the god's power for herself."

"Not so loud," Damon hissed. "That witch could be listening at the door."

Yes, Vincent. You don't know who could be listening.

"That's unlikely. I've stationed two members of my security team at either end of the hall. No one enters or exits without my knowledge." Vincent rubbed his bleeding knuckle. "We have plans to make. We will not take this deception lying down."

"While I'm all for putting Hermia in her place," Senator Hyde-Jones piped up, "I feel the release of the god is more important."

"We will do both at the same time," Vincent said. "The traditional memorial dance is coming up in a few weeks. Hermia has informed me that they have found a way to move the shadows from the gym, so it will be hosted there instead of the dining hall. This conduit we spoke of will once again connect the space to the god's prison."

"And?" Damon prompted.

Vincent stared pointedly at the fire in the hearth.

"Out with it, man." The senator boomed.

"It's simple. You all know what I'm proposing," Vincent shrugged. "They all need to die. It is what was supposed to happen in the beginning. We're simply finishing the job. They die and we use that power to break the god free from his cage. Then all the world will be ours for the taking."

"But Quinn…" Elena's hands flew to her mouth.

"He's been dead for twenty years," Vincent snapped. "Don't cry over him now."

She gulped back her sobs as Vincent raised his glass. A trickle of blood flowing over his knuckles. "I ask for a vote. Who is ready to close Derleth Academy for good?"

Once again, hands shot in the air – parents who were supposed to love their children barely even pausing to think before agreeing to kill them. The vote was unanimous. Even

Quinn's mother had her hand in the air while she wiped away her tears.

Vincent glanced at a gold watch on his wrist. "I'll make the arrangements. We should take our seats. The show will be starting soon. Remember, keep smiling. The last thing we want is the kids getting wind of any of this."

Heads bent together, murmuring and steadying their old bodies against each other, the Eldritch Club members exited the room. Vincent was the last to leave, closing the door behind him with a loud and final *CLICK*.

I let out a breath I didn't realize I'd been holding. My leg ached from kneeling in the cramped space. I turned to Quinn, gesturing for him to start moving. We had to get all the way back to the classroom wing to sneak backstage before the show started.

But Quinn didn't move. He didn't seem to have noticed me at all. He stared out at the empty room with glassy eyes. His body rigid, his heart in tatters.

He's just heard his mother give up on him.

"Quinn." I jiggled his thigh. "Quinn."

Still nothing.

I snapped my fingers in front of his face. He didn't even blink.

I held my hand out, palm up, and stoked the fire inside me. It wasn't difficult after everything we'd just heard to drag up a hot rage. A tall flame shot from my palm, nearly touching the ceiling of the passage.

That got his attention. Quinn leaped away, his eyes like saucers. In the flickering light, I could see the vein bulging on his neck.

"Fuck, Hazy." He clutched a hand to his chest. "You scared me."

"Yeah, well, you scared me, going all still and silent like that." I dropped the flame down to a tiny flicker, just large enough to light our way back.

Quinn raised his hand, cupping it around the flame as if warming his palm against a chill. He stared into that light for a long time. By now, my leg was screaming, the old burn agitated by the cramped conditions. I opened my mouth to tell him to move when he broke the silence first.

In a hard, cold voice that didn't sound like his own, he said, "I hope you burn them all."

CHAPTER THIRTY-THREE

We scrambled back down the passage and crawled out into the pod. Then it was a twenty-minute walk back through the forest to the tunnel, and then out into the basement. The whole way, Quinn didn't say a word or try to pinch my ass. That worried me more than anything.

Please, don't let this break him.

I wouldn't blame him if it did, but I needed him tonight. Now more than ever, we needed every student of Miskatonic Prep to see what their parents had done to them.

When we reached my old room, I was relieved to find it empty, all our bags of props gone. Quinn and I peeled off our sweaty clothes and changed into black from head-to-toe. I picked up my backpack with my supplies and slung it over my shoulder.

"When you first suggested this, I kept trying to think of ways to pull my mother aside so she didn't have to see it," he said, his jaw tight. "Now I hope she has a front-row seat."

Good. I gripped his shoulder. "I'm sorry you had to find out like this, but it's better you know. What they did isn't okay. We'll make them see that."

That's my promise to you. Whatever happens tonight, they will suffer for what they've done to you.

My heart leaped into my chest as we made our way through the deserted dormitory and locker-lined corridors to the auditorium.

At my old school in Philly, we didn't even have a space for productions. Plays, assemblies, dances, and other events happened in the gym, with everyone sitting on the bleachers or the basketball court. But at Derleth they spared no expense – the school's auditorium looked more like a Broadway theatre complete with bar and padded seats that stepped down toward an elaborate Moorish-inspired stage complete with gilded turrets, spires, and minarets.

A crowd of students and parents gathered at the entrance. It looked like the bar was already hopping. My heart hammered in my chest as I ducked behind Quinn. At any moment someone could look up and recognize me and this would all be over.

Quinn made it to the backstage door and yanked it open. I ducked inside, and we immediately separated – Quinn heading to the wings to start moving the set and props onto the stage while I scrambled behind the stacks of old set pieces in the corner, a hiding place I'd staked out in advance. I pulled my costume from my backpack and started to peel off my black hoodie and leggings.

From between Sweeney Todd's barber chair and a revolving bookshelf from Bugsy Malone, I had a small window to view the stage. Right now the curtains were drawn while black-clad figures moved around preparing the first set, but I could hear the trill of the audience as they took their seats.

They're in for a show tonight.

I smoothed down the front of my swirling ballgown, affixed the tiara to my head – hoping it wasn't crooked, as I had no way to check – and counted down the minutes. The last of the crew exited the stage. Feet shuffled across the floorboards as the actors and chorus lined up at the wings. I drew my head back as Tillie – who headed up the backstage crew – stomped past, barking orders into a walkie-talkie. The first ponderous notes struck from the orchestra, building into a crescendo as the curtains swung back and the lights went up on a busy Paris street.

Showtime.

Courtney strutted into the spotlight and spoke the opening lines. *My* lines. Not that I cared anymore. Applause echoed through the auditorium as the chorus came out and launched into a raucous number.

It was strange to watch something I'd worked on for months go ahead without me. Part of me knew what we were doing tonight was necessary, and that I'd never fit in at this school in the first place. But there was another part of me that wished I had the chance to have a normal teenage life – that I'd gotten to stand on stage instead of Courtney and play that part and have my mom in the audience laughing and clapping along with the music.

It's stupid to wish for things that can't happen. I clenched my fists, willing down the rush of heat pooling in my palms. *Tonight isn't about me – it's about making sure the Miskatonic students know the truth.*

The play chugged along at a decent pace. The audience seemed into it, laughing and clapping at all the right places. I was surprised – these were people used to Broadway shows and opera, and back in the meeting room they acted as if they were only here begrudgingly. Perhaps they were even better actors than their kids, or maybe they bought into this farce that they were normal, supportive parents. I wasn't sure which was worse.

Every second that passed brought us closer to our surprise. Tillie kept walking past with her walkie-talkie as sets flew in and out and actors scurried around the wings to meet their cues. The curtain dropped on intermission, and the audience exploded with conversation and thumping feet as parents made their way to the bar.

With what they were about to see, they were going to need those drinks.

My breath came out in ragged gasps as the second act began. The lights went down, and the first notes of a familiar song struck up. The song I danced with Trey. The song where I chose him.

Trey stepped out on stage. In his leather jacket and torn jeans, with his hair slicked back and a dangerous glint in his eye, he looked the epitome of the hot biker he portrayed. The music swelled, and he executed the first steps flawlessly, the way he did everything in his life. He finished on one knee at the front of the stage, his hand extended toward the wings, waiting for his leading lady to join him.

Courtney's cue sounded, but she didn't glide in to meet him. She couldn't. Andre had her locked in a closet backstage, knocked out with a mild sedative Quinn stole from Old Waldron.

A ripple of unrest echoed through the wings. Tillie stomped by, snapping into her walkie-talkie. "Courts, where are you?"

The orchestra repeated the bar, and the cue sounded again. That was *my* signal. I stood up, smoothing down the front of my costume, and bolted from my hiding place toward the wings.

The backstage students waiting with props looked up in surprise, but they'd barely registered my presence before I stepped out under the lights and glided into Trey's arms.

CHAPTER THIRTY-FOUR

I held my breath as Trey caught me, his strong hands on my hips steadying me. The orchestra swelled, and the song continued. The musicians had an awkward view of the stage – they hadn't noticed I wasn't Courtney. Trey and I moved together, leaping and flowing together as we danced our theme of seduction. All the moves we'd practiced came to me in a rush of heat and lust and fire.

While we danced, the lights swirled and shifted. In the lighting box, Quinn worked his magic, using a red-tinted spot to follow us across the stage. Murmurs rose through the audience as people started to recognize me. My shoulders prickled from the heat of their gaze, but no one left their seat. No one rushed the stage or used a comically-large cane to fish me off.

The whole auditorium teetered on a knife-edge, waiting to see what happened next.

Behind us, images flickered across the backdrop as Quinn turned on the projector. Faces twisted with innocent smiles while white mist swirled around our feet. Familiar faces of past scholarship students – each one with a cruel cross etched through their features by a King. The faces flickered over the walls and ceiling of the auditorium as Quinn swung the projector around.

The orchestra halted with a screech as the musicians realized something was seriously wrong. A cold hush fell over the audience.

Trey and I danced on, the only sound in the room the scrape of our dance shoes against the stage. Until a voice cried through the loudspeakers, startling even me with its fearful trill.

"My name is Freddie," a small voice whimpered. Trey really was good with voices. He'd recorded the tape earlier in the week, devising several different personalities – it was impossible to tell it was him. The reverb Quinn placed on the tape gave it an eerie, ghastly quality. "I'm John's younger brother. Now I'm his older brother because he wasn't allowed to grow up. We were going to work on our first cars together. He was stolen from me. I miss him."

"Hey, what the—" John Hyde Jones rose from his seat in the orchestra, his face red with anger as he watched his brother's face from his photograph flicker against the wall. He gripped his oboe like a baseball bat.

The light swirled, twisting away from his brother's image to another ghostly figure standing on the balcony, a blonde girl in pigtails and a white shroud torn to shreds.

"All my life I looked up to Amber. I wanted to be just like her when I grew up. But she disappeared. She never got to see me grow up."

Even though I knew the 'ghost' was just a cut-out head from the photograph beside Tillie's room glued on some cheesecloth, in the gloom it appeared quite spectral. I was starting to see how the charlatan medium Helen Duncan had won over all those followers with her fake ectoplasm.

"Bianca? What are you doing here?" From the audience, Tillie's mother stood up, her hand trembling as she reached out toward the ghost. From the wings, Tillie collapsed to her knees, staring up at the image with wide-eyed horror. "I told you Tillie was dead. I kept you from this for a reason!"

In a blink, Quinn flicked off the lights, plunging the room into darkness. Screams echoed through the audience. Backstage, students yelled at each other.

"What the hell is going on?" boomed Vincent Bloomberg above the rising din.

CLICK. A single spotlight came up, focused on another ghost hanging for the lighting rig. the image of Zehra's dark hair and penetrating eyes were visible against the backdrop of the gilded ceiling, her stare defiant as she looked down her nose at them all. A jagged cross marred her perfect face – the cross Trey had made over her photograph in Parris' book.

"You took my brother Ayaz from me," she declared. "Now I'm coming for every last one of you."

The lights went mad, dancing around the auditorium in a frenzy, bouncing from seat to seat as the projection flashed through a rapid succession of faces – sisters, brothers, friends, aunts, uncles, random people from the magazines we butchered. They swam in a tapestry of stolen futures across the stage, their limbs and smiles dancing over my skin as Trey and I held each other in silent reverie.

We danced on the ashes of our futures. We danced on the love that should have been ours.

More gasps and shouts rose from the audience. From the wings, I heard a commotion as students wrestled each other, but still we danced on. Trey's eyes burned into mine, flaring the heat that rose through my body, stoking the fire that lusted for vengeance.

"We miss our brothers and sisters!" the ghosts cried. "You were taken away from us. Do you know who took you away? Hazel Waite knows. She found out their secret, and they sent her away. But she's back now. She's back to return our brothers and sisters to us."

At the mention of my name, Vincent Bloomberg roared with rage. Tillie lunged toward us from the side of the stage, her fingers clawing for my face. Her nails raked my cheek as Trey spun me away. My head whirled. I caught a glimpse of Vincent out of the corner of my eye. He had a seat in the middle of the upper level, and he climbed over chairs and shoved people out of the way as he struggled to reach the aisle, not caring who he mowed down in his desire to reach the stage and choke me with his own hands.

That's not going to happen, Vinnie boy.

CLICK.

The image settled on the photograph of young Courtney I'd stolen from her noticeboard, posing for the camera in a shimmering dress nearly identical to the one I now wore. The projection zoomed in her gap-toothed smile while her father's inscription flickered across the stage.

"My beautiful Courts. You're going to be a star one day, just like your mother. Love, Dad," the eerie voices mocked. "Where is this star now? Why has she been locked away so no one can appreciate her? Is it so she will never outshine her mother?"

"Stop this at once!" Gloria Hayes bellowed from the back of the theatre, her voice rising with panic.

"You've been robbed of a future," the faces cried in unison. Quinn looped all our voices on the track to make it sound as though there was an army of broken children. "We are the ghosts of what could have been, and we will fight for you, even if you won't fight for yourselves. It's time to ask the question – who did this to you? The fire that took your lives was no accident, so who is pulling the strings of the god?"

"Get her off!"

Students spilled out on the stage, faces glowing red with rage as they closed in on Trey and I. I knew they'd do this – I showed them the truth and they blamed me for it. Luckily, we were prepared.

I whipped out my knife from my bra, but before I had the chance to use it, Andre barrelled in and tackled Paul to the ground. Derek wrapped a beefy arm around his neck, but Andre threw himself back, slamming the bully into the stage so hard the wooden boards splintered. More guys piled on top of him, but he was too strong. He kept them all at bay.

"Your parents!" the ghosts screamed over the fight. "Your parents sent you here to die for their own personal gain. So they could have more riches. More fame. More power."

"This is fucking bullshit!" Paul wheezed, trying to pull himself to his feet. Barclay grabbed my arm, but I broke his grip and landed a swift kick in his nuts. He dropped with a *THUD*. Trey shoved himself in front of me as more students poured toward me.

"She's trying to turn us against our parents!"

"She's just a fucking lying *gutter whore!*" A shrill voice screeched from the wings. I whirled around as Courtney staggered across the stage, her silky hair disheveled and her eyes hard as flint.

Shit. She must've got out of the closet somehow.

From her crooked walk, I guessed Courtney was still suffering the effects of the sedative. But she had one thing on her side – pure, unadulterated fury. I slashed at her arm, splattering her blood across my dress, but she didn't even slow down, Courtney tore the tiara from my head, taking a clump of hair with it. I howled as pain flared through my skull.

Courtney threw the tiara on the stage and stomped on it, breaking it in two.

"You never should have come back to my school," she hissed, advancing on me. Her words slurred from the drug. "You never should have tried to cross us with your lies. Now, I'm going to wring the life from you with my own hands. I don't care if it hurts the god. It will bring me great satisfaction."

She lunged again, screaming like a banshee.

Loretta appeared out of nowhere and tackled her legs, sending Courtney sprawling across the stage.

"How dare you touch me?" Courtney kicked and clawed at Loretta, but she didn't let go. A lifetime of abuse had hardened Loretta against pain.

That's my little murderess.

Quinn appeared at the wings, his face gaunt. He rushed to my side, backing me up toward the wings as he slammed a fist into Barclay's face. Blood spurted across the stage. John Hyde-Jones pulled himself up from the orchestra pit, swinging his oboe at Trey's head.

Trey caught the instrument easily, twisting it out of John's hand and laying him out with an uppercut. John hit the stage with a *THUD*. The students froze, unsure.

Trey's ice glare across the students – that same glare that once turned every one of them into his minions. His hand in mine burned with heat, matching the fire dancing in my chest. "You need to listen. Those ghosts or whatever they are... they're telling the truth about our parents."

"Tear that gutter whore apart!" Gloria Haynes yelled from the audience.

"She's not one of us," called out Senator Hyde-Jones.

"Don't listen to these lies." Elena Delacorte stood, her designer dress swirling around her as she held her arms out to her son. Tears streamed down her face. "My darling Quinn, don't believe this horror. It's not true. You know how much I love you. I would never dream of hurting you."

Beside me, Quinn's face paled. His eyes locked on his mother and his body jerked as her words hit him like a bullet exploding in his chest. All that rage he'd bottled up since seeing her in the meeting had fled him the moment he'd heard those magic words. *I love you.*

Those words held power over him. They'd once held power over me. But not anymore. My hatred for Quinn's mother burned bright. A small flame burst from my palm, but I snuffed it against my dress. *I can't lose control now.*

"See? No one's listening. You don't get a say anymore, Trey," Courtney sneered. "This little stunt only proves that you're not fit to lead this school. Ayaz is twice the man you'll ever be. He understands our privilege comes with responsibilities – namely, to exalt the glory of the Eldritch Club. Unlike you, I take that role seriously. You and your gutter whore aren't going to drag us through the mud any longer."

Ayaz? Where is he? I couldn't see him on stage or lurking in the wings. Why wasn't he here supporting his girlfriend and fighting for Vincent? My heart soared with forlorn, impossible hope. But not even that hope could extinguish the blaze that prickled against my palms, the growing heat of my simmering violence.

"Is that supposed to be a threat?" Trey's icicle eyes fixed on her, his shoulders tensing with rage. "I'm not afraid of you, Courtney. And as for Vincent, what can Vincent do to me that is worse than what he's already done? What you saw tonight wasn't a trick. It's a truth that's been lurking in the backs of our minds. Don't tell me you haven't already thought it. I know Tillie has because we whispered it to each other in the dark."

He whirled around to fix his gaze on his ex, who stood stunned at the edge of the stage. I could practically see the wheels turning in her head. Tillie flicked her head between Trey and her parents, in the third row. In a small voice, she asked. "Is this really true, Trey?"

"Of course it's true. Your mother confirmed it. You heard her say she told your sister you were dead. They inprisoned us because they wanted the god's power. Each family in the club chose one child to sacrifice. We have a list they made of all our names. I'll show it to you. Right now we all need—"

"That's enough!" Vincent boomed. He'd reached the front of the auditorium now, and the glow of the spotlight caught his eyes in the gloom – red with fury. As he gripped the front of the stage and tried to swing himself up, Quinn stepped forward and stomped on his hand, sending him reeling just as Ms. West swept onto the stage, a familiar dark figure at her side.

Ayaz.

He'd gone to find Ms. West. But why? He'd been at that meeting showing his loyalty to the Eldritch Club. So why had he brought the deadmistress into this?

Trey and Quinn squeezed close to me, their bodies my shield, their hearts the only thing keeping my fire in check. And even though I had the two of them, something still felt wrong. Incomplete. I knew what it was as soon as he stepped under the spotlight and his beauty drew my breath. His honey and rose scent slammed into me, knocking me back.

I missed Ayaz so much it was a physical ache that dragged in my limbs. I'd pictured him seeing Zehra's face on the projection tonight and running into my arms to kiss away all the pain. I kept hoping one day he'd wake up and remember. But that day was clearly not today.

Stay focused. Tonight wasn't about Ayaz and how I felt about them. Tonight was for the students of Miskatonic Prep. I forced a smile onto my face and addressed the deadmistress.

"Go on," I said, gesturing to the students gathering around her. "Tell them the truth. I know it serves your purpose. Tell them what their parents had you do."

"Don't say a word, Hermia," Vincent warned. For the first time, I thought I detected a hint of doubt in his voice. He managed to pull himself onto the stage. Quinn and Andre moved toward him, but four guys stepped in front of him, shielding him from us.

For now.

Ms. West swept her eyes across the students. "I must say, it has been quite the performance. One of the best productions this school has ever staged. I'm proud of all of you. Fifty merit points each. Except for Ms. Waite, of course. She's no longer a student here."

"Hazel ruined the show. She tried to make us all hate our parents. She drugged me and locked me in a closet and set up this ridiculous ghost show and sent her little minions to *attack* us." Courtney jerked her body like a worm, breaking Loretta's grip and kicking her in the face. Loretta staggered back, clutching her nose as blood trailed through her fingers. Courtney staggered to her feet and threw herself into Ayaz's arms. "You have to punish her. You have to give her to the god."

"I'm afraid Hazel isn't going anywhere near the god. Not now that I've figured out what unites her and Loretta." Ms. West's cold smile drove a dart of ice through my chest. From her pocket, she withdrew the stack of newspaper articles. "I can't believe that as long as I've had these, I didn't understand their significance until Ayaz here said something to me today. Loretta murdered her father, and you killed your mother and best friend. The two of you are the first murderers we've had as scholarship students."

No.

Don't you dare.

Don't you fucking dare say those words.

Behind me, students murmured, turning to each other to digest the news.

"Hazel didn't do it," Quinn said. "A gang set fire to the apartments—"

"Not according to this arson report, sent to me as Hazel's legal guardian." Ms. West removed another document from her robe, this one printed on crisp legal paper. "The police and fire department have conducted a thorough investigation. Hazel Waite had burns on her hands consistent with her starting the blaze. I'm disappointed in myself that it's taken me so long to connect the pieces, but now I understand everything." Her eyes narrowed on me. "*You* set the fire that burned Dunwich. You're *possessed* by fire – a conduit for power. And that is why you cannot leave this school. If I let you out, you're going straight to jail, and you won't do the god any good there. You're the key to getting us all what we want."

Trey's hand circled my wrist felt like a shackle. He pressed his thumb into the scar. "Hazel, is this true?"

"Of course it's not." Quinn dropped an arm around my neck. "Hazy would never..."

Quinn's words trailed off. He saw something in my face, in the flames in my eyes, in the defiant tilt of my chin.

I did it.

I killed them.

Memories of that day flew at me in a rush, riding the wave of the god's screams. Some kids from Dante's neighborhood kept trying to haze him into joining their gang. They would often follow us around his street, taunting us with slurs and spittle. That particular day, Dante hadn't been in class, so I walked over to his place to see if he was okay. He wasn't there, either. On the way back, four guys surrounded me. They tried to rough me up and take Dante's journal from my arms. The fight was a bit of a blur, but I kicked someone in the nuts, gave someone else a bloody nose, and ran for it. I raced home, lungs bursting. I thought maybe Dante might've gone there to wait for me. I thought my mom would protect me. That's what parents were supposed to do.

I rushed into our apartment to find the two of them together. On my bed. Naked and wrapped in each other's arms.

My mom.

Dante.

Betrayers.

I wanted to scream, but they'd stolen my voice. They'd taken everything I thought I could trust and torn it to pieces right in front of me. And so I gathered up all the screams that echoed inside me and I shoved them into the flame.

I ran.

I raged.

I *ignited*.

I watched from the street as the flames blew out the windows to dance in the crisp breeze, relishing their freedom. Black smoke spewed out as the building cleansed itself of treachery. People in the neighboring apartments rushed into the street. The kids who'd followed me tossed their Molotov cocktails into the empty parking lot and scampered into the night. I tried to pick one up and throw it after them and that was how I burned my hands.

My mother leaned out the window, a halo of fire wreathing her hair like an angel. Only she was no angel but a demon burning up in the inferno fuelled by her betrayal. She cried at me to help.

I watched her body collapse. I sucked in fresh air as the two people I loved most in the world breathed their last. The fire that possessed me burned like a warm comforter in my chest.

That is my truth.

That is the secret that possessed me, that made me a prisoner.

That is the lust fuelling the god's desire.

As the memories surfaced, the god came with them. He reveled in my secret, gorging himself on my crime like a kid loose in a candy store. A chorus of voices screamed in ecstasy inside my head. I clamped my hands over my ears, trying to push the sound back inside, but that didn't make the pain go away. I collapsed to my knees as my legs gave out and my body turned to jelly. Trey and Quinn let me fall.

Ms. West glided toward me, wrapping cold fingers around my wrist and holding my arm high. "Is this the girl you'd allow to lead you in rebellion? A *murderer*."

"That only proves my point further." Vincent stood on the side of the stage now, his hands in his pockets, a satisfied smirk playing across his lips. He thought he had me now. "That girl is trying to mess everything up for us. She must be got rid of."

"Hazy?" Quinn stepped away from me, his eyes wide. His face froze in the same expression he wore when he found out what his mother had done. It broke my heart to know I'd caused it.

"That's sick," Courtney gasped, clutching her stomach. "You burned your mother *alive?*"

They don't know you as I know you, the god spoke to me through the screams. How it was speaking to me while I was awake, I didn't know. *You alone can end this as it began. You alone can cleanse this place and do what I cannot.*

As the god spoke, I felt the black web of his power sliding over my skin. Wherever it touched, heat scalded me, turning my guilt into rage, tugging out all the memories of my torture at the hands of these students. I swam in the evil of their legacy, and in that dark place, I grasped for the light - the light of my own power. *My vengeance.*

Why was I trying to save them? They didn't *deserve* to be saved.

Trey shook my wrist, yanking me one way as Ms. West tugged me another. "Hazel, you fucking listen to me. None of that matters now. It's in the past. No one cares what you've done. We've all done horrible things. All I care about is what you do *right now.*"

"It matters," I whispered.

My words stoked the monster inside me. I'd tried so hard to hide it, to control it, but by exposing my secret, Ms. West had set it free. It whispered rage along my veins until the whispers became a roar – until my whole body swelled with a desperate, insatiable desire for release.

I was a caged bird, trapped by the guilt that held me down, by the wrath of the students I'd tried to help, by the elite who hated me because I represented their greatest fears. Most of all – I was trapped by my feelings for the Kings.

I may be trapped, but a song of freedom sings in my blood.

Ms. West whipped out a vial filled with amber-colored liquid. She slotted it between her teeth to pull the cap off the syringe. I didn't know what it was but knew it was going in *my* fucking veins.

Something inside me ruptured, and everything dark and hate-filled rose up through the fire.

My skin shattered as my rage broke through my palms, hitting the curtain behind Ms. West's head. She bellowed in surprise and leaped away, but not before the fire licked the sleeve of her dress, shooting along her arm. She dropped the syringe and beat at the flames.

"Fire!" Someone yelled as the flames consumed the curtain, turning into a column of orange light. Students screamed and scattered, scrambling for exits, for hiding places. This was their worst fear come to life once more.

Their fear only drove the flames higher as I shoved their fucking death in their faces.

From his cavern below the school, the god screamed in my head. It sensed the murderer in me rising to the surface, and it stoked that flame with its own desires. The stage buckled beneath my feet, trembling with an unbridled lust for destruction.

"Hazel." Trey shook my arm. His own fear had melted the ice in his eyes. "We have to get out of here."

"Go," I whispered through gritted teeth. "You can't be around me right now."

I was gone to him. I belonged to the god now, to the fire. The deity dug through my mind with threads of oily darkness, dragging up every loathsome memory, indignity, and torment done to me and others by this school. It sang a war tune made of broken dreams as it gathered all that power and all that hatred and poured it into my flame.

I am the conduit.

I am the righteous fire. I will sacrifice my soul to make sure you pay for what you've done.

Fire spewed from my palms, uncontrolled and unleashed. Students screamed and jumped away as I spun in circles, immolating everything I touched. Flames leaped across the sets and turned the orchestra pit into an inferno. In the audience, parents fell over themselves as I sent a ball of fire straight into their midst. Screams landed on my ears, dull and uninteresting, nothing compared to the screams that came from *inside* my head.

Betrayed.

Abandoned.

Possessed.

I'll show you fucking possessed.

Trey slammed into me. "Run!" I yelled, pushing him back toward the wings. "You can't be here for this."

You can't see what I'm about to do. Because there's one thing we never spoke out loud, one plan for tonight you never considered because you are many fucking things, you Kings of Miskatonic Prep, but you are not murderers. But if the Eldritch Club dies tonight, the magic binding the sigils will be broken. And if I burn every torturer and bully to ash along with them, so much the better.

A fresh flame danced in my hand. I stared into the orange flicker, and I thought I caught an image of my mother inside it, screaming through a wall of orange light, leaning out the window as the fire caught her hair. She looked like an angel in my visions, but she was just a seducer and a betrayer burning up in an inferno of her own sin.

Hazel Waite no longer existed.

I am the flame.

I am the monster.

"What are you doing?" Ayaz stepped toward me, his dark eyes wide with fear. He grabbed the strap of my dress and shook. "Please, stop!"

But I couldn't stop. I aimed one palm at Vincent Bloomberg's chest as he lurched toward me, one at Ms. West as she crawled across the stage. The god licked his lips.

Let them burn. Let them all burn.

TO BE CONTINUED

Secrets. Lies. Sacrifice. Find out what happens next in the chilling final book in the Kings of Miskatonic Prep, *Ignited*.

READ NOW
http://books2read.com/ignited

Turn the page for a sizzling excerpt.

.

Grab a free copy of *Cabinet of Curiosities* – a Steffanie Holmes compendium of short stories and bonus scenes when you sign up for updates with the Steffanie Holmes newsletter.

FROM THE AUTHOR

She is nine years old. Two girls at her school pretend to be her friends, but mock her and humiliate her behind her back. She confronts them one day, tells them she's sorry if she'd done something to upset them.

"I just want us all to be friends," she says.

Their faces break into smiles. "That's what we want, too!"

One of them says she has something awesome to show the others. "We just found it!" She drags the girl behind the school hall. "You'll love it." She tells the girl to bend down and look under the hall.

As the girl bends over, a hand grabs the back of her neck, forcing her head down. She twists away, but not before her face is pushed into a pile of dog shit.

She stands up and watches her friends double over with laughter, cackling like the witches of Macbeth. She floats outside her body, looking down on herself – this pathetic girl with dog shit all over her face. She runs. She runs from the school, their laughter following her down the road, around the corner, somewhere, anywhere away from them. She doesn't remember how far she runs or how her mum finds her. She just remembers running.

This is a true story. It happened to me.

I have a rare genetic condition called *achromatopsia*. It renders me completely colour-blind and legally blind. I was also a generally imaginative, weird, and introverted child. I was good at art and making up stories and terrible at sports. I wasn't like the other kids, so they ostracized me, called me names, deliberately invented games to humiliate me, locked me in cupboards, told me that I was stupid, useless, pointless, that I should just go away, that I should never have been born.

It took me years to learn to trust people, to let them see the real me. Social situations still make me anxious, and I've struggled with low self-esteem and internalising anger.

In part, this is why I put myself inside Hazel's head to write this book. But it's not the main reason.

I want to tell you a different story.

During my first year at university, I met this girl in my dorm. We bonded over a mutual love of *Stargate SG1* and Terry Pratchett and became fast friends. We moved in together and were flatmates for two years. We had many of the same classes together, we participated in the same clubs and societies, and she inserted herself into my growing circle of friends. She even started dating my BFF.

In my fourth year, the friendship started to unravel. I was doing postgraduate studies in a different subject to her. I'd moved out of our flat. I was making new friends and developing new interests. I started dating a guy she didn't like. She felt like she was losing me – this person who was so important to her life and her sense of self.

She was frightened, I think. And her fear pushed her behaviour to greater extremes. She became obsessive, demanding to know where I was every moment, controlling my life, forbidding me to go out without her. She accused me of lying, of stealing from her. She created elaborate scenarios in her head where I had wronged her and had to make amends. I moved her into my new flat, hoping that some proximity would help her to calm down. Instead, she grew more erratic and obsessive.

My boyfriend at the time saw all this happening. He watched me become fearful of this person who was supposed to be my friend. He noted me trying to appease her, cancelling plans because they'd upset her, choosing her over my schoolwork, retreating into my shell.

He knew I was giving into her because of my past, because I was so grateful to have a friend that I didn't want to lose her. He could see she was taking advantage of my nature to control me.

One day, my friend and I had a particular horrible fight about something. I was staying at his house, and I was terrified to go back to my flat because she was there.

My boyfriend couldn't watch me hurt anymore. He drove me to the flat. He insisted on coming inside with me. Just having him by my side made me feel stronger.

He marched up to her and he told her that she was going to lose me as a friend if she continued what she was doing. He didn't raise his voice. He didn't call her names. He calmly laid out how she was acting and what it was doing to me. He reiterated how much he cared about me and he wouldn't stand by and watch me hurt.

It was the first time in my life I remember someone standing up for me. Listening to him speak to her that day was like hearing him speak to every one of my old bullies.

Reader, I married him.

Time and again in my life my husband has stood up for me, stepping in where I wasn't strong enough. And I've done the same for him – I've been the lighthouse to his ocean when he needed me most. Now, I don't need him to fight for me, because he helped me uncover the strength to fight for myself.

I'm not Hazel, and she isn't me. She's way more badass. She says the things that I think of an hour after a confrontation and *wished* I'd said.

Hazel doesn't need no man to help her find her strength. But I hope as the series progresses, you'll see how Trey, Ayaz, and Quinn can become her lighthouses when she needs them most.

I know this note is insanely long. Bear with me – I just have a few peeps to thank!

To the cantankerous drummer husband, for reading this manuscript in record time and giving me so many ideas to make it better. And for being my lighthouse.

To Kit, Bri, Elaina, Katya, Emma, and Jamie, for all the writerly encouragement and advice. To Meg, for the epically helpful editing job, and to Amanda for the stunning cover. To Sam and Iris, for the daily Facebook shenanigans that help keep me sane while I spend my days stuck at home covered in cats.

To you, the reader, for going on this journey with me, even though it's led to some dark places. Warning: if this book had you on the edge of your seat, then the fourth and final book is probably going to give you nightmares. Grab *Ignited* now - http://books2read.com/ignited

If you're enjoying *Kings of Miskatonic Prep* and want to read more from me, check out my dark reverse harem high school romance series, *Stonehurst Prep* – http://books2read.com/mystolenlife. This series is contemporary romance (no ghosts or vampires), but it's pretty dark and strange and mysterious, with a badass heroine and three guys who will break your heart and melt your panties. You will LOVE it – you'll find a short preview on the next page.

Another series of mine you might enjoy is *Manderley Academy*. Book 1 is *Ghosted* and it's a classic gothic tale of ghosts and betrayal, creepy old houses and three beautifully haunted guys with dark secrets. Plus, a kickass curvy heroine. Check it out: http://books2read.com/manderley1

Every week I send out a newsletter to fans – it features a spooky story about a real-life haunting or strange criminal case that has inspired one of my books, as well as news about upcoming releases and a free book of bonus scenes called *Cabinet of Curiosities*. To get on the mailing list all you gotta do is head to my website: http://www.steffanieholmes.com/newsletter

If you want to hang out and talk about all things *Shunned*, my readers are sharing their theories and discussing the book over in my Facebook group, Books That Bite. Come join the fun.

I'm so happy you enjoyed this story! I'd love it if you wanted to leave a review on Amazon or Goodreads. It will help other readers to find their next read.

Thank you, thank you! I love you heaps! Until next time.
Steff

IGNITED

**I'll do whatever it takes to free them.
Even if I have to sacrifice my soul.**

The Kings of Miskatonic Prep have fallen.
Three arrogant, cruel, and broken boys defied an ancient god,
a faculty who imprisoned them,
and the parents who stole their future.
They were never going to win.

But they won't quit.
They won't stop fighting.
This time, it's not themselves they're trying to protect.
They fight for me. For us. For our future.

Pain. Pride. Temptation.
They rage against their inner demons.
While I embrace mine.

Shit's getting real at Miskatonic Prep.

I've got a heart made of fire, the wrath of an avenging witch, and
three Kings at my side.
You think you know monsters?
You ain't seen nothing yet.

One way or another, we're graduating from Miskatonic Prep.
Let's burn this motherfucker down.

Grab Ignited now!
http://books2read.com/ignited

EXCERPT: IGNITED
Kings of Miskatonic Prep 4

Enjoy this short teaser from book 4, Ignited.

"This party is awesome," Trey yelled over the noise as he danced in close. I relaxed into him, his body raising heat where it grazed mine. "There's only one problem – where's this pillar of ours? I thought you were going to do it when you swung at John – you looked angry enough."

I smiled. Beneath my feet, the god rumbled in anticipation. "Nope. I have another plan for pillar-raising."

I took Trey's hand, stroking my fingers over his knuckles. With my free hand, I picked up Quinn's wrist, draping his hand across Trey's. I looked up. Without me needing to do anything, Ayaz shoved his way through the crowd and stood before me, the corner of his mouth twitching into a smile. He laid his hand on top. Three pairs of eyes met mine – one ice, one warm amber, one dark as night.

I sucked in a breath. I deliberately hadn't told them about this. I didn't want to give them time to think it over, to back out, to come up with excuses. I didn't want them to wonder why I'd been pushing them away, only to draw them to me tonight.

I didn't want to explain that I wanted one last, wonderful memory to carry me across the cosmos before I said goodbye to the Kings forever.

My three bullies. My Kings. The three guys I loved more with every breath, who challenged me and infuriated me and made me giddy with the force of my passion.

"Come with me," I spoke my wish into the air.

"Where are we going?" Quinn raised an eyebrow.

"To the cabins." I met their eyes, letting my desire pool. "I need all three of you. Tonight. With me."

TO BE CONTINUED

Secrets. Lies. Sacrifice. Find out what happens next in book 4 of the Kings of Miskatonic Prep, *Ignited*

Read now:
http://books2read.com/ignited

Or devour the entire Kings of Miskatonic Prep series (with bonus POV scenes) in the boxset:
http://books2read.com/miskatonicbox

From the author of *Shunned*, the Amazon top-20 bestselling bully romance readers are calling, "The greatest mindf**k of 2019," comes this new dark contemporary high school reverse harem romance.

Psst. I have a secret.

Are you ready?

I'm Mackenzie Malloy, and everyone thinks they know who I am.

Five years ago, I disappeared.

No one has seen me or my family outside the walls of Malloy
Manor since.
But now I'm coming to reclaim my throne:
The Ice Queen of Stonehurst Prep is back.

Standing between me and my everything?
Three things can bring me down:
The sweet guy who wants answers from his former friend.
The rock god who wants to f*ck me.
The king who'll crush me before giving up his crown.

They think they can ruin me, wreck it all, but I won't let them.
I'm not the Mackenzie Eli used to know.
Hot boys and rock gods like Gabriel won't win me over.
And just like Noah, I'll kill to keep my crown.

I'm just a poor little rich girl with the stolen life.
I'm here to tear down three princes,
before they destroy me.

Read now:
http://books2read.com/mystolenlife

EXCERPT: MY STOLEN LIFE

Stonehurst Prep

I roll over in bed and slam against a wall.

Huh? Odd.

My bed isn't pushed against a wall. I must've twisted around in my sleep and hit the headboard. I do thrash around a lot, especially when I have bad dreams, and tonights was particularly gruesome. My mind stretches into the silence, searching for the tendrils of my nightmare. *I'm lying in bed and some dark shadow comes and lifts me up, pinning my arms so they hurt. He drags me downstairs to my mother, slumped in her favorite chair. At first, I think she passed out drunk after a night at the club, but then I see the dark pool expanding around her feet, staining the designer rug.*

I see the knife handle sticking out of her neck.

I see her glassy eyes rolled toward the ceiling.

I see the window behind her head, and my own reflection in the glass, my face streaked with blood, my eyes dark voids of pain and hatred.

But it's okay now. It was just a dream. It's—

OW.

I hit the headboard again. I reach down to rub my elbow, and my hand grazes a solid wall of satin. On my other side.

What the hell?

I open my eyes into a darkness that is oppressive and complete, the kind of darkness I'd never see inside my princess bedroom with its flimsy purple curtains letting in the glittering skyline of the city. The kind of darkness that folds in on me, pressing me against the hard, un-bedlike surface I lie on.

Now the panic hits.

I throw out my arms, kick with my legs. I hit walls. Walls all around me, lined with satin, dense with an immense weight pressing from all sides. Walls so close I can't sit up or bend my knees. I scream, and my scream bounces back at me, hollow and weak.

I'm in a coffin. I'm in a motherfucking coffin, and I'm *still alive*.

I scream and scream and scream. The sound fills my head and stabs at my brain. I know all I'm doing is using up my precious oxygen, but I can't make myself stop. In that scream I lose myself, and every memory of who I am dissolves into a puddle of terror.

When I do stop, finally, I gasp and pant, and I taste blood and stale air on my tongue. A cold fear seeps into my bones. Am I dying? My throat crawls with invisible bugs. Is this what it feels like to die?

I hunt around in my pockets, but I'm wearing purple pajamas, and the only thing inside is a bookmark Daddy gave me. I can't see it of course, but I know it has a quote from Julius Caesar on it. *Alea iacta est. The die is cast.*

Like fuck it is.

I think of Daddy, of everything he taught me – memories too dark to be obliterated by fear. Bile rises in my throat. I swallow, choke it back. Daddy always told me our world is forged in blood. I might be only thirteen, but I know who he is, what he's capable of. I've heard the whispers. I've seen the way people hurry to appease him whenever he enters a room. I've had the lessons from Antony in what to do if I find myself alone with one of Daddy's enemies.

Of course, they never taught me what to do if one of those enemies *buries me alive*.

I can't give up.

I claw at the satin on the lid. It tears under my fingers, and I pull out puffs of stuffing to reach the wood beneath. I claw at the surface, digging splinters under my nails. Cramps arc along my arm from the awkward angle. I know it's hopeless; I know I'll never be able to scratch my way through the wood. Even if I can, I *feel* the weight of several feet of dirt above me. I'd be crushed in moments. But I have to try.

I'm my father's daughter, and this is not how I die.

I claw and scratch and tear. I lose track of how much time passes in the tiny space. My ears buzz. My skin weeps with cold sweat.

A noise reaches my ears. A faint shifting. A scuffle. A scrape and thud above my head. Muffled and far away.

Someone piling the dirt in my grave.

Or maybe...

...maybe someone digging it out again.

Fuck, fuck, please.

"Help." My throat is hoarse from screaming. I bang the lid with my fists, not even feeling the splinters piercing my skin. "Help me!"

THUD. Something hits the lid. The coffin groans. My veins burn with fear and hope and terror.

The wood cracks. The lid is flung away. Dirt rains down on me, but I don't care. I suck in lungfuls of fresh, crisp air. A circle of light blinds me. I fling my body up, up into the unknown. Warm arms catch me, hold me close.

"I found you, Claws." Only Antony calls me by that nickname. Of course, it would be my cousin who saves me. Antony drags me over the lip of the grave, *my* grave, and we fall into crackling leaves and damp grass.

I sob into his shoulder. Antony rolls me over, his fingers

pressing all over my body, checking if I'm hurt. He rests my back against cold stone. "I have to take care of this," he says. I watch through tear-filled eyes as he pushes the dirt back into the hole – into what was supposed to be my grave – and brushes dead leaves on top. When he's done, it's impossible to tell the ground's been disturbed at all.

I tremble all over. I can't make myself stop shaking. Antony comes back to me and wraps me in his arms. He staggers to his feet, holding me like I'm weightless. He's only just turned eighteen, but already he's built like a tank.

I let out a terrified sob. Antony glances over his shoulder, and there's panic in his eyes. "You've got to be quiet, Claws," he whispers. "They might be nearby. I'm going to get you out of here."

I can't speak. My voice is gone, left in the coffin with my screams. Antony hoists me up and darts into the shadows. He runs with ease, ducking between rows of crumbling gravestones and beneath bent and gnarled trees. Dimly, I recognize this place – the old Emerald Beach cemetery, on the edge of Beaumont Hills overlooking the bay, where the original families of Emerald Beach buried their dead.

Where someone tried to bury me.

Antony bursts from the trees onto a narrow road. His car is parked in the shadows. He opens the passenger door and settles me inside before diving behind the wheel and gunning the engine.

We tear off down the road. Antony rips around the deadly corners like he's on a racetrack. Steep cliffs and crumbling old mansions pass by in a blur.

"My parents..." I gasp out. "Where are my parents?"

"I'm sorry, Claws. I didn't get to them in time. I only found you."

I wait for this to sink in, for the fact I'm now an orphan to hit me in a rush of grief. But I'm numb. My body won't stop shaking, and I left my brain and my heart buried in the silence of that coffin.

"Who?" I ask, and I fancy I catch a hint of my dad's cold savagery in my voice. "Who did this?"

"I don't know yet, but if I had to guess, it was Brutus. I warned your dad that he was making alliances and building up to a challenge. I think he's just made his move."

I try to digest this information. Brutus – who was once my father's trusted friend, who'd eaten dinner at our house and played Chutes and Ladders with me – killed my parents and buried me alive. But it bounces off the edge of my skull and doesn't stick. The life I had before, my old life, it's gone, and as I twist and grasp for memories, all I grab is stale coffin air.

"What now?" I ask.

Antony tosses his phone into my lap. "Look at the headlines."

I read the news app he's got open, but the words and images blur together. "This... this doesn't make any sense..."

"They think you're dead, Claws," Antony says. "That means you have to *stay* dead until we're strong enough to move against him. Until then, you have to be a ghost. But don't worry, I'll protect you. I've got a plan. We'll hide you where they'll never think to look."

MACKENZIE

(Four Years Later)

The thrumming bassline that rattles my bones and heats my veins with pure sex cuts off mid-riff, replaced by a tinny rendition of *Für Elise* blasting through the speakers.

Deedle-deedle-deedle-duh-dum-dum, duh-dum-dum...

The doorbell.

Shit.

I freeze mid-skank, one hand clutching my phone so tight my knuckles burn white, the other still gripping my ass like I'm a backup dancer in a Rhianna video. My eardrums shriek in protest at the piercing volume as the bell rings throughout the house's built-in speakers.

I listen hard. The jingle continues, and now it's accompanied by a loud thumping I can hear even though I'm miles from the front door.

Double shit.

It's been *months* since someone last approached the house. It's not an easy feat to achieve – you either have to scale the security gate with its iron spikes or clamber over the smooth limestone property wall in a Spider-Man feat of endurance. That is, unless you knew about my secret entrance, and no one does – only Antony.

The last time I had visitors, some drunk school kids managed to climb over the gate standing on each other's shoulders. They dared each other to run up to the door, ring the bell, and kick in the CCTV cameras while the rest hid in the garden and screeched like banshees.

I let them carry on with their games for a bit, but they were freaking out my cat, so I flicked the lights on and off and they ran screaming. One impaled himself on the gate spikes and ended up in the hospital. He gave a tearful interview in the tabloids about how he was attacked by the Malloy ghost.

Attacked by his own stupidity, more like. But I'm not calling in for a correction. It serves my purpose to have people believe I'm a ghost.

BANG BANG BANG.

Kids aren't knocking on my door at 10AM on a Tuesday morning.

No, this is the knock of someone who won't leave until they get answers.

I drop onto the rug of the media room and pull myself to the edge of the cathedral windows overlooking the sprawling front lawn. My all-black cat, Queen Boudica, leaps off her cushion and creeps along beside me, chest flattened on the ground and ears back. She thinks this is a game – we're working together to stalk our prey.

Perhaps there's truth to that.

At the window, I crane my neck to the side until I can see the figure standing on the porch, his dark uniform contrasted between the towering white columns. He looks completely out of place amongst the faux Grecian marble statuary and weird succulents in the garden – those stupid plants are taking over the place even though I never bother to water them.

Even from this distance, his uniform is unmistakable.

A police officer.

Triple shit.

Behind him, I can see the security gate swinging freely. The officer must have forced it somehow. I'll have to get Antony to come and repair it.

My fingers touch the glass as I study the officer – all square jaw and swaggering authority, one hand resting on his holster as he leans in to rap on the door again. In neighborhoods like this – a ritzy street of glittering mansions overlooking Emerald Beach from the top of Harrington Hills – police aren't feared. They keep the riffraff out.

But I'm not your ordinary Valley Girl – I have my reasons for staying hidden.

For now.

I trace the officer's outline on the glass, willing him to turn around and leave. Even though I haven't made a sound, the officer's head snaps up, his eyes landing on mine. I snap my head back from the window, my heart pounding.

It's too late. He's seen me.

"I know you're in there," he shouts. "Answer the door – it's the police."

His voice carries an unspoken threat. Queen Boudica tips her head at me and lifts a paw as if asking what I plan to do next. I debate my options. If I ignore him, he'll come back with reinforcements. But if I go down there, I might be able to bullshit my way out of whatever trouble I'm in. Antony does always say bullshit is my second name.

It's no problem. You can do this. You're Mackenzie Malloy.

I pull a Gucci hoodie over my workout gear and pad through the house. It takes me a good five minutes to navigate through the hallways to the grand staircase that leads down into the foyer. I pass gilded side-tables and weird blown glass art, all covered in layers of dust. Is it too much to hope that the cop will get sick of waiting and leave?

No such luck. I can see his shadow outlined through the frosted glass. He stands on the porch, arms folded, as I crack the door. The chain bites, and I give him the classic Mackenzie Malloy hair toss and withering stare.

"You've broken into private property," I bark at him – it's not a question. It's an accusation.

"Ma'am, I'm here to inform you that you're occupying this house illegally."

I toss my head so my golden blonde hair falls down my back, and I laugh. I laugh until my throat rasps, until the officer is squirming and looking unsure of himself. His fingers slip from his holster.

"This is a joke. Who's your superior?" I hold my phone up so he can see it as I tap the screen. "I'm going to report you for harassment. And for breaking my gate. You'll be paying for the repairs from your salary."

The officer's chin wobbles, and for a moment I think I've got him, but then he steps forward with a new determination. "I don't know what game you're playing, girl. This house has been empty for four years, yet neighbors have reported noises inside. Squatting in private property is illegal, and I'm under orders from the city to remove anyone caught on these premises." He shoots me a triumphant look. "Do you care to explain yourself?"

"Check your case law, officer. If I *were* a squatter, the owners of the property are required to send me a three-day written notice. But I'm hardly going to send one to myself." I lift my chin and meet his surly gaze with my own. "This is *my* home. I'm Mackenzie Malloy."

He staggers back, his hand flying to his chest as if I shot a dagger from my eyes that pierced his ribcage. It doesn't surprise me – my father always said my don't-fuck-with-me glare would topple kings. Glaring at people is my superpower.

"Miss Malloy, forgive me. No one has seen you for four years. Where are your parents?" He knows the stories. They all do. The rumors that flew around the world on the wings of the tabloids after my parents disappeared. After *I* disappeared. Rumors that the Malloy supplement company was involved in dark and nefarious deeds. That some rival had a hit out on us. That we returned as vengeful ghosts to haunt the hills of Emerald Beach.

The tabloids spin a web of lies so thick that even the truth gets trapped there occasionally.

"My parents are sequestered on our private Caribbean island. Mommy's last plastic surgery went wrong, and she vowed she wouldn't appear in public again until someone rebuilt her face. Her new surgeon uses this hormone from a rare species of Amazonian monkey, and it takes a long time to milk enough monkeys to fix the crater in Mommy's forehead." I shrug, the lie rolling easily off my tongue. "I'm looking after the property until they return."

"Your father is no longer the CEO of Malloy International. Doesn't that seem odd to you?"

I quirk an eyebrow at him. "It's illegal for a businessman to take a sabbatical now? Fine, I'll call our lawyers and they can come down here and explain to your supervisor that you broke our gate to harass me about my father's business decisions—"

He holds up his hands, unease flickering in his eyes. "That's not necessary, Ms. Malloy. If you show me some identification, I'll be on my way."

"Fine." I slam the door and march across the hall to where I left my ID in a bowl of glass apples that bore the mark of some fancy-ass Italian designer. My fingers seek the pendant around my neck – the gold locket hidden beneath my hoodie, thank fuck, because no way did I want that cop to see me wearing something so unfashionable. I tug at the heart charm on its thin gold chain, pressing my fingers against the familiar stamped surface and sucking in breaths until my heart stops racing.

This is it.

I knew the moment would come eventually. Luckily, Antony and I are ready.

Fuck, I hope we're ready.

I crack the door again. The cop holds out his hand for my ID, but I toss it at him. He has to stoop and pick it up, giving me ample opportunity to stare down my nose at him.

He frowns at my card, turning it over. "You're only just seventeen, Mackenzie. Why aren't you in school?"

I notice he uses my first name now. "I'm homeschooled. It's a free country. Shouldn't you be solving some actual crime?"

"Homeschool? A rich bitch like you? I don't think so." He notes something on his pad. "What institution? I'm going to check your enrollment."

"I'm not telling you anything without my lawyer."

"That line only works if you're suspected of committing a crime. We're just chatting."

"This feels like an interrogation to me." I fold my arms. "Don't make me call Daddy on the island to tell him about the trouble you caused just because some neighbors thought they heard a ghost. He's already going to be upset about the gate."

The cop sighs. He flips his pad shut and shoves it back into his pocket. "Very well, Mackenzie. I'll be checking up on you. You're still a minor, so if I can't see evidence that you're enrolled in school, I'll be sending around some CYF officers to talk to you."

Quadruple shit. I hunt around in my mind for something to tell him. I grasp for the memories tucked away into the corners of this impersonal home, the little touches that proved actual humans once inhabited it. My mind rests on the school prospectus in the drawer in the mahogany desk in the office. Students in sage-green uniforms, standing around under palm trees and grinning at the camera like smug bitches. "Stonehurst Prep. I'm about to start my senior year at Stonehurst Prep."

Keep reading:
http://www.books2read.com/mystolenlife

OTHER BOOKS BY STEFFANIE HOLMES

Nevermore Bookshop Mysteries

A Dead and Stormy Night

Of Mice and Murder

Pride and Premeditation

How Heathcliff Stole Christmas

Memoirs of a Garroter

Prose and Cons

A Novel Way to Die

Much Ado About Murder

Kings of Miskatonic Prep

Shunned

Initiated

Possessed

Ignited

Stonehurst Prep

My Stolen Life

My Secret Heart

My Broken Crown

My Savage Kingdom

Manderley Academy

Ghosted

Haunted

Spirited

Briarwood Witches

Earth and Embers

Fire and Fable

Water and Woe

Wind and Whispers

Spirit and Sorrow

Crookshollow Gothic Romance

Art of Cunning (Alex & Ryan)

Art of the Hunt (Alex & Ryan)

Art of Temptation (Alex & Ryan)

The Man in Black (Elinor & Eric)

Watcher (Belinda & Cole)

Reaper (Belinda & Cole)

Wolves of Crookshollow

Digging the Wolf (Anna & Luke)

Writing the Wolf (Rosa & Caleb)

Inking the Wolf (Bianca & Robbie)

Wedding the Wolf (Willow & Irvine)

Want to be informed when the next Steffanie Holmes paranormal romance story goes live? Sign up for the newsletter at www.steffanieholmes.com/newsletter to get the scoop, and score a free collection of bonus scenes and stories to enjoy!

ABOUT THE AUTHOR

Steffanie Holmes is the *USA Today* bestselling author of the paranormal, gothic, dark, and fantastical. Her books feature clever, witty heroines, secret societies, creepy old mansions and alpha males who *always* get what they want.

Legally-blind since birth, Steffanie received the 2017 Attitude Award for Artistic Achievement. She was also a finalist for a 2018 Women of Influence award.

Steff is the creator of *Rage Against the Manuscript* – a resource of free content, books, and courses to help writers tell their story, find their readers, and build a badass writing career.

Steffanie lives in New Zealand with her husband, a horde of cantankerous cats, and their medieval sword collection.

STEFFANIE HOLMES NEWSLETTER

Grab a free copy *Cabinet of Curiosities* – a Steffanie Holmes compendium of short stories and bonus scenes – when you sign up for updates with the Steffanie Holmes newsletter.

http://www.steffanieholmes.com/newsletter

Come hang with Steffanie
www.steffanieholmes.com
hello@steffanieholmes.com

Made in the USA
Middletown, DE
12 July 2021